THE LAST MONUMENT

By
Michael C. Grumley

ii

BOOKS BY

MICHAEL C. GRUMLEY

BREAKTHROUGH

LEAP

CATALYST

RIPPLE

MOSAIC

ECHO

AMID THE SHADOWS

THROUGH THE FOG

THE UNEXPECTED HERO

ACKNOWLEDGMENTS

To Gina.
For urging me to write this book.

Prologue

The explosion was deafening, propelling a barrage of earth and clay chunks in every direction. Five thousand pounds of steel wrecking ball erupted through the cloud of red dust like a beast freed from its cage, eventually slowing and beginning a gradual swing back into the billowing haze.

Overhead, the top of a white crane rotated backward, pulling the giant ball with it, only to send it swinging back again with another devastating blow—this time demolishing an entire wall of the ancient adobe building—walls that had stood the test of time for well over a century.

Walls of the last remaining original structure in the tiny town of Alerta, Peru, perched just five miles inside the Peruvian-Bolivian border, one of thousands of isolated South American establishments fighting to survive under the relentless advancement of modernization. With tiny Alerta, still deeply rooted in a ramshackle existence of tradition and heritage, beneath what seemed like an ever-encroaching blanket of poverty.

But today was different.

Today, the destruction of the town's only central building and ancient post office was cause for celebration after the government had allocated tens of thousands of Peruvian soles to build a new, modern administration building in its place. Officially delivering the town into an age of relevance within the great Republic of Peru.

The fourth blast from the giant, pear-shaped wrecking ball destroyed what was left of the north and west walls in one swing. In a shower of chunks, the impact caused the scarred, white-painted ball to twist slowly as it moved, before again pulling back from the arm of its overhead crane.

The last remaining section of wall was left wobbling before it tumbled inward, crashing onto the rammed earth foundation and what was left of the wooden flooring.

The ball was promptly dragged backward yet again when one of the nearby workers suddenly held up a hand and peered curiously through the red dust.

The crane's arm was halted, and two green-vested men climbed forward into the field of rubble. Scrambling over piles of broken bricks until one of the men pointed forward and waved off the crane operator.

***

Three hours later, Andre Lopez raised a hand and absently wiped away a bead of sweat from his forehead, a consequence of the old squealing air conditioner in the next room, which strained to stave off the summer heat and humidity every time the office's outside door was opened.

Puerto Maldonado was the capital of Peru's Madre de Dios region. Located in the country's southeastern corner, far from what most of the world would consider modern civilization, the city was still large enough to provide most of what Lopez ever needed growing up.

Now in his early thirties, Lopez worked for the local government as a freshly branded city planner, one of only three in the Department of General Services for the entire Madre de Dios region and currently responsible for distributing a round of several million soles in new government projects.

Under a thick head of dark black hair, he barely heard the outside door clang shut and only looked up when a figure appeared before his desk. The workman was dressed in dirty clothes and had his large hard hat tucked under one arm. Lopez remembered him as a foreman but struggled to recall the man's name.

Without a word, the older man dropped a stack of envelopes onto Lopez's desk, prompting him to glance at them curiously before spreading his hands in a questioning gesture.

"We found these in Alerta," the man replied. "In the old post office."

Lopez remembered now. The man's last name was Burga. Part of the project in Alerta, replacing the city's post office.

Lopez looked back at the envelopes. Perhaps two dozen, all stacked and bound with a single rubber band.

"What are they?"

"Letters."

Lopez frowned and picked them up. "I can see that. Why are you giving them to me?"

"We weren't sure what to do with them."

"Where did you find them?"

"In the remains of the old post office. Beneath the original flooring."

Lopez raised an eyebrow. "They were *under* the floor?"

The man nodded. "Looks like the place got a new floor a long time ago. These were scattered under the original subfloor. Probably fell between the gaps long before that."

Andre Lopez picked up the stack and flipped through them, releasing a tiny plume of dust. He then removed the rubber band and examined each one separately. "They look pretty old."

"Very."

"Any idea how long they've been there?"

"Dunno. A long time. Probably too long for anyone waiting for them to still be alive."

"Hmm." Lopez leaned back in his chair.

"Throw them away?" Burga asked.

He shrugged and fingered through them again. "I don't know. Leave them with me for now."

Lopez remained still, thinking, long after the workman had left. One at a time, he studied each envelope. Twenty-three in all. Most were addressed to other towns in southern

Peru. Four, however, were addressed to Bolivia. Three to Venezuela. And one, written in English, to the U.S.

Lopez briefly glanced at the steel wastebasket beside his desk. Burga was right. They were likely too old for any of the addressees to still be alive. He slowly lowered them into the mouth of the wastebasket but stopped when something occurred to him.

His mother.

Or rather, his mother's attic. She had been gone for several years, but a fleeting memory caused him to pause. One of his own nieces, only five years old, standing in his mother's dusty old attic barely a week after her death.

She had found a stack of envelopes written to his mother from Lopez's father years earlier. Correspondence between the two before they were married. Nothing sultry that would have made him regret reading them. Quite the opposite. Dozens and dozens of letters from two young people in love and separated by several hundred kilometers, while one worked and the other finished school.

The romance was endearing, punctuated again and again by their longing to be together. But for Lopez, there was something more in those letters. Between the lines, he had discovered a surprising, real-time peek into his parents' lives during those early years. An opportunity to see what their worlds were like as young adults. What they'd done, what they'd thought about, what they'd struggled with.

Lopez studied the letters in his hand. One never knew how history would reveal itself.

A trace of a grin crept around the corners of his mouth and he turned back to his desk, where he picked up a pen and began jotting down the addresses.

He remembered what one of his teachers had once said. *History is anything but predictable.* Who knew what surprises might be lying in wait, even for an addressee's descendants.

What Andre Lopez could not possibly know…was that

one of the letters in his hand would have the power to change the entire world.

1

Two Months Later

Known as the *Carnation City* in the early 1900s, Wheat Ridge, Colorado, had grown from a single stop along a Gold Rush travel route to a full-size suburb just outside of Denver. After incorporation years later, the small city in present day served as a prime suburban location for young families with parents commuting into downtown Denver, all against a perfect backdrop of the great Rocky Mountains.

The mountains towering in the distance were covered in white snow. At night, they faded into darkness and were replaced by another version of Wheat Ridge visible only under the bright glow of thousands of city streetlamps. Currently, they highlighted a curtain of fresh snowflakes, twirling quietly to the ground and marking the third official snowfall of the season, and enough to blanket the sounds of the late evening traffic.

The very same blanketing that helped muffle the sound of a large window sliding open just minutes after eleven p.m., beneath a cold dark sky now. Most of the small town was either close to or had already turned in for the night.

The thick double-paned window made no discernible noise as it slid open along a white vinyl frame. Now open, gloved hands appeared on the sill from inside, struggling to support a raised foot and the larger body behind it.

The exit wasn't smooth. Rather clumsy actually, considering it was the ground floor. When the figure reached the snow-covered earth, he briefly stumbled backward to regain his balance, leaving a wild scattering of footprints in the snow.

A large, dark blue duffel bag was then pulled out and dropped with a soft thud before the window was carefully closed again from the outside. The figure hefted the duffel bag back over his shoulder and scanned the street before ambling across the soft crunching blanket of snow and disappearing into the darkness.

2

For those who thought all government offices looked the same, the National Transportation Safety Board in Denver stood as a glaring exception. Located downtown, the single-story brown building looked more like a medical group than the regional office of a well-known government agency.

Officially separated from the Department of Transportation agency by Congress in 1975, the NTSB was run by a five-member board and tasked with investigating and reporting on all civilian transportation accidents in the United States. They also provided recommendations for systems or process improvements where necessary in an ongoing mission to improve public safety throughout the nation.

Something far easier said than done.

Like any other government agency, the NTSB was not

immune from scandal or controversy, leaving Assistant Director Kevin Wilkinsen thankful not to have been caught in the Federal Aviation Administration's public relations nightmare over Boeing's 737 MAX airliner accidents, including the painful revelations over the FAA's own negligence in the matter.

He knew several of the directors caught up in the scandal, and it wasn't something Wilkinsen would wish on his worst enemy.

The short and slightly overweight Wilkinsen hung up the phone and returned a pair of black-framed glasses to his nose, continuing through the report in front of him—one of several to be included in his weekly briefing to headquarters in D.C.

"Come in!" he barked, barely looking up at the knock on his door.

The door swung inward and one of his agents stepped in, along with a wave of loud chatter from those seated at the dozens of desks outside. "You wanted to see me?"

"Yes." Wilkinsen nodded and motioned him to close the door.

Joseph Rickards was taller than his boss by almost a foot. Twelve years younger, in his forties, he wore a somber expression under a full head of hair.

"Need a limited investigation. Small aircraft about forty miles south of here. Block and a half from an elementary school. Take Gutierrez and get it cordoned off as quickly as you can."

Silence filled the room, leaving the assistant director to glance up at Rickards when he didn't respond.

"Problem?"

"You sure you want me?"

Wilkinsen's reply was sarcastic. "It's a small aircraft. I think you can handle it." After a pause, he asked, "Can you?"

Rickards nodded. "Yeah."

"Good." Wilkinsen motioned him out and returned to

his papers, adding his signature to the first report. When the door closed, he stopped and looked up again, watching through the glass as Rickards crossed the open area.

Finally, he sighed. The situation was beginning to feel hopeless.

***

Outside, Rickards retrieved a few things from his desk and glanced up to see Dana Gutierrez staring at him.

"I take it he already told you?"

The younger woman nodded and passed him a folder.

"You ready, then?"

"Yes," Dana said, promptly rising from the desk and slinging a pack over her shoulder.

It took the agents over an hour—in complete silence—to reach the site through Denver's morning traffic. The crash site was a field just beyond a new housing development where they spotted several patrol cars positioned between the wreckage and nearby school. The blackened pile still smoldered slightly, leaving a thin trail of smoke ascending like a black snake, twisting upward before finally dispersing into the frigid mountain breeze overhead.

Exiting the car, the two immediately detected the all-too-familiar odor--a combination of fuel, charred metal and burnt bodies. It was a sickly stench no investigator ever got used to, no matter how long at the job.

Together, they plodded through foot-high snow until reaching the first pieces on the ground. There they were met by an approaching deputy sheriff.

"You guys NTSB?"

Rickards nodded and presented his badge, as did Gutierrez. Their gazes scanned the pieces scattered around the bulk of the mangled wreckage.

"What do you have so far?"

The deputy turned and looked at the wreckage with

them as he spoke, his breath visible in the morning air. "Still piecing things together, but we think it happened early this morning. Maybe two or three o'clock. Nobody heard the impact, but everyone noticed it on their way to work. We're checking Flight Service to see if anyone filed a flight plan."

Rickards frowned. "In the middle of the night?"

"Maybe they were passing through from somewhere else."

He looked up at a sky of muted gray clouds. "Not through this weather. Unless they were stupid."

Dana stepped forward. "We can take care of that. What else do you have?"

The deputy motioned forward and continued walking. "Only got a partial of the serial number, but it should be enough. We're running it right now. Four-seater and two bodies. Both completely burned. Probably going to take some forensics."

"Which means a lot of fuel."

"So probably took off from somewhere close," Dana finished. "Likely traveling south." She looked at Rickards. "Only a few major destinations between us and New Mexico."

"We'll check those, too."

The three reached the main pile of burnt aircraft, where two more deputies were examining pieces, careful not to accidentally touch or move anything.

"We're not sure what kind of aircraft—"

"It's a Cessna 182. Turbo," Rickards said. "Max range with two people in this weather, a thousand miles, give or take. Baggage?"

The deputy nodded. "Over there."

A chime sounded, and one of the other deputies several yards away pulled out his phone. "Looks like we have an ID on the plane. And the pilot." He looked at his superior. "It *is* a 182."

He stepped over a few pieces on the ground and approached, handing his phone to the senior deputy. He, along with Rickards and Gutierrez, squinted to see the tiny screen in the daylight.

After a moment of reading, Rickards and Gutierrez glanced at each other in surprise.

"You've got to be kidding."

3

They all turned when the sound of a distant vehicle rumbled to a stop behind them, a nondescript white Dodge van. A man and woman climbed out on either side. Both dressed in dark blue uniforms and moved back to open the vehicle's rear doors.

"Coroner."

Rickards reached for the phone in the deputy's hand and read the message again, more carefully this time. He then passed it to Dana, who read while Rickards wrote some things down on a palm-sized notepad.

"Pilot's name was Jim Huston," Gutierrez said. She peered closer at the screen. "Says the guy was eighty-six years old. What the hell is an eighty-six-year-old doing flying a plane?"

Rickards shook his head, watching the technicians approach toting a heavy duffel bag. "Don't know. But something tells me he hasn't flown in a long time."

***

Contrary to large commercial crashes requiring a major investigation with multiple teams, small private aircraft accidents required only a "limited" investigation, along with a limited amount of data collection and analysis, until a reasonable conclusion was formed--unless something unusual stood out to the investigators.

In the case of the Cessna 182, rough weather and poor judgment were both likely culprits. Why someone would take a plane out in the middle of the night like that made no sense. It indicated both people on board were exercising not only poor, but possibly compromised, judgment. It was not a huge leap for Rickards, given that the pilot was just a few years shy of ninety, which left him wondering if some forms of medication may have been involved.

He watched Gutierrez circle the smoldering wreckage, recording a detailed video on her phone, before he turned back to take several more pictures of the remaining fuselage. Large sections of its thin, white-painted aluminum skin were torn and ripped from beneath the frame.

The coroner's technicians had already extracted and bagged the remains, leaving him and Gutierrez to finish some documentation before the NTSB cleanup crew arrived.

If Rickards had to guess, rime ice, a form of ice created by supercooled vapor or droplets quickly freezing on hard surfaces, had played a part in what had gone wrong. An occurrence not entirely common, but deadly for small and medium-sized aircraft in unusually cold conditions. Most pilots were aware of the risks and avoided situations prone to creating it, making this particular crash even more puzzling.

Rickards scanned for more pieces and spotted a dark blue duffel bag crumpled on the ground, ripped and soaked from the moist snow beneath it. He walked over to it and took a picture before unzipping the pack and pulling out several pieces of clothing, followed by a bundle of documents, a vinyl case of personal items, a smaller black case containing bottles of pills and several books. Finally, to Rickards' surprise, he removed a thick stack of cash, which fell out when he unfolded the documents.

He was examining the bills when Gutierrez approached behind him.

"Smugglers?"

Rickards looked around and shook his head. "Not unless we find a hell of a lot more."

"How much is there?"

He flipped through several hundreds and fifties. "I don't know. Maybe ten grand."

"Maybe on their way to buy something?"

"Like what?"

Gutierrez shrugged. "I don't know. A car? Lot of these old guys like to pay for things in cash."

"Maybe." Rickards shrugged, then stood up and examined the rest of the papers. Without looking up, he handed something to her.

"What's this?" Gutierrez asked, flipping the small item over to reveal the front cover of a passport.

"It's our passenger."

4

Formerly known as the Tri-County Airport, the newly designated Erie Municipal Airport was north of Denver and situated less than forty miles from the crash site.

Rickards and Gutierrez arrived to find it home to dozens of small private airplanes, all carefully covered and winterized to protect them from the elements. The airport itself was little more than a cluster of individual buildings and hangars. A single fuel tank and pump sat nearby, covered in a thin white layer of snow.

According to the sign, it was closed during the peak winter months, and both agents had to squeeze through an opening near the gate--a feat easier for Gutierrez than Rickards.

Once through, Gutierrez answered her phone as they plodded forward toward the airport's small administration building.

After a short exchange, she ended the call. "The guy who runs this place is evidently out of town."

"For how long?"

"Till March."

Rickards rolled his eyes and continued forward, reaching the structure to find the door and windows covered from the inside. Outside the building, next to the entrance, hung a glass cabinet, enclosing a cork board covered with dozens of flyers and notifications.

Together, they turned and looked out at the tiny runway.

"No tracks."

"Covered up by now. When did the snow start falling last night?"

"After midnight, I think."

Rickards nodded. "Which means they probably took off before that. And still in the dark. Otherwise, the crash would have happened early enough for people to see it."

"So, they take off in the freezing cold *and* in the middle of the night?"

After a few minutes, Rickards sighed and stepped out from beneath the building's overhang. Snow crunching with each step, he walked out several feet and did a full 360-degree scan, his glance stopping again on the administration building.

Then something caught his eye.

An old, dull yellow light illuminated the wall just below the roof's ledge. And below that, a large round dial with big numbers. An outdoor thermometer, its red arm pointing at forty-four degrees Fahrenheit.

Rickards studied it curiously before withdrawing his phone from his coat pocket. He scrolled past several icons and tapped the weather app.

He stared at his phone for several seconds, then looked back up at the wall. He gave a sidelong glance at Gutierrez and walked forward again. Stopping under the light, he reached up and tapped the plastic face of the thermometer. When nothing happened, he hit it again, harder. This time the pointer suddenly jumped from forty-four to twenty-three degrees.

"Oh Christ."

5

"Looks like Jim Huston has no next of kin. Didn't have any children and wife died a few years ago," Gutierrez said, reading from her phone. Both agents were back in the warm car with the engine running. The younger read while Rickards stared ahead, watching fresh snowflakes dot the windshield.

"Says he was a pilot in Korea, then a commercial pilot here in Boulder until being forced to retire. After that, he was a part-time flight instructor around here for the last twelve years. Lived in Arvada with his wife, who retired as a schoolteacher."

"What about the passenger?"

"Gerald Reed. Ninety-one years old. Last known residence is a nursing home over in Wheat Ridge. Also a Korean War vet. And also a widower. Lived and worked in or around Denver his whole life. Looks as if he lost his wife several years back. Katherine Reed."

"What was the pilot's instrument currency?"

Gutierrez scrolled with her finger. "Last flight was eight years ago. Not current at all." She turned to her left. "So, what do you think?"

It took Rickards a minute to respond. "I think...we have a couple old geezers taking a trip under conditions the pilot thought were better than they were."

"Why would an eighty-six-year-old man still have a plane?"

"Because he was a pilot his whole life. And their plane is the last thing they give up."

"Even if he's too old to fly it?"

Rickards shrugged. "Could have been renting it to the school as a trainer."

"Okay," she said, following Rickards' gaze out the front window. "So how far do you want to take this? It's obviously a case of negligence. How deep do you want to dig before writing it up? I've got other cases waiting." The young woman's voice trailed off with her last sentence, forgetting she had other cases, but Rickards didn't.

If it bothered Rickards, it didn't show. Instead, he continued quietly staring out the window.

After a few minutes of waiting, Gutierrez raised her hands. "Hello?"

Rickards was still going over the facts in his mind. There were only two reasons he could think of why two old men would have done what they did. The first was simple stupidity. The second was desperation.

6

To Rickards, the entrance looked more like a small hotel than a nursing home. With a large circular driveway snaking under four giant gray pillars, the name overhead engraved in dark lettering was all that gave the building away.

Until they walked in.

When the double glass doors slid open, Rickards and Gutierrez were hit by a wave of warm air mixed with the distinct smell common in many nursing homes--a stench most identified as urine, but that was, in fact, something known as *nonenal*, a smell related to a chemical change in body odor in elderly humans. The clinical explanation in no way helped allay Rickards' distaste for the smell, and only partially distracted him from the short African American woman who quickly rose to her feet upon seeing them enter.

Dressed in a charcoal pantsuit and white blouse, the woman straightened her clothes and exited the glass office with a forlorn expression. "Are you the investigators?" she asked.

"Yes, ma'am," Gutierrez answered. She closed the distance and shook the woman's hand before turning to Rickards. "This is my colleague Joe Rickards."

The woman nodded and shook again, clearly troubled. "The sheriff's deputies just left. I can't begin to tell you how upset we are to hear about Gerald. What a horrible tragedy."

"We couldn't agree more," replied Gutierrez.

The woman shook her head. "We were afraid something might have happened."

"What do you mean?"

"Gerald's been missing since last night. We filed a police report early this morning when we discovered he was gone. But we never dreamed…" She put a hand to her mouth. "We just never could have imagined…"

"I know." Dana Gutierrez laid a reassuring hand on the woman's shoulder. "It's a shock." She looked at her badge. "Ms. Cannon, is it?"

"You can call me Kelly. I'm the assistant director. Ms. Macdonald is not here."

"We're sorry to bother you. We're just trying to get some answers as to what happened here." Gutierrez glanced back at Rickards, who was scanning the lobby. Well lit, it was filled with several brightly colored chairs, and tastefully painted pictures on the wall.

"How well did you know Mr. Reed?"

"Very well," Kelly answered. "He's been here for almost twenty years. One of our older residents. And very active. Everyone knew him."

"How did he disappear? Don't homes like yours always lock their doors at night?"

"He was a low-risk resident."

"Low risk?"

Kelly took a deep breath. "We have a number of elderly patients who try to escape. But he wasn't one of them."

Rickards turned around. "Escape?"

She nodded. "Not in the sense of what you might consider an escape."

"*Escape* to me means trying to get out of a place where you don't want to be."

"Of course. Forgive me. Escape was not the right word," she said apologetically. "You have to understand that many of our residents suffer from mental…challenges. Things like Alzheimer's or memory-related diseases, while others might struggle with accurate recall or mental anxiety. So, it's not uncommon that some patients feel a sense of anxiety or confusion and experience symptoms of panic. Sometimes it's because they haven't taken their medication, other times it's just part of…the disease itself. That's why we have the bus stop outside now."

Gutierrez smiled and began to ask another question when she abruptly stopped. "Wait, what?"

Kelly Cannon looked back and forth between them. "Pardon?"

"You said something about a bus stop."

"Oh, yes. Outside. In front."

"What does a bus stop have to do with Alzheimer's?" Gutierrez asked.

This time the woman grinned. "Sorry. It's new. Most people don't know about it yet. It's a type of safety measure."

Rickards raised an eyebrow. "A safe bus?"

"It's not a real bus stop."

This time Rickards stepped back and looked out through the double doors, spotting the small sign. He pointed to it. "That one?"

"Yes," she said, smiling. "Nothing actually ever stops there."

"Buses don't stop here?"

"No."

The agents looked at each other. "Why would you put in a bus stop if they don't stop here?"

Kelly walked forward and looked outside with them. "It's to keep the patients *here*. All nursing homes have the same problem. Patients who become disoriented and frightened and try to flee. But they don't know where they're going. It's more of an emotional trigger, still connected to old memories of having a home. We used to have to call the police once or twice a week to help find them. Often, they'd be found aimlessly wandering miles away. But since we put the bus stop in, we haven't had to call them once."

"Why?"

"Because what the patients are usually experiencing is fear, and short-term memory is often the part most affected with age. But long-term memories are still intact. And many have memory-association of waiting for a bus and going home. So now if someone manages to get out, that's where we find them. Waiting for a bus. Then one of us goes out and sits with them long enough for the anxiety to pass and then coax them back inside."

Neither agent spoke. They simply stared at her, fascinated.

"It's a gentler and far less frightening way to bring them back than in a patrol car."

"Who…in the world thought of that?"

"It started in Germany several years ago. Now a lot of homes are starting to do it. What can I say? It works."

Rickards shrugged at Gutierrez. "Wow."

The assistant director's smile faded, replaced again by her frown. "But Gerald didn't have that problem. His mind was as sharp as a tack. No mental health issues at all."

"So he didn't just wander out?"

"No," she said. "He *snuck* out."

Rickards stepped forward, stopping next to Gutierrez. "Snuck out?"

"Yes. When no one was looking."

"How?"

"Through his room's window."

"He climbed through his window?"

"Yes."

"What time was that?"

"We're not sure," Kelly answered. "But we found his room empty and window unlocked in the morning. After a complete search of the grounds, we called the police."

"And you didn't know where he was until…"

"Until the deputies showed up to tell us about the crash."

Rickards glanced over Kelly's shoulder. "Anyone else working today?"

"Yes. My staff is out double-checking the grounds. Including all the windows."

"Ms. Cannon," Rickards asked, "do you have any idea why Mr. Reed—Gerald—would do that?"

"I have no idea. No one does. He seemed fine. Happy. Especially lately."

"What do you mean?"

"Just that lately, he seemed quite chipper. Almost jubilant."

Gutierrez glanced at Rickards. "*Jubilant*? About what?"

"I don't know. I assumed it was because of the letter."

"Letter?"

"The letter he got a couple weeks ago. We assumed it was just some old letter from a distant relative. Lost in transit for a long time, but they finally tracked Gerald down.

They had a man from the post office deliver it personally. I think it was a fun PR thing for them to do."

Rickards' expression didn't change. "Who was the letter from?"

"I don't know who it was from or what it said. He wouldn't tell anyone. But it was clear he was very moved. Most of us figured it was a letter from an old friend. Perhaps one who had since passed away. Maybe an old girlfriend? I really don't know."

Rickards stared at the woman, then reached into his coat and pulled out an oversized plastic baggie. He opened it and reached in to retrieve the documents he'd recovered from the crash site. He unfolded them and searched through one at a time. Then shrugged at Gutierrez.

No letter.

"Ms. Cannon, is there anyone he would have told about the letter? Or shown it to? Friends or maybe family?"

"I don't know. I'd have to check. He was very good friends with Mr. Draper, but unfortunately, we lost him a couple months ago."

"What about next of kin?"

She nodded and walked back around the long desk, stopping at a keyboard and monitor. "He has a granddaughter in the area who we were just about to contact. Would you like me to call her?"

Rickards glanced at Gutierrez. "How about an address?"

7

"Anthropologists may differ in many subfields, but one commonly held belief is called…" The professor turned and looked back at her students. "Anyone?"

When no one answered, she turned back around to write on a giant blackboard. "*Human Universalism!* The belief that all people today are fully and equally human. This posits that people from all societies of the world are inherently equal, and that all cultures have value."

The professor turned again and smiled at her class. "No matter how much you might personally disagree. And no matter what you may think politically."

The class laughed.

"What I'm talking about is the belief that every human has the same physiology, dexterity, brain size and capacity for complex thought as anyone else. Which makes anthropology truly fascinating.

"Because," she said, pacing back and forth in front of her lectern, "if all anthropologists can agree on that, the true question then becomes: *What then makes us all so different?*

"But agreeing on that is something easier said than done. After all, not even some of history's greatest scientific minds could accept that premise. Even Charles Darwin, the father of evolution, a naturalist *and* biologist and arguably one of the most open minds of his century, could not accept the idea that all humans were equally capable."

One student raised his hand. "Well, but isn't he right to an extent? I mean, indigenous people all over the world are still living in huts. Or riding animals instead of driving." He smiled humorously and held up his phone. "And they don't use these."

Behind him, the class laughed.

Their female professor revealed an attractive smile and stared at him but said nothing. Instead, she allowed the laughter to fade and moved back to the lectern, where her computer was resting. She typed briefly on the keyboard and a picture suddenly appeared on the giant screen above her. A young, native African woman, with her dark head wrapped in a bright headdress, was sitting on a log, her feet bare. In her hand was a small phone with tiny wires running up to each of her ears.

The classroom fell silent and the professor shrugged. "She seems to be doing all right with one."

The student grinned back.

"There's a difference between inventing a tool and using a tool. We can all learn. Can't we?" She stepped forward with a piece of chalk still in her hand. "Are there people who are smarter than others? Of course. But on average, when adjusted for certain cultural biases, there is no indication that one society is significantly smarter than the others. In other words, we all have similar cognitive abilities, even if we don't all have the same means to apply them."

The professor's steady green eyes traveled across the faces of her students before stopping on two faces she did not recognize. They sat in the top row near the door. One was older than the other, and clearly neither was part of her class, but they remained listening intently.

She continued. "So, if we can accept that as a species we are equally capable, then anthropology, at its core, is the attempt to understand how we grew to be *so* different." She glanced at her watch. "Which is what we will be discussing next week." She returned her chalk to the blackboard. "You have your assignments. Ember, Ember and Peregrine. Read and be ready to discuss."

There was a rumble through the large room as dozens of laptop screens were closed at once and chairs slid back. Students began talking and standing up, dropping their belongings into backpacks.

At the front, the professor walked back to her own computer and killed the display overhead. She closed several programs before carrying her laptop to the table and setting it back down, noting the two she'd spotted above making their way down the carpeted steps past the students.

When they reached the bottom, they climbed three steps onto the raised floor. "Dr. Reed?"

The professor, in her early thirties with shoulder-length, dirty-blonde hair, smiled. "The good news is you've only missed two classes."

Gutierrez's face became serious. "Uh, we're not students."

"Really?"

She relaxed and smiled when she sensed the professor's humor.

"What can I do for you two?"

"Doctor, my name is Dana Gutierrez, and this is Joe Rickards. We're from the National Transportation Safety Board."

The woman paused and looked up. "That's a first. Don't think I've had one of you in here before." She opened her leather bag and slid in her computer. "Call me Angela. You two looking for help with an investigation?"

"You could say that," said Rickards.

She glanced at him, noting his lightly colored flannel shirt and tie. A little casual compared to the government employees she'd seen.

"What kind of help are you looking for?"

"Doctor," Gutierrez said and corrected herself. "Sorry, Angela. I presume we're the first to come talk to you today."

"Yes," she replied. "Why?"

The younger agent took a deep breath. "It's... about your grandfather."

Angela Reed froze. "What?"

Dana Gutierrez gave a slight wince. "I think you'd better sit down."

8

Angela Reed's face lost all color. She stared at both

agents, her expression suddenly nervous.

"Did something happen?"

Gutierrez nodded solemnly. "I'm afraid so."

"Is…is he…"

Gutierrez shook her head.

Angela brought both hands to her mouth. "Oh no."

"I'm sorry," she offered, with Rickards standing quietly behind her.

Tears immediately welled. The woman closed her eyes in a vain attempt to hold them back but couldn't. Instead, streams streaked down each cheek. "Oh my God. I can't—" Her mouth trembled and she stopped.

"I'm truly sorry," Gutierrez said again, glancing at the older agent. "We're both very sorry." Rickards nodded in agreement.

"It's not that," Angela said, half stuttering. "I just…I haven't…" She closed her eyes and squinted hard, forcing more tears to stream down her face. "Damn it."

For a full minute, she stared straight ahead, blinking, until finally composing herself and peering back up. "I…haven't…seen him in a while. We…" She inhaled. "I just haven't been to the home lately and—" After stopping in mid-sentence, she struggled, then looked at both of them with an odd expression.

"Where did you say you were from?"

"The NTSB."

Angela's eyes narrowed. "Why are *you* notifying me?"

It was a good question. Astute. Even overcome by grief. This kind of notification normally came in the form of a call from the nursing home. Or a visit from a police officer. Not agents from the National Transportation Safety Board.

She wiped her eyes with both hands and blinked. "What happened?"

"We're afraid your grandfather was in an accident."

"An accident?"

"An airplane accident."

Angela's expression turned to shock. "What?!"

Gutierrez nodded. "A small private aircraft."

"That's impossible." A quick glimpse of hope returned to her face. "You must have the wrong person."

"Why is that?"

"Because my grandfather hated to fly. And there's no way he would get into a small plane!"

Dana Gutierrez glanced at Rickards, who was listening quietly.

"I'm afraid it is him. I'm truly sorry."

"No." Angela Reed shook her head defiantly. "In a small plane crash? Not possible."

Rickards quietly handed the plastic bag of papers to Gutierrez, who then passed them to Angela. "We found some of his things."

She opened the documents and read, then shook her head again. "These are just travel documents. There could be other reasons why—"

Next came the passport.

Angela Reed halted again, examining the small book.

"There was more," Rickards said. "Including several bottles of medication, which we traced back to his doctors. Then his dentist. And from there, a copy of his dental records. The coroner just confirmed his identity."

The pain returned to Angela's face, along with another wave of tears. She continued shaking her head, not wanting to believe it. "But…what on earth was he doing in an airplane?"

"Actually, we were hoping you could tell us."

It was a rhetorical statement. There was clearly no way the woman knew why her grandfather was aboard that Cessna.

"Do you know a Jim Huston?"

"Yes." She nodded. "Wait. Don't tell me he was the pilot!"

"As a matter of fact…"

"This is impossible. I don't think he's flown in years."

"Yes, we know."

"Why would they both...?" She blinked incredulously. "It doesn't make any sense."

Gutierrez nodded sympathetically. "If it helps, that's more or less what we were thinking."

She stared at both agents. "What...exactly happened?"

"It was a small crash," Rickards said. "Just outside of Denver. Late last night."

"Last night?"

"Yes."

Angela Reed rolled her eyes. "At *night*, with Uncle Jim, in a small plane. That's just impossible. He wouldn't have done any of those. Let alone all three."

"You're sure about that."

"Yes, I'm sure," she said. "I think I know my own grandfather. The man raised me!"

"Is there anyone else in the family we should notify?"

"No. It was just me. And my grandmother, but she died several years ago."

"Were you close to your grandfather, Ms. Reed?"

Angela's gaze looked painfully at Gutierrez. "I used to be. But we haven't talked much lately."

"Why is that?"

"We had a falling out."

"Over..."

She shook her head. "It's a long story."

"When was the last time you talked to him?" asked Rickards.

"A little less than two years, probably."

"Any idea at all why he would try to fly somewhere in the middle of the night in bad weather?"

She scoffed. "I'm telling you he wouldn't have climbed into a small plane in the middle of the afternoon in *perfect* weather. He was scared to death of those things."

Rickards frowned. *Things were making less and less sense.* "Dr. Reed, do you know anything about a letter your grandfather received recently?"

"What kind of letter?"

"The assistant director at the home, a Ms. Cannon, said your grandfather received a letter a couple weeks ago--one that appears to have excited him."

"What does *excited* mean?"

"We don't know. But Ms. Cannon said there was a noticeable change in his mood."

Angela shook her head. "What did the letter say?"

"We don't know. Apparently, no one does. He didn't share its contents with anyone."

Angela folded her arms. "No one at all?"

"We couldn't find anyone who knew anything."

Reed's face seemed to harden slightly. She remained quiet, her lips pursed, until she finally looked around the empty classroom. "Did he...suffer?"

"No."

"But they knew they were going to crash. At some point."

Gutierrez shrugged. "It's hard to tell. Often in bad weather, things happen very quickly."

Angela nodded.

The younger agent frowned and turned to find Rickards quiet again. Motionless and stoic, as if studying Reed.

9

Rickards' stoic expression was very similar to that of his boss, Kevin Wilkinsen, now peering at the phone on his desk in a muted stare. But there was no disdain in his eyes. None at all. Wilkinsen had nothing but respect for the woman on the other end. His reaction was to the message, not the messenger.

"He won't talk." The woman's voice sounded through the speaker.

"At all?"

"He *talks*, yes. But not seriously. He's still holding it in."

"So, where does that leave us?"

"Nowhere good, I'm afraid. Some people are easier than others. Some just want to get it out. But others, usually men, keep things inside. Bottled up. Until…"

"Until what?"

"Until what he's holding in finally forces its way out. Into real, tangible problems. Manifesting in ways that may become not just his problems, but *your* problems."

Wilkinsen stared at the phone for a long moment. "So you're recommending what, then? Suspension?"

"What I really need is for him to open up. But you can't force that. You wouldn't want to even if you could. But, either way, the man is going to crack. They all do, eventually."

"Well, I'm not going to fire him. The guy's been through hell."

"Yes. Almost literally."

"Then what do I do?"

The psychiatrist on the other end of the phone pursed her lips, contemplating. "One thing that's clear is that he's holding on to one of the few crutches he has left, which is his job. It's a common reaction for people under this kind of stress. Focusing on something else to avoid the pain. Rickards is no different. If anything, he's worse. And taking that crutch away could result in unpredictable behavior."

"Wonderful." Wilkinsen frowned and turned to peer out his office window. His gaze returned with a tired sigh. "Are you saying this could turn violent?"

"That's a question I would ask you. You've known him longer."

Wilkinsen considered the question, and after a long silence, shook his head. "I don't know. I honestly don't know."

"He's going to have to face it sooner or later," the woman on the phone said. "Allowing him to keep this crutch will only prolong things."

"But putting him on leave and removing that crutch could be just as bad. Isn't that true?"

"Possibly, yes."

"So, I'm damned if I do and damned if I don't."

"Unless you think there's a possibility of violence. Then I have a legal mandate."

"A leave of absence."

"Yes, for starters."

"But you don't think he's violent."

"I haven't spent enough time with him yet," the doctor replied.

Wilkinsen shook his head. "So, according to the law, you'd have to put him on leave to protect him, even though it could be the very thing that sets him off."

"It wouldn't be to protect him," she said. "It's to protect everyone else."

10

Gutierrez peered at Rickards and spoke softly.

"What do you think?"

"About what?"

The younger agent raised her hands to her hips. "I feel bad for the woman, but let's be honest, this is getting beyond the scope of our investigation. Regardless of what motivated these old men to get in that plane, we have more than enough for the report. Pilot negligence and unsafe weather conditions. Pretty cut and dry."

Rickards glanced at Angela Reed, who was still sitting at the table, emotionally dazed.

"Maybe that letter made the old man do something desperate," Gutierrez said. "Tried to visit a dying friend or family member. I don't know. But I don't think it's going to change the cause of the crash. Besides," she said, glancing at her phone, "Wilkinsen says he wants us back."

The younger agent glanced sympathetically at Angela and continued in a hushed tone. "If you want to look into this more, be my guest. I'll tell him you're wrapping up some loose ends. But it sounds like we have most of what we need."

***

After apologizing and excusing herself, Gutierrez left Rickards quietly standing in front of Angela Reed, shifting uncomfortably.

The professor watched him for several minutes, wondering what had happened. The man was clearly capable. Intelligent. But something about him seemed off. Was he one of those quirky detective types who were uncomfortable around other people? No, his stance and demeanor appeared normal. Perhaps just irritated, or something else.

"Your grandfather was headed south. Did he have any friends or family downstate he may have needed to see?"

"Not anyone I can think of," she said in a slow, bereaved tone. "Most of his longtime friends were already gone. Jim--Mr. Huston--was one of the last."

"How well did they know each other?"

"Very well. Since the Korean War."

Rickards thought a minute and was about to reply when he suddenly stopped and looked back at the exit doors, frowning to himself.

"Something wrong?" When he didn't answer, Angela managed a polite grin. "Was she your ride?"

"Actually…yes."

"Didn't that come up when you two were over there talking?"

"We don't normally drive together."

"How long have you been doing this for?"

Rickards frowned sarcastically.

Angela Reed sighed and stood up. "I can give you a ride. I need to go to the nursing home anyway."

"I'd like to accompany you, if that's all right?"

"Fine."

She gathered her things and retrieved keys from her purse to lock the giant classroom, which was now eerily quiet.

***

The end-of-day traffic was already building, slowing cars on the I25 freeway to a near crawl, made even worse by the road's icy conditions.

From the passenger seat of the red Subaru, Rickards could make out several of Denver's two hundred renowned city parks in sight of the freeway, each covered by a pristine, untouched blanket of new white snow. Absently, he touched the side window with the back of his hand to feel the cold glass.

With the radio off and surrounded by dozens of cars inching alongside, Angela Reed remained quiet, clearly lost in thought. Or grief. Or both.

Having to face families of victims was one of the worst parts of Rickards' job. Completely devastated, always grappling, not just with the pain, but the emotional shock of not having the opportunity to say goodbye.

As if it would have made it any better.

"How long have you been at the university?" It was an obligatory question and one to which he already knew the answer.

"Twelve years."

"Why anthropology?"

She opened her mouth to respond and thought it over before simply saying, "It's complicated."

Rickards let it go and turned back to the window, watching the cars outside whose bottom halves were all caked with a thin layer of dirt and mud.

It didn't matter. He had long ago lost the desire for small talk.

11

Her grandfather's room had changed little in the time since Angela had seen him. He'd shared it with another man, Frank, who had already lost much of his memory and sadly was one of the beneficiaries of the nursing home's fake bus stop out front. He had gotten worse since she'd seen him last. She fondly remembered how her grandfather would patiently but constantly repeat himself to Frank.

Now the old, scrawny man lay silently on his bed, keeping to himself, lost in what few memories he still had left.

Outside, an occasional resident peeked in to sneak a look, sometimes stopping to give their regards. Angela only recognized a few of them.

"Looks like your grandfather loved history," Rickards remarked, noting the dozens of old books squeezed into a corner of the room. Neatly packed like a Tetris game within a cheap bookcase, bulging slightly at the sides.

"He'd taught at the community college since it was built," Angela said, glancing at the bookcase. "I guess I caught the bug from him."

"You said you grew up with him?"

"Yes." She returned her attention to some papers on his desk.

After a few moments, she handed Rickards a stack and moved to a new pile. They were all bills and magazines. The man evidently read a hell of a lot.

After a full hour, Angela had gone through every stack and every drawer. Even the tiny dresser and closet housing his clothes. But there was no sign--not just of the letter, but anything else hinting at needing to leave. No notes, no messages. No indication at all of what he had been planning.

Rickards noticed an elderly woman sneaking a brief look in before disappearing again.

"Did he have belongings anywhere else?"

"They have a small storage area in the basement, but he rarely used it."

"Any other ideas?"

She remained quiet, thinking, tapping a card on the desk which had fallen out of one of the magazines. Slowly a faint smirk appeared on her face. "Maybe."

Rickards stood expectantly waiting.

"Of all the people who have come by the room, there is one person I haven't seen." Angela looked up at him. "His girlfriend."

***

Lillian Porter looked to be in her mid seventies and was still quite attractive for her age. With straight dark hair sporting streaks of gray, her demeanor struck Joe Rickards as almost regal. But what surprised him most was an almost complete lack of excitement at seeing Angela.

She was, however, rather polite, inviting them both into her small room, despite her still red eyes.

"Nice to see you, Angela."

"Thank you, Lillian. How are you?"

"Not too well, I'm afraid. It's been a hard day for all of

us here. I'm sure you can imagine."

"I can." Angela nodded. "This is Joe Rickards. He works for the National Transportation Safety Board. He's investigating my grandfather's accident."

Lillian smiled politely. "Mr. Rickards. I wish I had something to offer you, but we don't have much in the way of amenities in these rooms."

"That's quite all right."

The older woman looked back and forth between them. "Is there something I can help you with?"

Angela's grin held more than a trace of sarcasm. "I don't know. Perhaps you can tell us why he did it?"

Lillian's eyes smiled politely, concealing her true reaction. She then allowed her smile to fade into a frown. "I'm afraid I don't know. Gerald didn't mention anything to me."

"He didn't tell you he was going to sneak out in the middle of the night, into a snowstorm, and fly out of a tiny airport that was closed?"

Next to her, Rickards remained silent, watching their cool exchange.

"No," Lillian replied. "He didn't."

"I find that hard to believe."

The older woman shrugged. "I find it…disheartening."

"Were you two still courting?" Her grandfather's term.

"As a matter of fact, we were. And *I* cared about him. Deeply."

Angela ignored the insinuation. "And he didn't tell you he might never see you again?"

"I'm sure he intended to return."

The conversation was devolving. "Excuse me, Ms. Porter," Rickards interrupted. "Your assistant director, Ms. Cannon, told me that Gerald appeared different lately. Would you know anything about that?"

She smiled at him. "He seemed the same to me. I'm sure if anyone would have noticed, it would have been me."

"Of course. Ms. Cannon also mentioned something

about a letter he'd recently received."

The woman thought for a moment and shook her head. "Not that I'm aware of."

There was a subtle shift in her expression. So faint that Angela appeared to miss it. But Rickards didn't. He had interviewed thousands of people, more than enough to know when something was not right. Or when someone was withholding something.

"When did you last see him?"

"Yesterday afternoon. At lunch."

"I see. Do you think you were the last person to talk to him alive?"

"I'm not sure. Possibly."

"And you don't remember him mentioning anything related to the events of last night? Anything at all?"

"No. Nothing."

Angela nodded, as though thinking. "That's odd. One of the staff mentioned they'd seen him with you last night at dinner. Perhaps they got the meals mixed up."

"I'm sure they did."

She continued thoughtfully. "The staff said they believed it was about 6:15 p.m. Seems a strange mistake to make. The time, I mean. Six is much different than, say, noon."

"I know what you're doing, Angela," the older woman said dryly.

"I'm sorry?"

"You're trying to bait me."

"I'm just trying to understand where the misund—"

"The bait only works if you're right." She crossed her arms. "Whether you believe me or not, I can assure you your grandfather told me nothing." Lillian stared at them for a moment before casually glancing out through her door. She then moved forward to close it.

For several seconds, Lillian's gaze remained facing the dark wooden door before she finally turned with a sigh.

She glared at Angela. "You should have been here."

Angela's eyes widened. "Excuse me?"

"Instead of abandoning him."

Angela's expression instantly hardened. "Well, maybe if you had actually *been there,* all those years."

"He told me everything," Lillian said, before turning her gaze to Rickards. "Gerald was a complicated man. Incessant. And naïve. But he loved her."

Angela's eyes narrowed. "The problem wasn't me."

The older woman didn't respond. Instead, she silently moved past them to her bed, decorated perfectly in a bright yellow-flowered comforter and pillows.

She bent down and pulled a metal box out from underneath. She opened it to retrieve a large manila envelope.

She stood up and almost reluctantly handed it to Angela. "He didn't tell me what he was going to do. But he did leave something with me. For you."

"The letter?"

"Yes," she sighed. "I knew about the letter. But I didn't know why he gave this to me until I heard the news this morning."

12

Angela remained frozen, holding the envelope between clenched fingers.

As if reading her mind, Lillian added, "He said it was an insurance policy."

"Insurance policy? For what?"

"I don't know."

Angela glanced at Rickards whose eyes were on the envelope.

She turned it over, tracing it, before sliding a finger beneath the sealed flap at the top and ripping carefully.

From inside, she withdrew two pieces of paper. Both were photocopies. The first was of a short handwritten note.

It was the second time Joe Rickards had seen the blood drain from the young woman's face today. This time it happened much faster.

Am alive.
Come quickly.
Alerta, Peru.
Almv10

-R.R.

Angela stood still, staring at the paper as if her body had suddenly petrified. Finally, she began to waver ever so slightly, but enough for Rickards to notice and instinctively step forward with a stabilizing hand. He backed her up and lowered her onto the soft, neatly made bed. "You all right?"

Angela didn't respond. She merely stared at the paper with a look of bewilderment.

"This can't be what I think it is."

Behind Rickards, Lillian said nothing.

"It's...impossible." The younger woman fumbled absently, separating both sheets to see the second was a copy of the envelope. Handwritten, with no postmark.

She stopped at the bottom of the page. Another copy of some writing from another piece of paper. A single paragraph. Neatly printed in what appeared to be German.

"When was this sent?"

Lillian shook her head. "He didn't know."

"Do you read German?" Rickards asked.

Angela shook her head.

"We have someone in the home that does."

"Did that person read it for my grandfather?"

The woman nodded.

Angela remained silent for a long time. *"This...is impossible."*

"What is?" Rickards asked, folding his arms.

Angela shook her head, partly in disbelief and part denial. "R.R.," she whispered.

"Who was R.R.?"

"His brother." Angela's eyes were back on the first page. "His older brother. My God." When she finally tore her gaze away, it was to look at Rickards.

"You were right with what you said in the car. It *was* desperation."

13

"What do you mean?"

Angela's expression was still transfixed. "My God," she mumbled. "*My God!*

"I didn't believe him," she finally said. "I didn't believe him." Her eyes rose and found Lillian. "Did he tell you?!"

"He told me it was from a friend. And that he wanted me to keep these copies for you. But wouldn't tell me why."

"He didn't tell you about his brother?"

"Of course he did. When we first met. He said he died in the war."

Angela turned again toward Rickards. This time absently, as if she were speaking to herself. The words forming on her lips felt strange. Somehow hollow. Empty. "What if he was right?"

"Right about what?"

"But he was in Europe," she whispered. "Not South America."

"Angela, what are you talking about?"

"I didn't believe him."

"Your grandfather?"

She nodded, still on the bed. "I believed him when I was young. Along with my grandmother. But as I grew up..." She flashed them both a guilty look. "It was only her."

"Believed him about what?"

"That his brother was still alive." She held up the paper. "His older brother was named *Roger Reed*. He was killed in the war. Missing in Action during World War II. At least, that's what the Army said."

"His brother was in World War II?"

"Yes."

"And died."

"Yes."

"But now you're saying he didn't?"

Lillian spoke up. "Gerald didn't believe he'd died. That much he did say. He thought the Army was lying."

"Why?" asked Rickards.

Lillian shrugged.

"Because he thought they were covering something up," said Angela.

"So...you're now saying that they were?" Rickards asked.

"I don't know." She handed the second photocopy to him. "I don't know how old this is, but there's no way it was before the war. It had to have been sometime *after* the war, After the Army claimed his brother had died."

"Was he in a battle or something?"

"No, that's just it!" Angela exclaimed. "He was a Monuments Man."

Rickards frowned. "A what?"

She took a deep breath and repeated, "A Monuments Man."

"What's a *monuments man*?"

Angela stood up from the bed. "Follow me."

Back in her grandfather's room, Angela moved to the bulging bookcase in the corner, stopping in front and scanning the spines of the books, before removing one, worn and tattered, and flipping through the pages. Without a word, she handed it to Rickards.

He read a few sentences from the open page and turned the front cover over to see the title. "What's the *Roberts Commission*?"

"One of two commissions appointed during World War II. The first had to do with Pearl Harbor. The second was appointed to help the U.S. Army protect cultural works of value in Allied-occupied Europe." Angela continued searching through the rest of the books, turning several to see their spines. Finally, she removed another, less worn but resembling something more like a military manual or handbook.

Rickards read the title of the second book aloud. "American Commission for the Protection and Salvage of Artistic and Historic Monuments in War Areas." He gave her a confused look. "And what is that?"

"That," she said, "is what all this is about." Angela glanced briefly at Lillian, who was standing quietly at the door. "This is what gave birth to the project my great-uncle, Roger Reed, was a part of."

"Your grandfather's older brother was part of a secret war project?"

"Not secret," she corrected. "Just quiet."

"A quiet project to do what?" Rickards asked. "To save monuments?"

"Not just monuments. To save the history of Western Culture itself!"

"What does that mean?"

"Culture, at its core, is the very embodiment of a

society's intellectual achievements. Of our identity. Of our existence! Records of culture portrayed and communicated throughout centuries in things such as art that tell us about history, of the values and beliefs that came before us. That kind of culture!"

Rickards put a hand over one of his eyes. "I'm beginning to feel like I'm trapped in a riddle here."

"There was a lot going on in World War II," she explained. "While millions were fighting in battles, others were fighting for something different--something arguably even more important. For our identity and our culture. And for the very history of who we are as a species."

"That doesn't sound dramatic at all," Rickards said, shaking his head. "So, that's what your great-uncle was doing?"

"That's right. He was part of the Monuments, Fine Arts and Archives program. A group of men and women from different countries who were quietly fighting to save millions of pieces of Western culture taken by the Nazis."

"You mean like paintings."

"I mean like *everything*. Over five million items of historical significance. Paintings, sculptures, statues, scrolls, ancient texts, you name it. Items stolen from every place the Nazis conquered. All across Europe. Museums, personal collections, even stashes meant to keep them safe. They were all found and raided for Hitler and his Führermuseum."

"His what?"

"His Führermuseum," she repeated. "The giant museum he'd planned to construct in his hometown of Linz after the war. Didn't you ever take a world history class?"

Rickards frowned at her sarcastically. "Yeah, like twenty years ago. And I don't remember covering Hitler's personal dreams."

She ignored his response and moved on. "The group trying to save it all was called the Monuments, Fine Arts and Archives program. The M.F.A.A., or more commonly known as the Monuments Men. They made a movie about it, but it was only a glimpse of what the program really was."

"Meaning?"

"Meaning, there were actually several dozen soldiers involved in it from countries all across Europe, methodically tracking down and cataloging stash after stash hidden by the Nazis. Sometimes monuments were found in caves or salt mines, and others in castles or even jail cells. Anywhere the Nazis could hide them before fleeing."

"So, your great-uncle was one of the people trying to find this art and save it? One of these Monuments Men?"

"That's right. He was one of them."

"And he supposedly died?"

"That's what the Army claimed. They said he was Missing in Action. They didn't change that to Killed in Action until sometime in the 1970s."

"And how did one get to be part of this project?"

"He was a college history professor. The Monuments Men were all museum curators or historians, often from universities. People who knew art better than almost anyone else on the planet."

Rickards nodded. "And wasn't your grandfather also a professor?"

"Yes. He'd followed in his brother's footsteps. But he never joined the military. By then, the war was over." Angela looked up at Lillian. "Nor did he ever believe the Army when they said his brother was dead."

14

Rickards was finally beginning to understand. "And

now, you're saying this letter proves your great-uncle didn't die?"

"I'm not positive. But on the surface, that's what it looks like. Which could also explain why my grandfather did what he did."

Angela reached out and pulled another, thicker book from the case. Opening it, she lowered a hand onto the thick red blanket of her grandfather's bed and suddenly stopped. She looked down and gently ran her hand back and forth over the soft material. The same bed he had slept in just two nights before. And now he was gone. Forever. Without her ever having a chance to say goodbye. Or to explain. Or apologize.

In that moment, it became clear how petty life was. How superficial most arguments really were. All just opinions and beliefs that in death simply disappeared into the ether, as though they never existed.

She wondered how many pointless arguments, how many fights, had taken place throughout the lives of all humans who had ever lived.

And God, how many wars?!

Angela remained silent with her head still down, gently smiling at the soft feel of her grandfather's old blanket. She was suddenly overcome by an almost sickening feeling of guilt for not trying harder. For not realizing sooner. Loss was painful, but *regret* was forever.

"Angela?"

She looked up at Lillian.

"You know he loved you."

She frowned. "I know."

"And he *knew* you loved him."

Angela blinked and suddenly began to tear up as she stared back.

Lillian smiled. "He knew without a doubt that you loved him."

She bit her lip. "Are you sure?"

The older woman nodded. "He did. And told me. Many

times." Tears formed in the corners of Lillian's eyes. "He never stopped loving you. You were his daughter," she said. "Just like your mother was. He always called you his daughter. Always. Even when you weren't speaking to him."

They were the last words Angela heard before tears poured from her eyes, running down her cheeks. And she wept.

In front of her, Joe Rickards remained quiet. Lillian lowered herself down and wrapped an arm around a sobbing Angela. Her pain was obvious to all, as was the look of regret on her tear-streaked face.

But it was only the first stage. Next would come waves of sadness and remorse. Then, if deep enough, depression. And much further beyond that, at the very end of the darkness, was misery, where days were devoid of any real purpose or meaning.

It was a place Rickards knew well.

15

The long, tense moment was eventually interrupted by a loud *ding* from Rickards' phone.

With a quick apology, he pulled it out of his pocket and read the message, then glanced at Angela, who looked up at him.

"I'm sorry," he said again. "I need to get back to the office."

He stepped forward and tried to add a comforting hand to her shoulder.

"Don't you need a ride?" Angela asked through her tears.

"I'll get a cab."

With only a slight hesitation, he turned and left the room, exiting through the narrow door and turning right into a long, beige hallway.

When he reached the front lobby, he continued briskly outside beneath the entrance's overhang, where at the end, he turned and walked past a lonely pole, prompting him to pause and peer up at the generic *Bus Stop* sign, and then down at the small stone bench below it. Thinking about what the woman inside had explained to them, he wondered, just for a moment, what kind of patient he would be when the time came.

***

Rickards knew what was coming the moment his boss asked him to meet.

He spotted Wilkinsen immediately after stepping through the restaurant's oversized wooden doors. His boss still in his suit as he quietly waited in a high-backed booth, watching several patrons as they squeezed, laughingly, through the crowded aisle.

As he approached, Rickards eyed Wilkinsen's empty bottle on the table, which was promptly replaced by a young server immediately after he sat down.

He watched silently as Wilkinsen raised the second bottle and drank.

"Everything okay?"

The bottle came down with a clunk. "No, Joe, it's not."

"What's the matter?"

He looked at Rickards sarcastically. "Health and Human Services. That's what's the matter."

"This about my sessions with Dr. Merritt?"

"It's about everything," Wilkinsen answered, lowering his gaze and staring through the bottle's colored glass. "It's going to wreck you. And me. And I think you know it."

Rickards leaned back. "I'm fine."

"No. You're not."

"Okay, fine. What do you want me to do?"

"*Talk* to them. Let them help you. Let *someone* help you. What you—" Wilkinsen shook his head. "Look, I don't blame you. And I sure as hell don't like therapy any more than you do. But Jesus, you've got to let her help you. Otherwise…"

"Otherwise, what?"

He took a deep breath. "Otherwise, you go on leave. For your own good. And better that I do it before they do. Because that'll be a whole different kind of problem for your career."

"What does that mean?"

"Being put on leave for mental health reasons never comes off your record. Assuming you even care about that anymore."

Rickards didn't reply, watching as Wilkinsen took another drink.

"What *do* you want, Joe?"

His gaze dropped. "I don't know."

"You've got to try, man."

"Do I?"

"Yes. You do. Otherwise, what's the point?"

Rickards' voice abruptly fell, almost to a growl. "What *is* the point?!"

"To get through this."

"For what? Get through it for what?"

"To—" Wilkinsen suddenly stopped, realizing he didn't have a good answer. "To…survive."

"Survive?" said Rickards. "For what? A better life? Happiness? What will that give me?" He leaned forward. "Tell me exactly what that will give me?!"

Rickards' words quickly faded between them like a spear through the chest of reality. Wilkinsen stared at him for a long time, finally picking up his bottle and emptying it in one long gulp.

He had nothing to offer. Nothing at all.

16

The knock on the door was loud, jolting Rickards from his thoughts. He blinked and turned his head before standing up from the couch, flipping on a small table lamp on the way to his front door.

His tired expression was replaced by surprise upon opening it, followed immediately by confusion. "What are you doing here?"

Outside, the shadowed face of Angela Reed stared up at him, frowning. "Is that how you greet everyone who comes to your door?"

"No one comes to my door."

A forming smile halted and she suddenly found herself unsure how to respond. "Uh, I'm sorry to bother you then. I just wanted to tell you something."

With a squint, Rickards' gray-blue eyes peered out over her head. "How did you figure out where I lived?"

"It doesn't matter," she said, changing the subject. "I need to talk to you about my grandfather."

"Why?"

Now Angela looked confused. "Because…it's your case?"

"It *was* my case."

"What does that mean? It's not your case anymore? Why not?"

"It doesn't matter."

Angela frowned. "Why? Did you get fired or

something?"

"Or something."

"Oh my God. Did you actually get fired? I'm sorry. I was only joking."

"I said it doesn't matter. Just call down to the office in the morning and they'll tell you who it's been given to. Whatever it is you think you have you can tell them." He began to close the door when Angela reached out to stop it.

"Wait! I still want to talk to you."

"I just told you I'm not the one writing the report anymore."

"It's not about that," she said, then tilted her head. "Well, maybe a little. But I found something out. Something important."

Rickards looked at her and sighed. "Honestly, lady. I don't really care right now."

"You cared this afternoon."

"No, I was just curious."

"And now you're not?"

"Not really." Rickards frowned. "Look, I'm sorry about your grandfather, but my partner was right. Whatever the reason was for him and his friend last night, it's not going to change the conclusion. Pilot error. With a hell of a lot of stupidity thrown in."

"About that," Angela Reed said, inching closer to the door. "May I…come in?"

If she was put off at Rickards' delay in answering, she didn't show it. Instead, she waited patiently until his glowering face reluctantly receded and he opened the door wider.

"Fine."

Angela promptly stepped in from out of the cold, dusting snowflakes from her black coat's thick lapels as Rickards closed the door behind her.

The entryway was neat and empty. Clean, with nothing hanging on the walls. Just a set of light brown stairs leading up, with an accompanying white railing. To the left was the living room, sparsely decorated with a few well-styled pieces of furniture and a single table lamp struggling to light the entire room.

"Am I disturbing you?"

Rickards shook his head and motioned to the couch while moving to an upholstered chair on the opposite side of the barren coffee table.

Angela grinned wryly. "Were you just sitting here in the dark?"

"No. That would be weird."

She laughed at his attempt at humor, then removed her coat and folded it, placing it next to her on the couch as she sat down, along with a small purse.

It was clear Rickards' mood had changed. And not for the better.

"Are you okay?"

He nodded.

"Well, I hope you're still at least curious because I discovered something strange."

"How strange?"

"Strange enough to come here." She reached into her purse and retrieved several folded papers. "Remember the German writing on the papers Lillian gave us?"

"Gave you," he corrected.

"Gave me. Well, I had them translated." She handed him a sheet. "Would you like to read it?"

Rickards blinked and reached out, taking it and flipping it open to read the handwritten text, this time in English.

Easy as it was to conquer the Empire of the Incas, this was not so as regards to the region east of the Andes (known commonly by the designation of La Montana) owing to the impenetrable forests which cover its surfaces.

When he finished, Rickards looked back at Angela with a blank expression. "Am I supposed to know what this is?"

"No. I certainly didn't."

He handed her the paper and eased back against the chair. "This is what you wanted to tell me?"

"I wanted you to see it."

"Because…?"

"Because this is the first piece in what I believe may be a bigger puzzle. And frankly, having someone else see it makes me feel a little less crazy."

"Why is that?"

"Because that text was written by the one and only Percy Fawcett."

"Who?"

"Colonel Percy H. Fawcett," she said. "You've never heard of him?"

"Should I have?"

"Probably not. Sometimes I forget not everyone was raised by an obsessed history professor. Surely you've heard of Indiana Jones."

"From the movies?"

"Yes, from the movies." She nodded. "Played by Harrison Ford. The fictional character of Indiana Jones was based on the *real* character of Colonel Percy Fawcett, a famous British explorer."

Rickards' eyebrows finally rose. "No kidding."

"Colonel Fawcett was a legend around the turn of the century, and arguably one of the greatest explorers of his time. Right up there with Lewis and Clark."

"Those names I've heard of."

"Fawcett was one of the earliest explorers ever to venture into South America and what we know now as the Amazon."

"The rainforest."

She nodded. "Until the turn of the century, very little was known about huge stretches of South America--or the Amazon, where Colonel Fawcett ultimately disappeared in

1925."

"So how is he connected to your grandfather?"

"This paragraph, copied from Percy Fawcett's own writing, was in the letter my great-uncle sent to my grandfather. But it was written in German."

"Okay?"

"I'm wondering if it was some kind of message. To my grandfather."

Rickards shrugged. "It talks about the Incas."

"I don't think that's it. As far as I can tell, it's a small fragment from a book Fawcett wrote about some of his exploits. I looked it up. The rest of the page this came from just talks about how dangerous the area was at the time."

"So, you're wondering why your uncle would send that quote to his younger brother."

"Exactly."

Rickards thought for a moment. "Well, the other piece of paper was telling him to come quickly. Maybe that paragraph was his way of saying 'be careful.'"

"Maybe," she mulled. "But Fawcett was talking about Brazil in his book. My uncle's letter was sent from Peru. They're on opposite sides of the continent. And if that was true, why would he cite something from Fawcett's book instead of just saying *be careful?*"

"Beats me."

After a long silence, Rickards reluctantly asked, "You still don't know when the letter was sent?"

"No."

"Maybe you should find out."

She studied another of the pages, the copy of the envelope itself. "I don't know how I would do that."

"I may know someone who can help."

"Really?"

"He's a friend at the post office."

"Can the post office figure out when it was sent?"

"I don't know. But this isn't just anyone," Rickards replied. "He's an investigator. A specialist in things like this."

"Do you think a date might reveal something?"

He tilted his head, his eyes gradually growing less indifferent. "It might. If nothing else, it may shed some light on what could be the more interesting question: Why was this guy Fawcett's quote, from his own book, transcribed into German?"

17

The casa, or *house* in English, was small by most standards, even for Puerto Maldonado, Peru. But it was more than enough for a young, single man in his thirties, though this was something Andre Lopez was hoping to rectify soon. He was following loosely in the footsteps of his father by being engaged to a woman living several hundred kilometers away, working her residency in one of Peru's state-run hospitals.

The casa was not much, but Katia loved it and thought it had charm, her way of saying *potential*. Meaning something to be improved upon. This didn't bother Lopez in the slightest. It was his pleasure, his honor, to build Katia a castle. Even from the inside out.

Still outside, Lopez unlocked the door and reached to retrieve the bag he had set down. Pushing the front door open with a foot, he stepped inside into a darkened interior with old tiled flooring. The room instantly provided a cool respite from the early evening heat.

Bumping the door closed behind him, he sauntered down the narrow hallway into the kitchen, where sheets of plastic covered the kitchen floor. Cupboard doors were removed and the frames sported a fresh coat of yellow paint, giving the room a noticeably lighter feel. Next would come the doors, then counter and sink, and eventually the floor.

Lopez experienced a pleasant feeling every time he looked over the disarray of his kitchen. After absently putting away groceries in the small refrigerator, he turned toward his bedroom to change out of his clean clothes.

He stopped abruptly.

In the small room opposite the kitchen sat his office, neatly packed with most of the items from his cupboards. But the room looked different.

It took Lopez a moment to notice what was missing. His computer. His *entire* computer, from beneath his desk, leaving a web of tangled cables resting on the dusty tile floor.

He blinked, momentarily unsure of what he was seeing until after several seconds, he stepped forward and peered more intently at the floor.

"*Qué*—" was all he managed, when suddenly, he spotted a person standing to the side and nearly jumped out of his skin. Lopez's eyes bulged as he instantly stumbled back, looking for a weapon. "*Vete! VETE!*" he screamed, turning and finding his hammer behind him.

The other man remained as calm as ice as he watched Lopez stumble around one edge of the doorway, dodging for safety.

"*Sal de aquí!*"

Still, the man dressed in plain clothes did not move, just stared intensely through cold blue eyes. Finally, as Lopez continued to scream, the man raised his hand and placed a finger over his lips.

Lopez frantically looked back down the hallway. Seeing no one else, he switched to the other side of the doorway, pointing his hammer at the intruder.

"*Silencio,*" the stranger said, lowering his hand. With the other, he deliberately raised a black gun with an unusually long barrel.

Lopez froze when he heard someone behind him.

18

The dark hood was ripped off in one forceful motion, instantly exposing Lopez to the bright room and glaring lights overhead. A tuft of his hair stuck straight up and a trickle of blood had dried beneath his left nostril.

He looked around fearfully before his gaze settled on the table directly before him.

Long and clean, with a single person sitting at the other end.

The man was old. Very old. Perhaps in his eighties, with little of his white hair remaining. He had a lean face, with tan, taut skin that left little imagination as to what his skeleton would look like.

To Lopez's right, one of the men he'd seen at his casa emerged and stood to the side as if waiting for instructions.

"*Qué está pasando?*" Lopez mumbled, almost crying.

The old man showed no expression and spoke slowly.

"I know you speak English," he replied in an unfamiliar accent.

Lopez's jaw trembled. "A little."

"Your name is Andre Lopez?"

"*Sí*," he mumbled. "Yes." He looked pleadingly at the man standing nearby. "What...did I do? I don't know."

The old man calmly stared at him, still without expression. "You are not here because of what you did. You are here because of what you know."

Still frantic, Lopez looked back and forth between them. "I don't know anything! I swear it!"

The old man stared at him, uncaring, and then turned in his seat to a door behind him, which was as featureless as the wall and the rest of the room, except for a single doorknob.

The old man snapped his fingers and the door quickly opened. The other man from Lopez's house appeared and extended something. The old man took the object and let the door close again.

It appeared to be a computer tablet.

The man inhaled but said nothing as he studied the screen, flicking lightly with his finger.

"This is information from your home computer," he said. "And it says you were doing some research."

"What…what research?"

"You were looking for something."

"I don't," Lopez stammered, "I don't know what you mean."

"You were searching for something rather specific two months ago. Ring a bell?"

Lopez was desperately trying to remember. "I don't know."

The old man peered over the screen in his hands. "Yes, you do." He glanced at the other man, who moved back behind Lopez.

"I don't! I swear I don't know what you are talking about!"

"Where do you work?" the man asked.

Lopez jumped at the chance to tell him something. Anything. "For the government. In Puerto Maldonado!" He paused, trying to think of the right words, settling on, "Planning jobs."

"Then tell me, Mr. Lopez. What happened two months ago?"

"I…I don't know." He clenched his jaw. With his arms bound, he was nervous at not being able to see the man behind him. "I will tell you everything I know if you tell me what you are talking about!"

"Did you receive or come across something unusual?"

"I don't—" Lopez suddenly paused.

"Perhaps something," the old man continued, "written in German?"

Andre Lopez became still, quickly thinking back. *Could that be it?*

"L-letters," he stuttered.

The old man's expression finally showed a hint of emotion. "Letters?"

"Yes. Yes! Very old letters. From a…" He didn't have the words in English. "*Oficina postal.*"

The old man looked at the man behind Lopez. He had shoulder-length dark hair and a grizzled chin. "Post office," the man translated.

"Old letters from a post office. Where?"

"In Alerta!" Lopez blurted.

***

The old man stepped outside into a bright but fading sun. The afternoon heat was still as heavy in the air as a thick blanket, causing his aged system to begin sweating again in the several steps it took to reach the waiting car—a gleaming black Town Car. He gratefully sank into the soft leather seat, instantly relieved by the interior's air conditioning.

The door was quickly closed behind him, causing him to glance back and view several of the locals who were inching forward, squinting, trying to see who it was inside the government car.

Another man, in his sixties and dressed in a Peruvian uniform, was already waiting inside the car, and raised a glass to his lips as he watched the old German pick something off his slacks with aged, spotted fingers.

"I told you."

The old man stared back with an expression impossible to read, a gesture with which he had become an expert. Something of which he'd been forced to become an expert at. *How many years has it been now? Sixty?*

Six decades…searching for something without allowing anyone else to know what it was. Not granting anyone the ability to know more than was absolutely necessary. Only the smallest bits of information, so nothing could be pieced together.

All for what appeared to be a hopeless mission.

An utterly fruitless pursuit spanning most of his adult life. Half from desire, half loyalty. And all for something that would likely never be found.

There were only three copies in existence. Copies of something that was beyond extraordinary. So incredible, in fact, that at least one of them simply had to resurface.

Eventually.

Because they would be dearly protected by anyone who had the faintest understanding of what they were. Or even a fraction of what they meant.

"You were correct." The old man finally nodded and retrieved a handkerchief from his pocket, dabbing his forehead. "And you will be paid for it."

The officer grinned and tipped his glass of scotch.

"After which, you will retire and leave the continent."

The man froze, staring over the top of the fine crystal. "The continent?"

"Correct."

"You said no communication."

"That's right," the German said. "And I require assurance."

The look of surprise on the officer's face eventually faded before he finally nodded. "Fine."

It would be well worth it, the officer mused. Besides, he knew nothing lasted forever, especially given how old this employer was.

The car pulled forward and smoothly accelerated, prompting the old man to reach back for the seat belt, pulling it over his lean chest and securing it with a click.

He had waited a lifetime for this. Sifting through

hundreds of false leads which had proved one by one to be no more than ghosts in the end, leaving him embittered and hopeless, sure that what he longed for would never resurface again within his waning lifetime.

But someday it would. Of that he was sure. At least one of them. No doubt long after he was dead. Falling into a new set of hands, and then another, until someone was bright enough to put things together.

The steady aging of the document, combined with German writing, would be enough to make someone curious enough to search for the text online, eventually using enough of the exact German wording to separate it from the millions of searches of similar variations or coincidental fragments. After all, a sentence in any language with more than twenty words was virtually guaranteed to be unique enough to isolate it from the minutiae.

And that's what he had been waiting for.

The old man had paid good money to a well-known German hacking group to monitor thousands of servers and networks around the globe for the exact phrasing. Phone calls, text messages, search engines. All digital channels for modern eavesdropping. The old man was no expert, but he knew people who were. And they assured him that if enough of those exact words were entered, their software would spot it.

It was his last-ditch effort--a desperate, even paltry attempt to learn whether anyone would find one of the copies before he took his last breath. Which was not far off. But he never imagined the tip he was hoping for would come from a city worker in tiny Puerto Maldonado, Peru, a region he considered to be one of the armpits of the world.

The car accelerated again, passing through a busy intersection with dozens of poor Peruvians milling about, working meager jobs and living miserable lives. Wearing faces dirtier than their clothes, convinced they somehow mattered in the world, in this tiny, meaningless place.

He hated South America. A filthy, utterly impoverished

existence barely a step up from Africa. A place in which he hated spending time. A place that could never hold a candle to the pristine beauty and rich culture of Europe.

It was an extreme irony the old man was now being forced to endure that very thing. *One of the areas he abhorred the most, being the place his lifelong search had finally turned up.*

19

The nearest metropolitan airport, if he could call it that, was over the Bolivian border in La Paz, a slightly less abhorrent locale and fifteen hours away by car. Almost half the distance it would have been to Lima. Making him hate Puerto Maldonado even more for its isolation.

But a man like him flying into such a small town would have attracted far too much attention, forcing him to instead land in La Paz and make the long trek by car, all the while being assured by the officer sitting across from him that the city worker Lopez was a legitimate mark.

Of course, it had been worth it. A total of thirty hours in a car was an easy trade for sixty long years of his life, giving the old man plenty of time to think, and even smile, about what to do next.

"What are your instructions, Señor Bauer?"

The old man almost didn't respond. Deep in thought, he had forgotten the Peruvian officer did not know his real name.

"What?"

"How are we to proceed?"

For the first time in years, the elderly German found himself caught slightly off guard. Not by the other man emptying another bottle of scotch single-handedly, but by the revelation. Even though he had been assured it was legitimate, the German was expecting it to be another false lead. And now that it appeared real, he had to think...carefully.

The officer across from him was named Fernandez. A common Spanish surname in Peru, dating back to the decree of Phillip II in 1568. Though this Fernandez was different than most. A former colonel in Peru's national intelligence service, he now worked outside of an official office or department, reporting directly, and covertly, to the Peruvian president's intelligence council--when he wasn't selling his talents and knowledge elsewhere.

Fernandez was a deeply corrupt man, but extraordinarily useful--at least to the old man he was addressing as Bauer, who now sat quietly staring back at him, contemplating the question. There was so much to do now. The information they had gleaned from the peasant Lopez was just the tip of the iceberg.

"Orders?" Fernandez asked again, now that he had his attention.

"Give me time," he replied.

Fernandez still had a role to play. For some time. Until he too had to be silenced. But he had several more weeks, at least. Far better than Lopez, whose body should have already been disposed of by now. The old man briefly wondered just how many vital secrets throughout history had been permanently sealed through death.

20

Joe Rickards studied the paper again, then peered

curiously at Angela. "Why do you think the passage in the letter was written in German?"

"I have no idea." She shrugged.

"Did your great-uncle speak German?"

"A little. Taught to him by the Army before being sent over with the rest of his group."

Rickards kept thinking.

"Do you really think the date of the letter is that important?" she asked.

Now it was his turn to shrug. "I don't know. But it seems a little coincidental."

"Coincidental?"

"That something of such importance happened in South America, at least as far as your grandfather was concerned, could possibly be related to that German passage."

"Why do you say that?"

"Because South America was where a lot of the Nazis escaped to after the Second World War."

"That was Argentina. With the Peróns."

"A lot of them went to Argentina. But some ended up in other South American countries."

Angela thought for a moment. "I forgot about that. You think it's somehow connected?"

"No idea. I just said it was coincidental. Unless the letter was sent before the end of the war, in which case maybe there's no connection at all."

Angela nodded and turned to look out the side window of Rickards' car. They were parked, and the corners were already forming bits of frost on the other side of the glass. "I feel like we're on a stakeout."

"We're not on a stakeout."

"I know. It just feels like it. Sitting in an empty parking lot, in the dark, waiting."

"You must watch a lot of TV."

Angela laughed. "I do."

Rickards peered out the windshield pensively. Denver's main facility on 53rd looked more like a giant warehouse than a postal center. Dozens of large USPS semitrailer trucks lined the outskirts of the huge lot, all parked neatly at 45-degree angles. The building itself was bathed in an ambient glow of bright overhead LED lamps with a long wall of enormous shipping doors all closed tight. Above them, but beneath the black roof, was a row of long rectangular windows stretching the entire length of the building, all illuminated brightly from within by the center's interior lights.

Outside and closer to the giant building, Rickards and Angela sat, watching employees occasionally exit from a side entrance.

"When is he supposed to be here?"

"Any time."

"And how do you know him?"

"He's helped me with a few other investigations. A while ago. Don't worry, you'll like him."

"What does that mean?"

Rickards frowned. "What does what mean? The word *like*?"

"No. That *I'd* like him."

Rickards grinned. "Because everyone does."

She let it go and looked around again, glancing at the giant gray doors lining the face of the building. "He's a postal inspector?"

Rickards nodded. "And then some."

Angela turned to him with a sarcastic grin. "Anyone ever tell you that you're a hard man to get to know?"

He reached for his paper coffee cup and took a sip. "Everyone."

"Do you have any kids?"

He paused before answering. "No."

"Married?"

"Next question."

"Where'd you grow up?"

"Milwaukee."

"Wisconsin?"

66

"Mm-hm."

"How'd you come to work for the NTSB?"

"I was trying out for the FBI. After college."

"And?"

"Had trouble with the fitness test. It appears I have some bone spurs. I scored well enough on the rest that I got a recommendation from one of the officers to the NTSB."

"So, no running with this job."

She was surprised when he laughed. "Not generally."

Rickards changed the subject before she could ask another. "And you?"

"Kind of boring," she said. "Archaeologist turned cultural anthropologist. Lived here my whole life."

"And raised by your grandfather?"

"Yes."

"How come?"

Her face drew tight. "My mother died when I was young. During childbirth."

"Having you?"

Angela nodded.

"I'm sorry to hear that," Rickards said, peering through the windshield.

"Thanks. Fortunately, there's not a lot of pain there since I never knew her."

"And that's fortunate?"

"Well, probably more regret than anything else. At never having the chance to meet her."

Rickards nodded silently.

"I was raised by my grandmother and grandfather. And I actually had a great life. I also like horses, pizza and watching TV."

Rickards managed a brief grin. "So, what do you think the letter means from your grandfather's older brother?"

Angela inhaled, contemplating. "Honestly, I still don't know what to make of it. I keep playing different scenarios over and over in my head."

"Like that paragraph in German?"

"That's one of them. My guess is that it's some kind of cryptic message. Why else would he put it in there? Maybe something from an old Nazi project referencing the Incas. Hitler was a nut about all kinds of things."

"But you said the paragraph was a quote from that guy Fawcett's book."

"Yes."

"That was written before the war?"

"Long before."

"Seems strange," Rickards said, taking another sip of his coffee, "that the Germans would use something like this as one of their codes. A reference maybe, but a code?"

"And then there's the bigger question of how my uncle came to be classified as dead by the Army when he was really in South America."

"Secret mission, maybe?"

"There was no U.S. Army presence in South America during World War II. I checked. In fact, most of those countries didn't follow the world's lead and declare war on the Axis powers until 1945. And Brazil was the only one to ever send troops. So there wasn't anything happening in South America until after the war, when the Nazis were looking for a place in which to vanish."

"Enter Argentina."

"Exactly."

"Then why would your uncle be there?"

She shook her head. "I think it all depends on *when* he was there. Because if he was there after the war, that could mean the Army may not have been involved at all."

"But that would mean he was there on his own accord."

"Potentially."

"Which means..."

"That he *wanted* to go there."

Rickards gave her a doubtful look.

"What if," she said slowly, "he wanted them to *think* he was dead?"

Rickards blinked and leaned back again.

"Think about what the Monuments team was doing there--searching for some of the most important and most sacred artifacts in all of human history."

"You think he found something." It was a statement, not a question.

"Does that sound crazy?"

"No crazier than everything else that's happened so far."

Rickards glanced up at a pair of approaching headlights, winding around a row of parked cars before pulling up into one of the open spots near the building, not far from them.

The driver's side door opened and a man of average height stepped out, dressed in a thick blue coat and red knit cap. He immediately saw them and pushed the door shut, covering the short distance and smiling at the sight of Rickards climbing out of his car to meet him.

"Nice night for a stakeout," he said, smiling.

Rickards looked sarcastically at Angela, who was grinning. He rounded the car and shook the younger man's hand. "Ken, meet Dr. Angela Reed. Angela, the one and only Ken Stives."

"Come on now." Ken shook his head, revealing a handsome smile below a set of green eyes and dark eyelashes. "You'd think I pay this guy or something."

"Thank you for meeting us." Angela reached out and shook the young man's hand. He was attractive and relaxed in appearance, and much younger than she expected.

"My pleasure," Ken said. "It's the least I can do for Joe."

"Don't believe it," Rickards said coolly. "He owes me a favor."

"That's true. Now come on, let's get inside."

The place appeared even larger from the inside. It was packed floor to ceiling with giant bins, large metal shelving units, what Angela guessed to be hundreds of giant bags of mail and thousands of brown boxes.

Farther in were absolutely enormous machines

stretching as far as she could see, with thousands of parcels moving along belts and rails almost too fast to follow. And among them, countless uniforms of men and women moving in and out, attending to the machines or piles of mail which were being pushed around in mobile bins.

The two followed Stives as he walked along an endless row of towering metal shelves before ducking down a small aisle to a flight of stairs. There, heading up to a second floor, they found dozens of offices and administrative cubicles stretching toward the front of the building.

Down one aisle and after a sharp turn, they reached a small, nondescript door displaying Ken's name on a thin brown placard.

Stives glanced over his shoulder while unlocking the door. "Welcome to the Jungle."

Jungle was apt, if perhaps a bit overstated. His office was messy, but still retained a faint hint of organization. Stacks of papers, interspersed with letters, and packages, littered every available surface, including two desks, two tables and a tall double-wide filing cabinet.

"Looks cleaner than last time."

"Really?"

"No. Not at all."

The younger man frowned at Angela. "I'm pretty sure I'm the only one who takes his calls anymore."

With that, he emptied two chairs of their papers and walked around the larger desk to sit down. "All right, so what do you guys have?"

Rickards turned to Angela, who fished the photocopy from her purse, allowing Stives to study it.

"Do you have the original envelope?"

"No."

He nodded and opened a window on his computer screen, then typed the addressee's name. *Gerald Reed.* When a screen filled with information, he began reading.

"Hmm."

"What?"

"Just reading some notes. Looks like we had to track down your grandfather to deliver this. Says here, this came in a larger envelope postmarked from Puerto Maldonado." He glanced back. "Isn't there a baseball player named Maldonado?"

"On the Astros."

Stives nodded and continued reading. "The sender's name was Lopez. Andre Lopez. Departamento de Servicios Generales."

"What does that mean?"

"Department of General Services," answered Angela.

Stives turned back to her piece of paper. "I'm not sure what we can glean from a copy. With the original letter, we could take UV and chemical samples. But not with this." He pulled a magnifying lens closer and flipped on its light, using it to study the paper. "Doesn't look like a very good copy, either. Did Joe take it?" he asked with a grin.

"No. My grandfather did."

Stives nodded, then pulled the paper in closer and back out multiple times. "Well, the postmark is barely visible. And only partly at that. Not enough to make out a date."

"No dice?"

"I didn't say that," he replied, staring at the corner of the image. "If we can't scan it, we still have our powers of deduction." He grabbed the computer mouse, then logged into the postal database. "What we can see pretty well is the stamp."

"Do you recognize it?"

"No. But we should be able to find it. There are dozens of historical collections cataloging stamps from all over the world. Even from countries that no longer exist. The Stanley Gibbons Catalogue, for example. But those were of the earliest stamps, back in the 1800s. Today most have been put into computer databases." Stives continued typing, then switched to his mouse when he found the correct listing. He began scrolling. "Peru...Peru..."

His mouse suddenly slowed. "Okay, here we are." He studied the stamp on the photocopy again and returned to his screen. "This looks like your stamp. A dedication to the very first postage stamp of Peru. Circulation 1957."

Angela and Rickards looked at each other.

"Are you sure?"

"That's what it says." He turned his screen so they could see. "The original is in color, but you can see it's the same one."

"And it was issued in 1957?"

"No. It was in circulation in 1957. It could have been issued up to a few years before that. And probably used for at least a decade after, as the currency slowly lost value. I seem to remember reading that Peru suffered from hyperinflation sometime in the eighties." He switched windows and ran a search in his browser. "Yep. Look at that. 1985."

"What's hyperinflation?"

"It's when a country's debt finally catches up with its currency, first causing inflation, followed by very high inflation, then finally hyperinflation. Usually takes a few years to play out, but when hyperinflation finally hits, it goes quickly. Just like what's happening now in Venezuela."

"And then what?"

"They replace the currency," Stives replied. "In Peru, the sol was replaced with the inti. And they started over. It happens a lot more often than people think."

Angela picked up her photocopy and studied the tiny image of the stamp. "This was in their original currency."

"Yep."

Rickards folded his arms, peering at the screen. "So chances are this letter was sent around that time?"

"Correct. Most currencies lose a certain amount of value every year. More now than in the old days. Which is why there are clearer usage trends when it comes to stamps. Used more when they're first issued and less and less over time as postage rates increase. If I had to guess, I would say your letter was most likely sent sometime between 1955 and 1960. For anything more exact, we would need the original envelope itself."

"Right."

"So," Stives said, swiveling around in his chair. "You guys gonna tell me what was in the envelope?"

Rickards glanced at Angela. "We're working on that part."

21

The female customs agent studied the German passport carefully before looking up to study the man's features again. Middle-aged, average height and build. Somewhat attractive despite a strong, oversized Roman nose. The man bore a pleasant expression, peering through the bulletproof glass with a pair of gray eyes surrounded by a dozen wrinkles. Waiting. Patiently.

"What's the purpose of your stay, Mr. Fischer?"

"Business."

"And what sort of business are you in?"

"Finance. My company has several American branches here."

The woman glanced at the briefcase clutched in the man's left hand, then slowly reached for her stamp. "How long are you staying?"

"Just until Friday," he replied with only a hint of an accent. Never losing his smile. "Too cold, I'm afraid, for anything longer."

"And where are you staying?"

"The Embassy Suites near the convention center."

She nodded through the glass and let her right hand hover briefly over the passport before finally dropping and stamping the small page. Her eyes remained friendly but attentive while she slid the passport back to him through the opening. "Enjoy your stay."

"Thank you."

He took the passport and slipped it back into his suit's vest pocket. He did not linger, nor did he move too quickly. Nervousness was an easy tip-off, and one any decent immigration agent would be watching for.

Instead, he continued forward, casually relaxed, with briefcase in hand, passing through the double doors in front of him along with several other passengers.

Outside, the full breadth of Denver International Airport instantly enveloped him with the building's massive, stunning design. High overhead, a ceiling of giant, sculpted white canopies stretched into the air, both artfully mimicking the state's snowcapped Rocky Mountains and providing homage to Native American Teepees from centuries past, flooding the entire terminal with bright morning sunshine.

But unlike most other passengers, Fischer barely looked around, instead walking directly toward the baggage claim where his carousel had just begun moving.

The immigration system would soon link him to the corporation and his hotel. But that was as far as it would go. There was nothing even remotely suspicious under his passport to flag anything with their computers. No recent, unusual destinations, no intelligence or social connections to persons of interest, and nothing else in the public domain or other media sites. Nothing to prevent their automated system from quickly moving on to the tens of thousands of other passengers traveling through Denver International that day.

There would be absolutely nothing to link Fischer to anything at all--until, of course, he had already left. And even then, it was highly unlikely.

This was not Fischer's first rodeo, as the Americans liked to say. He had made many such trips throughout his career, under different names, circumstances and slightly different appearances. That was something which was becoming increasingly more difficult to do with tracking techniques like the FBI's facial recognition systems in place. America, China and even the Russians were doing it. Analyzing and recording millions of faces in thousands of locations every year. Quietly, and with cameras that went largely unseen to the human eye.

Soon they would be everywhere, giving Fischer yet another reason to be relieved this whole mission was finally near its end. At least according to the man who had employed him for all these years.

It was astonishing, really, especially since Fischer didn't think the old man would survive much longer. Death couldn't be more than a few years away. At most.

But evidently, he had finally located what he'd been looking for. Or so he'd said.

To Fischer, it made no difference whatsoever. He was merely doing his job. *On the clock*, to borrow another American term. He didn't care whether the old man was right or not. All he cared about was when the funds would appear in his account and how soon he could walk away from all of this, spending the rest of his days sipping wine in the peaceful sprawling vineyards of Tuscany beneath a melting orange sunset.

No, he was not an assassin. Which, frankly, was little more than a cultural caricature now, anyway. Mindless sheep, all watching the same movies and television shows displaying stories about how mindless sheep thought these things worked.

But it wasn't anything of the sort. Fischer had no gun. No long blades or killing instruments. Nothing that could be identified or tracked in the blink of an eye. No high-tech electronics to cripple a building's security system or synchronize some elaborate detonation sequence. He had nothing.

Because he didn't need anything.

Fischer was no assassin. Not specifically. His job was much more general than that, yet specialized at the same time. If anything, he was more of an extractor, of whatever needed to be extracted, and by whatever means necessary, be it information, possessions or the risk of someone talking. Fischer would merely learn and secure what he needed to, regardless of how he did it.

He carried nothing because the extent that he needed to go along with the resulting outcome was almost entirely dependent on the target and their environment when he found them. It was all about improvisation. Something, even Fischer had to admit, he had become exceedingly efficient at.

Because he always found them.

22

Upon retrieving his bag, Fischer left the area and stopped before a wall of glass windows near the airport's exit, where he summoned an Uber car from a prepaid phone, purchased in cash with an untraceable credit card.

Ironic, really. As wholly digital as the world had become and how easy it was to trace everything and everyone, the onerousness of that same system had in many ways achieved exactly the opposite of its intended result.

Thanks to organizations like the FBI, NSA and CIA, as well as private corporations such as Google and Apple, everything was being captured. Not just personal information, but *everything*. Every scrap of human information and activity. Every place, every parcel, every byte, at every location. All tracked and logged and permanently saved in gargantuan datacenters with almost unlimited storage. All supposedly in a greater effort to make the world not just more efficient, but safer.

But with every strength came a proportionally opposite weakness. A vulnerability that could be exploited and used. The modern systems were no different. Because ultimately, in all of that colossal amount of data, resided the same simple dependencies that linked their purposes together in the first place.

Humans. Or more specifically, human labor.

All the information in the world still required someone to make sense of it. To analyze. To study and derive real and accurate meaning. Even those who worked tirelessly to eliminate that human variable with things like artificial intelligence remained dismissive that even the smartest computer programs ultimately still needed human brains and hands to program, test and maintain them.

The wondrousness of *unlimited* information had now become *too* much information. Yes, passports and cell phones could be tracked and eventually pinpointed. Credit cards, driver's licenses, electronic devices, even automobiles.

Unless those targeted items continually changed. Unless they were routinely being rotated, creating endless problems for the trackers who had to then find out what the next related credit card number was, what the next street bought phone number was, or the newly fabricated name, all swirling endlessly in a never ending expansion of more data.

Every time a variable changed a human brain would eventually be required to verify whether the links were valid. To analyze yet another routine in a computer search algorithm.

As the cloud of digital tracking grew infinitely larger, Fischer knew it was just as quickly making things vastly more complicated, allowing someone like him who understood it to become lost in an increasingly hopeless game of *Where's Waldo.*

His car arrived less than two minutes later. A white Ford, driven by a pleasant man in his sixties with a Korean accent whose conversation was promptly stifled by Fischer's visible lack of interest.

Instead, in the back seat, he studied the phone to ensure he had completely memorized the information so the device could be discarded when necessary.

One way or another, everything was tracked. If not with a barcode, then by some other means. Which was another irony of modernization. If governments and corporations could track everything, so could the people Fischer worked for. With the right access, and the right system...anyone could be found.

23

Through a wide window, Angela watched Rickards traverse the sodden, muddy parking lot and step over an icy puddle less than ten feet from the door. Once inside the diner, he scanned the large room until he found her waiting in a vinyl-padded booth with a cup of coffee in front of her.

Winding between tables to reach her, he removed his coat, revealing a larger than average frame, relatively well-built, but reflecting a certain physical demeanor.

Something that felt almost...surly. Or perhaps morose. Or something else. She couldn't decide.

Rickards looked down and noticed the second coffee cup.

"Thank you."

"I thought we could both use one."

He sat heavily and took an appreciative drink.

"How'd you sleep?" she asked.

"Okay. You?"

Angela raised her own mug. "Didn't get much myself. I can't seem to turn my brain off."

"Think of anything new?"

She stared at him for a moment. "Think. No. Find? Yes."

"What does that mean?"

"Are you sure you want to know?"

Rickards scowled, still gripping his coffee cup.

"I take it you don't like suspense." With that, she turned and unzipped her purse, pulling out two envelopes and dropping them on the table.

"What's this?"

"Two more letters. Postcards actually. From my great-uncle, shortly after he joined the Monuments Men and went to Europe."

"To your grandfather?"

"No. These were addressed to my *great*-grandmother. His and my grandfather's mother. I found them in my grandmother's old boxes. They must have been passed down."

Rickards looked curious. "And?"

"Nothing special. Just the standard *Hi Mom, I'm okay. Everything is fine in Europe* letters."

He reached out, opened the top envelope's flap and slid the card out to read.

"I didn't see anything useful in them. Except..."

Rickards' gaze captured hers. "Except?"

A grin crept back across her face. "Except for the handwriting. The handwriting matches what turned up in the mail for my grandfather a few weeks ago."

She added the photographed copy to the pile in front of Rickards so he could compare.

"I'm no expert, but I'd bet dollars to doughnuts that's a match."

"Dollars to doughnuts?"

"My grandfather used to say it." When Rickards' expression didn't change, she folded her arms. "It's a thing!"

"So, does this mean you're officially a believer?"

"I think so. Yes," she corrected. "It does."

"So, what now?"

"I'm not sure."

The two sat staring at each other silently, until Rickards' phone rang from his front pocket. He answered, his attention still on the letters in front of him.

"Hello, Ken."

After a moment, his gaze became still.

"Yes. She's here with me now. We're having dollars and doughnuts."

Rickards paused again, this time much longer. His eyes moved to Angela. "Are you sure?"

The last pause was almost a full minute. "Okay. Thanks. I'll pass it on."

He glanced down to end the call before looking back up, finding Angela impatiently waiting.

"In case you hadn't guessed, that was Ken Stives. He said he found out something interesting."

She shrugged as if to say, *What are you waiting for?*

"Ken said he tracked down the mail carrier who delivered the letter to your grandfather."

"Really?"

"He talked to him this morning."

"And?"

"The man remembered your grandfather. Distinctly."

"He did?"

"Not surprisingly, your grandfather was pretty shocked to get that letter," Rickards said, nodding at the photocopy.

"Did my grandfather say anything to him?"

"Not at first. But the carrier said your grandfather had difficulty calming down. And when he finally opened it, the carrier said he went silent on him pretty quickly."

"Silent."

"Uh-huh. Until…"

Angela's eyes widened even further. "Until? Until what? What are you waiting for?"

A small grin emerged from Rickards. "What's wrong, you don't like suspense?"

She got the joke and scowled. "Fine. I'm sorry. Tell me!"

"Ken says that your grandfather only started talking again when the carrier mentioned he'd noticed something interesting about the envelope. The one we don't have."

"Something about the envelope? What?"

"This carrier told your grandfather that it looked as if the letter had already been opened. And resealed."

24

Angela sat still, pensive, thinking about what Rickards had just said. If the letter had already been opened, what did that mean? And when had it been opened? Fifty years ago, or more recently? Either way, she was sure it would have only exacerbated her grandfather's sense of urgency.

Across from her, Rickards broke the silence. "Are you going?"

"What?"

"I said, are you going?"

"Going where?"

"To Peru."

"No, I'm not going to Peru!"

"Why not?"

"I—I don't," she stammered. "I mean…what? No! No,

I'm not going to Peru. I'm just…I'm trying to understand what happened and why. Not run halfway around the world."

Rickards shrugged with coffee cup in hand. "I disagree. I think you have long passed trying to understand what happened. You're now firmly into *why*."

"What makes you say that?"

"Because I have two eyes. And can fog a mirror."

She did not answer.

"Anyone can see it. You want to know *why*. It's what we all want eventually. Knowing *what* is never enough."

"Even investigators?"

He nodded. "Especially investigators."

With a furrowed brow, she slowly began shaking her head. "I can't go. For one, I have a job."

"You work for a university. I'm sure you could get some bereavement leave."

"And two," she continued, "is that I don't exactly like to travel."

"You don't like to travel?"

"No." She leaned back in her seat against the vinyl backrest. "I don't do well traveling."

"What does that mean?"

"It means I *don't do well*."

"I thought most women liked to travel."

"Not all."

"What happens if you travel, do you explode or something?"

"Very funny. It's not that I can't. It's that," she paused, visibly struggling. "I can't."

Rickards took a sip of his coffee. "Well, that clears it up."

"I know. I know. It's just…not…easy for me."

"To travel?"

"No! To tell you…*why*."

Rickards leaned back in his own seat against the squeaking vinyl. Angela was suddenly very uncomfortable. And he had no desire to push her.

"You don't have to tell me anything. Everyone has their own issues and I'm not trying to get into your head. Whatever your reason is, I'm sure it's valid."

"It's not you. I just—" She stopped and took a breath.

"I shouldn't have said anything. It's really none of my business. I just don't know how much more you can learn about this letter from here."

"What do you think happened?"

"To your uncle? I have no idea. But I think I believe you about him writing that letter. *Why* is the real question."

Angela frowned, thoughtfully. "What would you do?"

"What would I do about what?"

"Would you go?"

Rickards shook his head. "This is not about me."

"But if it was, would you go?"

"I don't know. The reason for him sending it appears to be somewhere in Peru. But on the other hand, any details surrounding that letter sixty years ago are probably long gone."

"What if there really was a secret mission?" she asked. "The Nazis had secret missions all over the place, all the way to Antarctica. What if the Monuments team found something, or even discovered that some Nazis had carted off something important with them to South America?"

Rickards considered it. "It's a possibility."

"What if there was a small part of the Monuments Men team who didn't go back with the others, but continued to South America after the end of the war?"

"Also possible."

"And my uncle somehow died in the process? But not before he got a letter off to his brother. Which, for some inexplicable reason, disappeared for half a century."

"It's a plausible scenario."

She paused for a long time before taking a deep breath. "Listen, the reason I don't travel well has to do with why I switched my focus."

"Switched your focus?"

"From archaeology to anthropology a little over ten years ago."

"Angela," Rickards said, "you don't have to explain anything."

It was the first time he'd called her by her first name.

"No. I want to tell you this. I need to. I need to tell someone."

"Angela. Really—"

She cut him off. "Just…let me finish. I know what you're going to say. We've known each other for what, three whole days?" She sighed. "For some reason, I think it feels easier to tell someone I don't know very well."

Her eyes fell to the cheaply made laminated table between them, her hand reaching forward and fingering a small chip in the veneer. "Just a few years after finishing my degree, I was part of an archaeological dig in Bolivia. Just outside of Tiwanaku. I was in a small group of fifteen Americans who'd joined a Bolivian team for a three-month research excavation. Not my first, but probably my most exciting.

"I was one of seven women on our team, along with eight men. Mostly graduates like me, with a few grad students and two professors. Living conditions were not exactly the Ritz but we were used to that. Living in tents since most digs tend to be in remote areas."

She took another deep breath. "We were there for almost two months…when we were attacked one night. Out of nowhere."

"By who?"

"We think it was a group of men from a nearby village. They stole most of our equipment, beat up several of the men, including the Bolivian team, and raped some of the female archaeologists."

Across the table, Angela watched as Rickards' eyes narrowed.

"The truth is," she said gravely, "I came very close to being raped myself. Too close. And…it changed me. A lot.

And not for the better. The excitement and sense of adventure that I used to feel being out in the field died. Completely."

Rickards frowned. "Shit."

Angela's eyes began to well. "It's funny. You can spend years cultivating a dream, working toward your goals, turning it into reality. Toward the one thing you think you're meant to do. Only to have it decimated in a single night. In mere *hours*. Leaving you not even wanting to think about that dream again for years."

"I'm sorry," Rickards said.

She feigned a smile. "Thanks. But it's not your fault."

"Doesn't mean I'm not sorry it happened."

"The worst part is that it leaves you hiding a piece of yourself. In shame, from everyone you know. Afraid, and knowing deep down that someday it may somehow seep out."

"You haven't told anyone?"

"I told my grandmother. And a psychiatrist."

He nodded and turned to gaze out through the large window. "Did it help?"

"I guess. I'm functional," she said with a grin.

"We're all functional."

"Probably true. For me, though, it feels as if it's always there."

"I can understand that."

She gently flicked the handle of her coffee cup, turning it slightly. "So, anyway, I went back to school and switched my focus, which was also a passion of mine. It makes it a lot easier to avoid traveling, allowing me to stay here and teach in my own little bubble of safety."

"Is that what caused the rift with your grandfather?"

"No. He knew something had happened to me in Bolivia, but that I didn't want to talk about it. The problem he and I had was with my grandmother. She became sick about a year after I got back, at the same time I had a lot of anger swirling around inside of me.

"When I was losing my grandmother, I began to really see what kind of marriage he had given her. A life filled with his own self-absorption. Correction, self-obsession. All he ever cared about his entire life was finding out what had happened to his brother. He was always studying, always searching. Whenever they traveled, it always had something to do with a place he wanted to investigate. And she always obliged."

"Always?"

"I'm sure she thought his obsession would eventually die out. But it never did. Just always continually about him and the preoccupation with finding out what happened to his brother. The Monuments Men and their—"

She suddenly stopped.

Rickards raised an eyebrow, waiting. When she didn't continue, he looked behind him to see if something was happening. "You okay?"

"That's it."

"What?"

"The Monuments Men."

"What about them?"

Angela blinked and stared excitedly at him. "My grandfather knew absolutely everything about the Monuments Men! He studied and researched them his entire life."

"So…"

"So," she said, "if they *had* been in South America, for any reason, he of all people would have known about it."

25

Flakes of snow blew sideways in the icy wind, making

their long winding journey to Earth before suddenly being whipped up in a frenzy of turbulence near the ground, a few landing and sticking to nearby objects instead of the wide concrete sidewalk.

Hundreds more tiny flakes still caught in the breeze whirled up and around and stuck to the soft fibers of Fischer's heavily lined coat as he stood outside, peering at the nursing home across the street.

A car was necessary. Rented from a small agency, it allowed him to move more freely without being tracked. Car services like Uber tracked each ride through GPS, which created a digital trail that could eventually be traced, if someone were to look in the right direction, even by accident. Far better to risk a credit card connected to a third-rate rental car that was not tracked at all.

To Fischer, the building resembled a hotel more than a nursing home, complete with a covered circular driveway in front and small bus stop near the sidewalk.

Fischer was waiting on the opposite side of the street under a larger building's short overhang, near a single-door entrance to a legal firm, the lettering on the glass indicating a small, one- or two-man operation. The office next to it appeared to be chronically empty.

Fischer was waiting outside to ensure he could see clearly. Or at least as clearly as possible through the falling snowflakes.

According to his sources, the nursing home was the current address of the person to whom the envelope had originally been addressed. A Gerald Reed. Ninety-one years old. A retired war vet who had apparently been killed in a plane crash a few days before.

He glanced at his watch when the person he was waiting for finally emerged from the front entrance of the home, barely ten minutes after speaking to Fischer on the phone and just seconds before her taxi turned and rounded the small driveway. She walked briskly to the car, bundled in a thick black coat and matching headscarf.

The woman's name was Lillian Porter.

A friend of the old man's, the nursing home had referred him to her when he called, posing as an investigative agent. Though the way she spoke of Gerald Reed suggested the two had been more than friends.

His first call had been to get the name of the NTSB agent involved in the airplane crash. A woman named Gutierrez, who during his conversation with her revealed she was one of two investigators originally assigned to the accident. An older agent had apparently left the case for unexplained reasons.

Neither was it difficult to find out who the mail carrier was who had delivered the letter to the old man in the first place. That required only a quick call to the station manager at the post office, posing as a new resident and asking the name of their carrier, leaving no sense of suspicion on the other end of the phone. After all, whoever targeted the messenger?

Now, however, Fischer lingered in the bitter cold, waiting patiently for one simple reason--to see what Lillian Porter looked like.

She was not at all surprised on the phone when he gave her an alias as a reporter working on the case. Her reaction told Fischer she had already spoken with the police or NTSB. Perhaps even the older agent from the case named Rickards. Something he would need to ask her.

"Lord knows the residents have been through enough," were the words he'd used. *"Better to avoid yet another anxiety-ridden visit from the press."*

Fischer stepped back into the law building's entryway as the taxi rounded the remainder of the nursing home's driveway and turned right onto the main street, headed downtown.

When they were out of sight, he stepped out again and quietly walked the thirty or so yards around the corner to where he'd left his rental car.

Choosing what he thought would be the least frequented

coffee shop in the area may have been risky. The Porter woman sounded slightly cautious. But this was to make things easier.

For him.

This wouldn't take long.

26

Angela lowered the first of three cardboard boxes onto her dining room table with a thump. Her grandfather's most important documents, given to her by Lillian Porter before she'd rushed out for something. Which was fine for Angela, given how cool the woman was still acting toward her.

Angela was now alone and able to relax as she sat down and pulled the cover off the first box, sifting one at a time through dozens of old manila folders.

Her grandfather's records were meticulous, spanning his brother's early childhood, friends, schools and education. Then college, his first job at the university, and finally his acceptance letter to be part of the Monuments team in September of 1942. She was unsurprised to see notes from the postcards she'd found in her grandmother's things, and even a few more from her great-uncle from Kassel, Germany, and then later from Innsbruck, Austria.

After an hour and a half of reading, she reached her grandfather's Monuments files, taking up the last third of the first box and some of the second. Thick folders were filled with articles, letters, stories, and, surprisingly, notes from discussions he had received directly from what appeared to be other members of the Monuments team years after their return from the war.

Angela leaned back and stared at the boxes for a long time.

What was she doing? More importantly, what was she prepared to do? Was she really willing to get on a plane? Rickards was right. Anything having to do with this letter was probably long gone. Sixty years was a long time. Hell, almost seventy. Which had to mean her great-uncle was already dead. Maybe long dead. Was whatever he knew really that critical? To anything anymore?

She could feel her blood pressure rising at just the thought of getting on an airplane. Especially going back to Bolivia. She'd spent years trying to forget that horrible event. Trying to put it behind her and focus on a life ahead. Peace. Happiness. Only instead to find that she'd grown more spiteful over her own past, and now her grandfather's.

This whole thing was just so bizarre. So surreal. And now she'd managed to tangle Joe Rickards up in it. Yes, he could make his own decisions, but it was she who'd shown up on his doorstep, almost forcing her way in. Forced a man who was already deeply wounded from God knows what. What kind of person was she to get him tangled up in her mess? Just because he had been interested didn't mean he wanted to be part of it—whatever *it* was. Part of something she wasn't even sure *she* wanted to be part of. But in the end, he was right. Knowing what had happened was not enough. Ultimately, she had to know why.

At eight a.m. the following morning, she did it again. With eyes red from lack of sleep, Angela knocked on the door and waited. After getting no response, she knocked louder and stepped back, crossing her arms in front of her.

It took several minutes for Rickards to answer. He opened the door with a drawn, tired expression, dressed haphazardly in sweatpants and a wrinkled T-shirt.

Angela didn't wait for him to speak. "There was no mission in South America during the war. I'm sure of it. And no Monuments Men reported ever seen outside of Europe. None."

He raised his eyebrows and nodded.

"And yes. I'm going!"

27

The elderly Bauer listened carefully to the cell phone in front of him, hands resting calmly and deliberately over both arms of his chair. His suite in La Paz, Bolivia, where he had spent the last two days waiting for Fischer's call was spacious and opulent. Behind him, the room was furnished with white leather couches and chairs with matching white plush carpet. The picturesque oversized window behind him displayed the rest of the bustling city against a backdrop of the lightly colored Andes Mountains.

Fischer's voice blared loudly over the phone speaker in native German. "Gerald Reed is dead. Killed in a plane crash."

"Confirmed?" If old man Bauer was surprised, he didn't show it.

"Yes. I saw the site myself."

Bauer remained quiet, waiting for more.

"However, it seems he made a copy of his letter and gave it to a female companion."

"Have you retrieved it?"

"Not yet. It has since been given to Reed's granddaughter."

"Do they understand what it is?"

"I'm not sure. The letter was sent by Reed's brother Roger Reed." Fischer paused only slightly before adding,

"He was a member of the American project known as the Monuments Men."

Bauer's eyes widened. "Say that again."

"The sender of the letter was a Monuments Man. One who did not return home with the rest."

Bauer was stunned, immediately leaning in toward the phone. "Impossible!"

"It's true. I have verified. Reed's companion knew much about the brother."

Bauer remained still in his chair. A Monuments Man! From the war. Which meant he must have found something. Perhaps one of the two missing documents. But if so, which one? Bauer had what was left of the third.

"She confirmed he received the letter a few weeks ago. From Peru."

That made it consistent with Lopez's interrogation. The government worker said the letters had been found in an old post office beneath the rotting floorboards. A concept too difficult for Bauer to believe at first. The odds of something so profound being accidentally lost seemed impossible to accept.

But if it was true, when was it originally sent? And what had this Monuments Man found in the troves of German artifacts during the war? More importantly, had he acted alone?

As if reading the old man's mind, Fischer answered his question. "The woman thinks the sender, his brother, was acting alone."

"How do you know?"

"There was no indication otherwise. The letter appeared to be for Gerald Reed and him alone. No one else."

"Tell me more about the letter."

"Just as Lopez described it. A short message stating for the younger brother to come quickly, with the name of the town--Alerta. On the second page was part of the British explorer Percy Fawcett's book, copied in Deutsch."

So it was true! Bauer could feel his aging heart begin

beating faster. The Monuments Man had found something in Germany. The pieces were finally coming together.

"Where is this female companion?"

"Gone," replied Fischer.

"Good. Anyone else?"

"The mail carrier."

"What does he know?"

"Nothing anymore," said Fischer. Inside the car, he glanced absently at the passenger seat and then down at the dark floor. He studied it a moment before reaching down and plucking something from the matted carpet. A strand of hair.

"The carrier remembered delivering the letter to Gerald Reed but didn't know what the old man was so animated about. He did say he noticed the envelope had been opened previously and mentioned that fact to Reed."

"That's all?"

"Yes."

"And what of him?"

"He's gone too," said Fischer. "I'm now looking for the granddaughter."

28

"You're actually going?"

Angela nodded, still standing on the icy porch.

Rickards blinked and ran a hand through his tousled hair before stepping back to allow her in. She quickly stepped in out of the cold and watched Rickards shut the door.

"I thought you had trouble traveling."

"I do."

Rickards stared at her. "So, when are you going?"

Instead of answering, she pulled a slip of paper out of her pocket and presented it to Rickards. It was an airline ticket.

"Today?!"

"That's right."

"Wait a second," he said, holding up a hand. "Why today?"

"Because if I don't go now, I'll probably talk myself out of it."

"So you're doing it before you change your mind?"

"Yes."

Rickards frowned at the thought. "That's not the best way to make decisions. Just think about this for a minute."

"I did. All night. And you're right. I want to know why. I want to know why my uncle was in South America when everyone else said he was dead. I want to know why he sent that letter. And I want to know why my grandfather risked everything to get there as quickly as he could, even after all these years!"

"Okay, okay." Rickards nodded. "I get it. But that was sixty years ago, Angela. *Sixty years!* A lot happens in sixty years. In fact, no one who was around back then probably remembers anything. Hell, they may not even be alive, unless they were a child."

"Maybe. Maybe not."

"Wait." He looked at her suspiciously. "What does that mean?"

"Do you know the population of Alerta, Peru?"

"No."

"Four hundred and seventy-five people. It's tiny. It's smaller than tiny. And anthropologically speaking, I'm willing to bet that most, if not all, of those residents were *born* there."

"So what?"

"The smaller the tribe, the less it changes. Including its history," she said. "Anthropology 101."

Rickards opened his mouth but said nothing.

"A small town like this would be our best chance of finding someone who still remembers."

"Wait a minute. *Our* best chance?"

Angela froze. "Did I say *our*?"

"Yes."

"I meant *my*. My best chance."

"Is that right?"

"Yes?" Her tone sounded more like a question than an answer.

"Just to clarify," Rickards said, "you are in no way expecting me to go with you."

"Um."

"You cannot be serious."

She held up both hands and stepped forward. "Okay, listen. I know we've only known each other a few days. I get that. Believe me. I get it. But you are the only person I've talked to about this. And something tells me I probably shouldn't be telling anyone else at this point. You're the only person I've confided in."

"I don't care. I'm not flying to Peru, Angela. And I'm sure as hell not doing it tonight."

"Wait, wait. Just hear me out," she stammered. "Let me explain my reasoning."

When Rickards fell silent, she realized she hadn't practiced this part in advance. "Well…why not?"

"That's your pitch?! *Why not?*"

Angela shrugged. "Kind of?"

Rickards rolled his eyes and shook his head at the same time. "Lady, you don't know anything about me. Christ, I could be anyone. I could be some kind of maniac for all you know!"

"Don't you go through a lot of testing for the NTSB?"

"Yes."

"And a background check?"

He sighed. "Yes."

"Some kind of character assessment?"

"Yes," he replied through gritted teeth.

"You're right. I don't know you, Joe. But I don't think you're a maniac. I see it in your eyes. In your body language. You have some issues, that's obvious, but you're not a maniac."

"You don't know anything about me."

"It's true, I don't. All I know is that you've helped me. Selflessly. And that underneath it all, I think you want to know *why,* too. You said it yourself--all investigators do. And also," she said, looking around his living room, "you keep an oddly clean house. But more than that, I think you're an ethical person."

"You don't know me," he repeated.

"I don't," she acknowledged. "But for some reason, I do *trust* you."

"Angela, listen to me—"

"Please."

Her plea stopped him in mid-sentence.

"Please," she said again. "I know you don't think it's a good idea, or even worthwhile. But I told you about my problem. I told you why I've never gone back to South America. Or anywhere, for that matter. I told you how hard this is for me, but in spite of all that, I'm *still* willing to do it anyway. I'm willing to try. Doesn't that say something? Not just for me, but for my grandfather. And even for my grandmother."

Rickards continued staring at her, his unshaven jawline tense. "What do you mean, for your grandmother?"

Angela looked around before turning and walking to the couch. She sat, poised, looking back at him. "I told you I stopped talking to my grandfather out of anger for the life my grandmother was forced to endure because of him. The woman who was essentially my mother, wasting all those years over my grandfather's fixation."

"You did."

"Well, what if it wasn't all wasted after all? If this whole thing is true, or even part of it, then what she put up with all those years would just be wasted if I don't go."

For a long time, Rickards stared at her skeptically. Finally, he lowered his shoulders with a sigh. "I cannot believe this."

29

Bauer was now having trouble calming himself, unable to stop the faint trembling in his fingers when he stood and moved to the expansive window.

It is real. It is all real.

He peered out with both hands on the glass, taking in the city. Over 3,500 meters above sea level and the highest capital city in the world, it rested upon the famed Andes Altiplano Plateau, the most extreme section of the mountain range and home to pre-Columbian cultures such as the Chiripa, Tiwanaku and the Incan Empire.

He continued staring until with a sudden impulse he turned around. Leaving the window, he walked back to the other side of the room, where he moved a painting to reveal a large digital wall safe—owned by the hotel but secure enough to satisfy his needs for the time being.

He punched in a six-digit code, followed by a thumbprint, upon a small screen of illuminated glass, until he heard a loud *clunk* behind the door.

Bauer twisted the heavy handle downward to pull the door open and reached in to withdraw several large, thick pieces of acrylic plastic, which he carefully laid on the table behind him.

Five pieces in all, with dimensions just larger than a standard typewritten page. Protected between thick, sealed panes, each was a single sheet of paper, or rather, remnants of one.

Each of the sheets appeared to have been badly burned and sported large dark, burnt holes with crinkling borders. Between the holes remained line after line of handwritten text, written in German and once covering the entirety of each page.

But unlike the first three, the final two of the five pages, also permanently sealed under glass, had been almost entirely destroyed. Of those two, what few pieces remained also had small patches of German writing, but not enough to provide any meaning.

Bauer stood, staring at them. They'd been immortalized under the clear panes since he was a young man. First under glass, then later under plastic. He'd carried them with him most of his adult life and had read them thousands of times. Perhaps tens of thousands.

They were the only remaining pieces of the third set of documents.

He still couldn't believe the letter to tie them all together had come from an American. The town of Alerta he already knew of from Lopez, information given to him shortly before the young man's death. But a *Monuments Man* was something Bauer had never expected.

It was a mistake which vexed him greatly, although in hindsight, it would not have made a difference. Not to him anyway, or his search. Because the documents were clearly not where they were supposed to have been.

Bauer had been told that the first two sets of documents had been delivered to the top two leaders of the Nazi party--Adolf Hitler and Heinrich Himmler--and had been intended for their eyes only.

But clearly, at least one of those documents had not been delivered. Meaning either Himmler or the Führer himself had likely not been made aware of what had been found near the end of the war. Something they had been desperately searching for. Something of extraordinary importance. And the reason most surviving senior Nazi officers were given instructions to avoid capture and flee to South America immediately.

But if the Americans had gained possession of one of the cases, or *aktentasche*, it meant either Hitler or Himmler had not. Because even while mad, both men would have been smart enough, or paranoid enough, to destroy them before letting them fall into American or Russian hands.

It was a puzzle Bauer may never solve. Not now, all these years later. Nor how the secret had ended up with the Americans. But one thing he did know was that *it was not the fault of the messenger.*

That man had done everything humanly possible to get the information to both leaders in time. He had personally delivered the packages to both aides-de-camp--Martin Bormann and Werner Grothmann, with urgent instructions to present them to Hitler and Himmler.

Whatever the ultimate fate of the documents, it was *not* the messenger's fault. Because the messenger had been his own father.

Bauer already had a man in Alerta who was looking for information, but with great difficulty, lacking the name of the sender on the original letter. They had only initials and did not know who R.R. was.

But now they did. *Roger Reed.* Older brother of Gerald Reed and missing Monuments Man.

Now Bauer needed to find out what Roger Reed had discovered and what he'd been trying to convey to his brother. Was it just the documents--or had he actually used them? Had he used them to find what Hitler and Himmler's men were supposed to? And what the explorer Percy Fawcett had also been scouring South America for in the 1920s?

Perhaps he might still learn how the documents delivered by his father had been lost before the war was over. It was a burning question whose elusive answer now appealed greatly to Bauer. Because his father had made the last and final copy for himself, using the very best Jewish counterfeiter he could commandeer from the Nazi Party's Operation Bernhard.

Flawless copies with no errors, no unreadable words or markings, not even an accidental pen stroke, ensuring absolutely nothing from Percy Fawcett's secret letter was lost.

Three perfect copies. The last had been destroyed in a fire that claimed the life of Bauer's father, leaving only remnants of the secret pages he could never reconstruct, until now.

Of course, Bauer was not the real name of the now old man staring out over the city of La Paz. Nor had it been his father's name. Their actual name was recognizable to anyone familiar with the artifacts for which the Germans were really searching during the war. Both the old man and his father were known by the name of Ottman.

30

Ottman.

A name only one other person knew to be Bauer's real name. At least the only one still living. That man was sitting quietly in a small, nondescript rental car, waiting.

Fischer sat motionless, parked just a block and a half from the main opening to the apartment complex, his eyes glued to the front entrance. He occasionally glanced at the rearview mirror when someone passed.

It was always surprising to Fischer how few people ever

scrutinized a parked car with someone sitting in it. Notice? Yes. But actually take a good look inside? Rarely. And for the extreme few who did, all it took was Fischer to raise his phone and appear to be talking to keep them moving.

Like being good drivers, most people thought they were attentive, but they weren't. Even watching people enter or exit the apartment building over the last two hours had resulted in only one person so much as glancing at Fischer or his car. And even then without the slightest look of suspicion. A world filled with sheep happily satiated in their bubble of false security.

His gaze remained trained on the entrance, as well as the driveway next door leading down and into the underground garage, while he thought about Ottman. He wondered what the old man would do with the information he had provided him.

Even as emotionless as he was, Fischer could not help but feel a slight hint of satisfaction for Ottman. With everything he had done, after waiting this long, he almost deserved it--if one excluded the murders.

But to Fischer, it still meant nothing. It was merely a job. All Fischer cared about at the moment was finding who he was waiting for.

Forty-five minutes later, Fischer's phone rang. He immediately recognized the number even without a name associated with it. Another of those in Ottman's employ.

"Yes."

"I have something," a voice said in German.

"What is it?"

"A hit on her credit card. Three hours ago."

"Where?"

"The Denver International Airport. Seventeen hundred and twelve dollars."

Fischer leaned forward in his seat. "Are you sure?"

It was a rhetorical question. The person on the other end

was rarely wrong.

"Yes."

"Where is she going?"

"I don't know yet."

Fischer blinked twice. "Where is she now--her cell phone?"

"I'm working on that. But it takes time. Those are private systems."

"I don't care. I need to know right now."

"You'll have it as soon as I do."

Fischer ended the call, eyes still on Angela Reed's apartment building. *Joe Rickards. Gerald Reed's girlfriend said Joe Rickards was with Angela when she came to see her.*

He quickly straightened and doubled-checked Rickards' address on his phone, sent earlier by the same person to whom he'd just spoken on the phone.

Starting the car, Fischer thrust the gearshift into reverse and backed up enough to turn out, mashing the gas pedal.

***

He could tell the Porter woman was sharp. It hadn't taken her long to become wary of Fischer. Perhaps even leery. She'd asked him seemingly innocent questions to test his knowledge of the case.

But eventually, she told him everything, even if it was under extremely physical duress when he'd finally had her alone.

Joe Rickards' residence was fifteen minutes away through afternoon traffic, prompting Fischer to dial the same international phone number back.

"Still nothing on her phone."

Fischer's eyes flared in frustration as he stared down a line of cars waiting between him and a stoplight. The cross streets were no better. "Where's her goddamn car?!"

"Don't know."

He knew that, too.

"Do you have anything new?!"

"No."

"Then call me when you have her location. Especially if it's anywhere close to Rickards' address."

31

"This is insane. You understand that."

Angela nodded and watched Rickards drop his duffel bag onto the floor with a loud thud. She remained still in his living room, standing sheepishly with her hands behind her back.

"I wouldn't have asked if you weren't, you know, not working."

He turned from the staircase and narrowed his eyes on her. "Don't start that again."

"It wasn't derogatory. I was just saying."

He approached and dropped his hands to his hips. "I agreed to go, but here's my condition. If we don't find anything solid, and I mean *solid*, from your uncle in Alerta, I'm turning around and coming back."

"How will we know if something is solid?"

"Trust me," he said. "I'll know."

"Do you speak any Spanish?"

"No." Rickards suddenly gave her a concerned look. "Do you?"

"A little. But it should be enough."

'Fine. I'll be ready in twenty minutes. Your place next?"

"I'm already packed."

"Already?"

She shrugged. "I couldn't sleep. My bags are in my car."

Rickards looked curiously at her. "What time did you decide you were going?"

"About three-thirty."

"Did you sleep at all?"

"Not really."

He passed her and walked into his kitchen, which was illuminated by natural light from a small skylight in the middle of the ceiling.

He opened the refrigerator and looked inside before pausing and turning back to her, now standing in the doorway. "Have you eaten anything?"

"No."

"Do you want anything?"

Angela glanced at the dark table near the doorway. Small and simple, with four chairs neatly pushed in. The top held not so much as a saltshaker.

"Do you actually have any food here?"

"Not a lot."

"Then I'm fine."

He closed the refrigerator door. "Suit yourself."

"We can get something at the airport. My treat."

"Yay."

This was insane. Utterly insane. He barely knew the woman, he had no personal connection to this case, and he had no clue what he might be walking into. For all he knew, this was all part of an elaborate hoax, made up by some delirious explorer at death's door from a jungle-born illness.

It was also a fourteen-hour flight. Fourteen hours. For what? To find out why an old man died in a plane crash?

Somberly, Rickards studied a shadowed reflection of his face in the polished refrigerator door. She was right, though. He had to give her that. He was curious, at the very least. The investigator in him did want to know what happened. And thanks to her irritatingly astute observation, and as much as Rickards didn't want to think about it, he literally had nothing else to do at the moment. What else was there to do, sit and wallow?

He stopped shaking his head and looked at Angela. "This is insane."

All she could do was grin and nod. "You might have mentioned that."

32

Fischer stomped on the accelerator again, careening down a narrow street and swerving around a parked car before letting up and rounding the next corner. He was too close to worry about police. Barely three blocks.

He accelerated faster down a short block before slowing hard again for another turn.

As recently as fifteen minutes ago, Angela Reed's cell phone was within one hundred and fifty meters of Joe Rickards' house. Which meant they were together.

The last two people to know anything about the letter.

Fischer punched it again, approaching the final turn, instinctively dodging a car when a driver's side door opened. He yanked the screaming vehicle back into his lane and braked even harder this time, bringing the small compact car down to a slow twenty miles per hour at the last minute--just before reaching the last corner.

Once on Rickards' street, he slowed further and scanned the houses as he passed, counting addresses.

The numbering indicated he wasn't more than six or seven houses away, prompting Fischer to look for an open place to park with enough room to allow for a rapid departure.

Neither Reed nor Rickards should be expecting him. Or

anyone, for that matter. The two previous victims had no sense of fear when asked about the letter or its contents. Which meant Reed and Rickards were most likely still in the process of trying to understand exactly what they had.

Fischer was sure he had reached them in time. He spotted the house, followed by a space large enough for his car farther up the street. Another hundred feet, at most, from Rickards' driveway.

He slowed further and casually glanced at the front of the house as he passed, noting the location of the front walkway and door. In plain view and unprotected. Which also meant visible to everyone else. He was going to have to make this—

Fischer nearly jumped when he suddenly spotted something close to him, almost stomping on the brakes out of instinct.

Instead, he continued, and through his side mirror could make out two figures in a car he had just passed. Both occupied the front seats of the vehicle, which was parked directly in front of Rickards' house.

Fischer continued rolling forward until reaching the open spot. He casually eased in, leaving the engine running while he shifted into park. *How could he have missed the woman's car?*

"Ready?"

Joe Rickards blinked at the open dashboard in front of him, trying to think of an excuse not to go. Finding none, he reluctantly nodded his head.

Angela reached for the gear shift and paused with her hand on top of the round knob. "I really appreciate you doing this," she said. "I mean it. I honestly couldn't think of anyone else to ask."

"Lucky me."

She glanced at him and smiled at his joke. "At least it's a

distraction from, you know."

He glared in response.

"Hey, there's no shame in getting fired. It happens to everyone sooner or later."

"I didn't get fired."

Angela turned back to face forward. "Of course you didn't."

She waited for a car to pass on her left and pulled the gearshift back one notch into reverse, slowly inching backward before switching into drive and turning her front wheels outward. With a final look in her mirror, she pulled out into the street and accelerated.

Rickards took a deep breath and glanced outside as the car sped up, briefly noting a car that stopped in front of them with its brake lights still on.

This was a bad idea. He could feel it.

33

He missed them by seconds.

A glowering Fischer watched the red Subaru continue ahead, partly obscured by the large truck in front of him. Just in time, he noted which direction it turned.

He pulled out again and glanced at his watch. Almost 3:30 p.m.

Next to him, his phone vibrated, having already been silenced, prompting him to reach over and accept the call.

"What."

It was the same voice. "Rickards is now on the plane. Same flight as Angela Reed."

Fischer accelerated, careful not to lose them, but also not

to get too close. Any decent federal agent would notice a tail if he was looking for one. Fischer needed some cover.

"They're both on their way to Los Angeles," the voice said. "Then to Mexico City and on to Lima."

Fischer nodded, spotting Angela Reed's car making a left-hand turn. He conveniently slid in behind another vehicle. "They're heading east."

"Toward the airport," confirmed the voice.

Fischer slowed to allow a third car between them. Unless they stopped, he would have little opportunity before reaching the airport with a thousand bystanders.

"Traffic?"

"Heavy. Rush hour. I70, the main route to the airport, is heavily congested. Under construction."

"Other routes?"

"Nothing helpful," the voice said after pausing. "Even in this traffic, I70 still provides the shortest travel time."

A car merged out of Fischer's lane, forcing him to ease back farther while both lanes of traffic promptly slowed to a crawl. Less than a tenth of a mile away, he could see the car.

There was no way. No appreciable scenario that would allow Fischer to get to them without dozens of witnesses. And yet how ironic his situation was. The German's lip curled. The airport was the same place he had returned *to rent his car.*

"Is it a full flight?"

The voice on the phone paused.

Perfect.

"Reserve me a seat," Fischer said. "My visit here is over."

34

It took Angela barely ten minutes to fall asleep after takeoff, long before the Airbus A320 finally reached its cruising altitude and leveled off. Across the aisle and back two rows, Rickards noticed the top of her blonde head fall limply to one side.

He was still telling himself it was nuts, but Rickards knew deep down there was something else. Another silent thought that had gotten him on that plane. Something he hadn't told Angela. He didn't have to. It wouldn't have made a difference, at least not to her.

The simple truth was that Rickards didn't believe in coincidences.

Very few good investigators did. Because in the end, there was always a reason for everything. Every action, every connection, every relationship—all could be traced back to cause and effect, if the layers of circumstance were peeled back far enough.

Especially when it came to people. Human beings never made decisions inside a vacuum. There was always a reason, no matter how complicated. No matter how convoluted.

All human behavior happened for a reason, regardless of whether the person or persons were aware of it

To Rickards, this was no longer just about his curiosity. Yes, as with all humans, he wanted to know what had happened. He wanted to know the truth. The explanation.

Whether it was inquisitiveness or something more academic, like a child wanting to know how the magic trick was done, he didn't know. All he knew was what he had learned from over twenty years on the job. Nothing was random.

He didn't know what it was, what specific detail he had learned about the mysterious letter sent decades before. But something was not right. Something was off. Like a small door, plain and nondescript. Overlooked, while hiding something truly surprising behind it. There was something here that Joe Rickards couldn't put his finger on. But knowing what he did about people, he was gradually becoming more convinced that the note was somehow just the tip of the iceberg.

Regardless of whether anything they'd already learned was accurate. Or even true.

Every person and every person's actions were part of a larger, more complex puzzle spanning thousands of people over thousands of years. Human lives, whose decisions and actions were interwoven into one giant, unimaginably complicated web of events and human interactions. And then there were secrets, some of which were important and some not. But everyone played a role.

To Rickards, the hints already uncovered were undoubtedly connected, slowly arranging themselves into something he was sure would eventually fit together, even if most of the other pieces were lost forever. The question for Rickards was whether enough still existed to present a picture, or an answer, of what really happened. Or was it too late?

Joe Rickards closed his eyes and tried to relax enough to sleep. *There were no coincidences.* Of that he was sure. Which was ironically the very same reason he would never be able to get past what had happened to him.

As he gradually drifted off, the last thing he would have expected was that one of the puzzle pieces was sitting just twelve rows behind him.

Staring quietly at the back of his head.

35

The sounds in the distance were growing nearer, day after day--a frightening reminder of what many considered inevitable. Explosion after explosion, tainting the air with an ominous feeling of advancing obliteration as Nazi strongholds continued to fail across the pockmarked face of northern Germany. It was an inevitability that would one day soon deliver either death or salvation.

A feeling in the air, mixed with the strong scent of explosives.

They were losing—a concept almost unimaginable only eighteen months earlier. But now, the German forces were slowing. Struggling. Trying to fight multiple fronts at once, where many units, disorganized and underequipped, were being eviscerated one by one. Despite what their Führer chose to believe.

But many Germans refused to believe as well—that defeat may be inevitable. They fought now with even more ferocity and conviction, utterly persuaded that even surrounded they had the upper hand.

Erhard Ottman was one of them.

Dressed in a worn, dusty uniform now hidden beneath a heavy black coat, Ottman intently marched beneath the brick entrance of the Mauthausen-Gusen internment camp, passing by several Nazi guards, all running in the opposite direction. Ottman momentarily turned to watch them, only to have his tired gaze drawn up and out at the distant smoldering horizon. Dark streams of smoke mixed unevenly amongst the gray clouds of an otherwise beautiful North European winter.

There's still time.

Ottman whipped back around and continued forward, boot heels pounding noisily over hand-laid bricks. His hat was firmly tilted over a hastily washed forehead with black double lightning bolts emblazoned on one shoulder of the coat. A leather satchel tucked tightly under his left arm.

Ottman's face remained resolute, without the slightest reaction from the stench permeating the entire base. Instead, he marched diligently forward, heading directly for the SS administration barracks.

The front room was empty and smelled no better than outside. Intermittent shouting seemed to come from all directions, but not quite close enough to be intelligible.

It didn't matter. He could have guessed what they were saying.

Ottman slammed the wooden door behind him, prompting an immediate sound of scrambling boots and a young guard to appear. His hat was missing, and he was dressed in a shabbily worn uniform. Barely seventeen from the looks of him.

The teenager immediately saluted.

Ottman rolled his eyes and scanned the rest of the room. "Where's Krüger?" he asked in German.

The boy stammered something unintelligible.

"Krüger!" he barked.

"I-I don't know."

"Then find out!"

It was happening everywhere. Communication was already beginning to break down, driven by rumors that the war was slowing and a mounting fear of what would happen to them. Especially at a place like Mauthausen, where tens of thousands had been cleansed.

Ottman watched as the young soldier disappeared out the back before he stepped around the large counter and ambled past two rows of empty metal desks, each strewn with stacks of papers and folders.

Near the back of the room, filing cabinets lined the entire wall, some with several drawers dangling open.

Empty.

Ottman turned and peered outside through the glass window in the middle of the rear door and saw several guards rushing to and fro. Further in the distance, he could see a few others pushing wheelbarrows.

Rushing to the ovens. Ovens no longer being used to burn bodies, but evidence.

Several minutes later, a visibly irritated officer, older but still younger than Ottman himself, followed the teenager back into the office.

"Yes, yes," he shouted. "What is it?"

"You're Krüger?"

The officer nodded, unconsciously running a hand over his thin black hair to straighten it. "Yes. What do you wan—" He stopped in mid-sentence upon seeing the pin on Ottman's lapel, made of bright, shimmering gold. But not a pin displaying rank. Instead, it was a large letter "A," causing the younger officer to audibly inhale.

"Forgive me, Herr Hauptscharführer. I was…I was just tending to… Things are hectic." He cleared his throat. "My sincerest apologies."

"Quiet," Ottman said, ignoring his sputtering. "And listen carefully. You are to find your best forger and bring them to me. Now."

Krüger blinked. "Forger?"

"The best you have. Quickly!"

"T-they are on the truck. I've been instructed to take them to Redl-Zipf."

Ottman's eyes narrowed and became icy. "Then get them *off* the truck!"

Twenty minutes later in a small empty room, save only for a table and chair, Ottman removed his coat and stepped behind a sitting woman. Her eyes were filled with fear as she looked nervously from Krüger at the door, to the man now behind her.

A moment later a knock sounded, prompting Krüger to open and let in a guard, who promptly crossed the room without a word and placed a box of supplies in front of the nervous woman.

The guard never looked up, nor waited for instructions. Instead, he immediately turned and exited just as quickly as he'd arrived.

Ottman lowered himself closer to her ear. "Do you have all you need?"

"I'm not sure," the woman's voice said feebly. She leaned forward and examined the items. "What am I to do?"

Ottman's eyes rose to Krüger, who was still standing next to the door. "Get out."

The younger officer almost jumped, gripping the knob of the door before hesitantly turning back. "Herr Hauptscharführer, I have been ordered to leave this afternoon."

"You will stay until I release you."

With that, Ottman rounded the table and stood before the woman, waiting for the door to close after Krüger. When it did, he swiftly removed the satchel from under his arm and unbuckled two thick straps across the top. He delicately retrieved several papers and placed them on the table in front of her.

"I need replicas of these," he said. "*Perfect* replicas. In every way."

The woman examined the pages, studying them carefully.

"In every way," he repeated.

Obediently, the woman dropped her gaze back to the

table and reached down to scoot her chair closer. She was the best of the group. A former printing expert from Poland, she was one of the first twenty-six Jewish prisoners to arrive.

The project was called Operation Bernhard and operated for years as one of the Nazi Party's many secret plans to destabilize their enemy. Originally named Andrew, the operation was born from an idea in 1938 as a means to undermine Great Britain by decimating its economy and destroying the British pound as the world's reserve currency.

Economically, the plan was simple and terrified the British. But the actuality of counterfeiting enough notes to airdrop over the country proved more difficult than expected, causing the project to grind to a halt after a falling out between the egos of two high-ranking Nazi officers.

But the plan was later brought back to life by none other than Heinrich Himmler himself--this time, not as an attack on Britain, but as a more practical means of helping Germany finance its runaway costs of war run amok.

Now, in early 1945, Germany was reeling, out of money and trying desperately to find any resources or other means to continue. Which was exactly what Ottman had just accomplished.

His own project had been initiated several years before, also in 1938, and also by Heinrich Himmler, head of the SS and second in command to Adolf Hitler.

And it all began with the city of Troy.

The fabled city of Troy, described in Homer's *Iliad*, had long been considered to be exactly that. A fable. Nothing more than a mythical story born not from Greek history, but from the imagination of Homer himself...until it was actually discovered in 1868 by a German archaeologist named Schliemann. But what made the discovery so profound to the Nazis was not *where* Troy was found, but *how.*

For years the story had been dismissed by the world's greatest scholars as a fable. A myth. Fabricated as part of a fictional story.

But Schliemann did not believe it. He remained convinced that Homer's setting of the Trojan War was, in fact, true. Even accurate. He searched for years, by ignoring the historians and trusting in the written words of Homer. Studying every detail of the *Iliad* and Homer's descriptions of ancient Troy. Painstakingly piecing the clues together until he believed he knew where it was.

And he found it. A city that no one believed existed--proving not only was the legend true, but that many of our oldest written records were likely based on *facts*.

It was a form of archaeological inspiration that fueled men like Erhard Ottman, men assigned to track down critical religious or historical artifacts to ensure victory for the Nazi party.

Just as Herman Wirth was searching for Atlantis to trace their superior Aryan ancestry back to its roots, or Otto Rahn searching for the Holy Grail near the remains of fortress Montségur, each of them took their lessons from the great archaeologist Schliemann, by studying the world's great religious texts very carefully.

Unfortunately, Wirth had failed. And Rahn was now dead. But Erhard Ottman was not. Ottman had not only survived, he had *succeeded*. Succeeded in finding what he had set out to discover. What he had been assigned to locate by whatever means necessary. No matter what it took or where it ultimately led.

What he was searching for was not in Asia as they had originally thought, but in South America, buried deep in the forests of the Amazon where few dared venture and even fewer survived. Where innumerable ways existed to befall a man, all of them lying in wait in dark jungles, like predators ready to strike.

Enough death to keep all but a few foreigners away for

generations. Except one man by the name of Percy Fawcett, a British explorer and resolute believer that the rumors were true. Legends which were little more than faint whispers among tribes that something truly extraordinary lay hidden deep within the dense, almost impenetrable walls of the Amazon, waiting to be discovered after centuries of obscurity.

The same Percy Fawcett who'd finally found it. And as his fellow patriots would later prove so utterly adept at during the war after cracking the Enigma code, Fawcett kept the secret quiet, telling absolutely no one about the discovery until his untimely death--with the only exception being his *family*.

In a separate piece of correspondence, hidden away by Fawcett's family for years, it was the explorer's youngest son who finally cracked, handing it over to SS Officer Erhard Ottman after a rather intense episode of persuasion.

Now, just as with Homer's *Iliad*, Ottman had finally hunted down and attained a detailed description in Colonel Fawcett's own handwriting, revealing the final location of what Ottman had long been searching for.

A handwritten letter that one of Krüger's forgers was now making an exact replica of. Three copies. One for the Führer. One for Heinrich Himmler. And a third for Ottman himself, who was now watching while absently fingering the golden letter "A" on his coat--the pin for a founding member of the terrifying *Ahnenerbe,* later to be known as the Nazi SS.

36

Three-quarters of a century later, Erhard Ottman's son was still standing and peering out over the city of La Paz,

Bolivia, the first city in South America ever visited by Percy Fawcett. The giant window now reflected a faint image of the old man's face, worn and tired, but with eyes ablaze with life. With hope. That he had finally found what his father had instructed.

A great secret that could have saved the war if it had not somehow mysteriously vanished into history. The same secret his father had died trying desperately to preserve when their house had caught fire in the winter of 1949.

Karl Ottman studied his face in the window. Tanned, with tight leathery skin. Deeply set and intense blue eyes, gleaming even in the reflection.

He could still see remnants of his father in the glass. The eyes and heavy brow still matched parts of his last paternal image. Writhing on the ground, coughing and belching out smoke and blood from severely burned lungs. Trying to speak, but unable, while clutching the panes of cracked glass tightly in his charred hands. His own copy, created by the female forger at the Mauthausen concentration camp, irreparably burnt.

Karl Ottman could still hear his father's words. *Lass es nicht mit mir sterben.*

"Don't let it die with me."

Ottman stepped back and watched his reflection disappear into nothingness. He stared down thoughtfully at the plush white carpet beneath him.

So, they were coming to Peru. The Monument Man's great-niece, along with a U.S. federal investigator. Which meant they must know something. But what? What could they possibly discern from two handwritten paragraphs? The answer was *nothing*.

Ottman inhaled and raised his head. He was ready. After a lifetime of waiting, he was ready. He would do whatever was necessary and use the entirety of his resources if need be. Copious resources, thanks to something else his father had revealed to him.

A federal agent from the United States would require caution. Nothing insurmountable. Not in the least, with a little planning.

The woman, from Fischer's description, sounded inconsequential: a teacher from the local university. Hidden away in an ivory tower, no doubt preaching about how the world should be, instead of how it truly was. *Brutal and unforgiving, beneath a thin veneer of civility.* And outside of places like the United States, in places such as South America, that veneer was even thinner.

Ottman glanced at his watch.

He had mere hours to prepare before the Americans' arrival, to make arrangements and get money into the correct hands. To ensure that whatever measures were necessary would go unquestioned and forgotten. Long enough for Ottman to get what he needed.

After all, smaller countries knew exactly how to deal with giant elephants. More than enough experience managing great and powerful nations, especially the giant and very bureaucratic United States.

They are coming to Peru, Ottman thought with a confident smile. And the best part was that Fischer was on the plane.

37

The second leg of the flight was much longer. Sixteen grueling hours out of Los Angeles, allowing Angela to get more than enough sleep. But not Rickards. He'd never been able to sleep on a plane and was now sitting several seats up and to the right, flipping quietly through some of the information she'd given him.

The constant roar of the engines had him wishing he'd bought some of those expensive noise-canceling headphones, especially given a tiny seat that periodically prompted him to shift in the dark to get comfortable, while glancing around the cabin.

This time he noted a mother playing with her young child to keep him distracted. Rickards watched, wondering how long the mother had before the boy finally caught on to her game.

Rickards lowered his head again and continued reading through the journals Angela's grandfather had kept over the course of fifty some odd years, searching for answers to his older brother's fate.

What Rickards was becoming increasingly interested in, though, were the details surrounding the Monuments Men as a whole.

It was a fascinating mission. One of a very small team of volunteer soldiers who, just as Angela had explained, quite literally saved the entire world. Or more specifically, the history of the entire world. Paintings, sculptures, shrines, even churches in some cases, from the insatiable and tyrannical clutches of Adolf Hitler and his Nazis, a group whose ruthlessness knew no bounds.

Rickards stopped on one of the journal's pages, where Angela's grandfather had jotted down an old quote. It was a quote from a name Rickards recognized as one of the most powerful leaders of the Nazi Party.

"It used to be called plundering. But today things have become more humane. In spite of that, I intend to plunder, and to do it thoroughly." — Hermann Göring.

To destroy another country's army or government in war was one thing. But to destroy the very identity and history of the citizens themselves was akin to cultural genocide. For Hitler, killing millions of innocent victims was not enough.

He also wanted to destroy their culture and the very souls of those who might survive. To plunder and confiscate human history itself. And destroy it if need be.

Saved by approximately sixty overweight and out of shape volunteer soldiers who laid their lives down to find and protect it all.

It was an extraordinary effort that few alive today fully appreciated or even understood. And yet it was one that ironically left Rickards with a strange feeling of guilt. Because as powerful as the story was, for Rickards, there was a slow, inching worry about Roger Reed himself. A man about whom he still knew very little. Where he was from, yes, but virtually nothing else that spoke to what kind of man he was.

Because what Rickards knew was that no matter who they were or what they did, *all* men were fallible. All were vulnerable. And there was an important element in Reed's story that he and Angela had only briefly touched upon.

Joe Rickards was now wondering about the other side of Roger Reed. And that place that existed beneath every man's exterior. Even heroes.

After all, not every man could simply disappear from the planet for an entire decade, then suddenly surface again to send a single letter. And then disappear again.

What was it, exactly, that drove Reed to do it? Had he been instructed by his government? Or had he acted alone? Because if he'd acted alone, a darker explanation of his motives had to be considered.

When all was said and done, Rickards' ultimate question was: *Was it possible that Roger Reed, a distinguished Monuments Man, had been involved in something darker? Something unethical? Or worse, illegal?*

The last thing Rickards needed was to walk into something that could inadvertently make him an accomplice.

38

Less than two hundred feet from the ground, the large Airbus A319 suddenly rolled hard, frightening several passengers before the pilots quickly corrected, fighting to keep the aircraft level against unusually strong crosswinds. Hardly uncommon for the Jorge Chávez International Airport, which lay just eleven kilometers outside of Lima, Peru, but the conditions were as bad as anyone had seen in a year.

The massive aircraft rolled again, this time almost violently, and was once again jerked back by its pilots. Overhead, the seat belt sign glowed bright red, and passengers were being instructed in both Spanish and English and in no uncertain terms to hold tight and not remove their belts under any circumstances.

Another hundred feet and the turbulent winds grew even worse, rocking the plane from side to side.

Sitting in a different seat from the previous flight, Rickards turned and peered between the seats at Angela, who had her eyes closed and was grasping the arms of her seat with white knuckles.

Another sudden drop and roll gave Rickards a momentary glance of the earth directly below them through a side window, followed immediately by several soothing words overhead by one of the pilots, spoken in rapid Spanish.

Finally, less than fifty feet from the surface, the plane leveled long enough for the pilots to force the craft down onto the asphalt runway. The impact caused everyone to jerk forward in their seats, followed instantly by the deafening reverse thrust from both engines outside and forceful shaking as the entire craft rapidly slowed.

Angela's eyes reopened and she looked around the cabin, finding Rickards, who raised an eyebrow at her through the narrow opening. She nodded and tried to smile, even with her hands still firmly wrapped around both metal arms.

The braking eased and everyone leaned back again in relief, many murmuring in nervous tones while others made reassuring jokes to each other.

Rickards, however, knew what kind of stress testing these planes were subjected to and the limits before metal fatigue or failure normally appeared. The wings themselves would damn near flap before they would break. But the sudden impact of the ground was different, and why his blood pressure was up just like everyone else's. Knowledge only went so far in moderating a human body's natural anxiety.

After a few minutes, the lumbering craft came to a full halt. Dozens of passengers stood up at once, filling the aisles. For Rickards, standing up, even in a hunched position, was a godsend and allowed him to get a better look at Angela, who this time gave a nervous but genuine smile.

It had been years since he had experienced a landing like that.

***

Once off the plane and inside the airport, a sullen Angela caught up to Rickards, who was waiting near a row of plastic seats.

"Well, that wasn't *awesome*."

"You okay?"

She nodded. "As you can probably tell, I'm not a huge fan of flying."

"I'm sure a lot of people on that flight are thinking the same thing about now."

"I think I officially owe you *big* now for coming with me."

"Yes, you do."

He began to turn when Angela reached out for his arm. "So, have you ever been to Peru before?"

"No."

"Anywhere in South America?"

"Nope."

"Anywhere outside the country?"

"Hawaii."

Her eyes narrowed. "That doesn't count."

"Alaska?"

"Forget it."

"Canada?"

Angela shook her head. "Listen, there are some things you should probably know in terms of local customs and what to expect."

"Such as?"

"As you might have guessed, not everything is like the U.S. down here. Or even Canada. There are a lot of things you need to be careful of."

"Like...?"

"For starters, like being careful not to offend anyone. Don't talk about certain things that may upset them. Number one is no politics."

"What do I know about Peruvian politics?"

"How should I know? I don't know anything about you."

"Fine. So, don't insult their president."

"That's a good start. You also need to remain very respectful of the native peoples."

"Check."

"Don't call them *indios*. Call them *indigenas*. And don't worry, them calling us gringos is not an insult."

"Anything else?"

"Yes. But later," she said, watching the direction of the other passengers. "Let's get our bags."

Customs was cleaner and more efficient than Rickards was expecting, especially given the modest size of the airport.

Angela could see the look of surprise on his face. "What did you expect, people carrying caged chickens?"

"Something like that."

She laughed. "I shouldn't joke. There *are* places like that." She reached into a pocket and withdrew her cell phone. "No signal here."

Rickards bumped her with his arm and motioned toward a sign on the wall, banning cell phone usage in the area.

"Why don't they want people to use their phones?"

Rickards shrugged. "Probably freaks out the chickens."

About thirty feet behind them stood Fischer, calmly, quietly watching both as they inched forward in the line. Rickards carried a large duffel bag and the Reed woman towed a stylish green and white rolling suitcase.

His eyes shifted to the customs agents, searching for any signs of an alert, but found none. His boss Ottman would not be foolish enough to use his connections and stop the Americans at the border. Too many people and too many agents. Where they needed them was a more secluded environment.

They would wait. Until the time was right.

39

The flight from Lima to the smaller city of Puerto Maldonado was even worse. This time they were aboard a smaller prop plane that had seen better days, highlighted when the main door failed to close without the help of both the attendant and the pilot. Angela and Rickards were both relieved to be back on solid ground just forty-five minutes later.

Outside the large one-building airport, the hot, humid afternoon air absorbed them immediately upon exiting, a welcome to the tropical Amazon Basin, promptly made worse by a brief but harrowing bus ride to the car rental agency. The young bus driver appeared to believe they were on the autobahn and speed limits were merely suggestions.

Clutching the chrome handrails firmly, Angela and Rickards both glanced at each other repeatedly, surprised that none of the other passengers seemed to notice. It was just a quiet busload of locals all moving and swaying in unison while looking at their phones.

The end of a long journey that prompted them both to sit quietly in their rental car for several minutes just to relax.

Rickards studied the instruments of the automobile. A French design painted bright yellow.

"At least they drive on the right side of the road."

"Don't get too excited," she said, winking. "You're still going to need your defensive driving skills."

At that, Rickards reached back and retrieved his seat belt.

"Welcome to Puerto Maldonado. Just like your football player."

"Baseball."

"Whatever."

***

An hour later, Rickards crossed the hotel's shabbily carpeted hall and knocked on the opposing door. He waited only a few seconds before Angela pulled it open. She was freshly showered and dressed but wore a worried look.

"What's wrong?"

She pulled him in and closed the door while holding up

her phone. "I just connected to Wi-Fi and had a voicemail come in."

"And?"

"It was from one of the staff at the nursing home."

"In Wheat Ridge?"

She nodded. "They can't find Lillian Porter!"

Rickards raised both eyebrows. "Your grandfather's girlfriend?"

"Yes! They can't find her anywhere."

"For how long?"

"Two days. I just called them back."

"How did they sound?"

"What do you mean?"

"How worried did they sound?"

Angela paused. "I don't know, not overly. They said this happened before when she went to visit her sister. She lives in the mountains where the phones had gone out. And they're out again."

"Did she let anyone know?"

"Not that they can find."

Rickards thought it over. "When was the last time you talked to her?"

Angela moved to her bag and pulled out one of her grandfather's journals. "The evening before I came to your house. When she gave me these and some other boxes."

Rickards frowned. "Hmm."

"And that's not all. She was getting ready to go somewhere."

"When you saw her?"

"Yes."

"Where was she going?"

"She wouldn't say. But I could tell."

"Maybe to her sister's?"

"Maybe."

He stared at the journal in Angela's hand. "Could someone else know about this?"

"I don't know. I don't see how."

"The mail carrier said the envelope looked like it had been opened before." Rickards walked past her to the window, peering out through a set of thin, faded curtains.

"Do you see anything?"

After a pause, he nodded. "Yes. Cars. People. Some mountains."

"I'm serious!"

He didn't look away. "Nothing unusual."

Angela plopped down onto the bed. "What do you think we should do?"

"About what?"

"Lillian."

He let go of the fabric and looked at her. "I think if the nursing home isn't worried, then we shouldn't be. And being thousands of miles away, there's not a lot we can do at the moment."

Angela nodded. "Right. Okay. Then what now?"

He glanced at his watch. "It's almost four o'clock. And I'm going to be dead tired in two hours, three tops. It's a small town. Let's put your Spanish to work."

"You mean Andre Lopez?"

"Andre Lopez," he nodded. "At the Department of General Services."

40

From the back of a black Mercedes, Karl Ottman watched from a safe distance as the two left the hotel. Not through his window, but from a book-sized screen in his hands. He watched Angela and Rickards exit from beneath the old building's narrow arch, chipped and faded, the walls on either side covered by patches of half-dead ivy.

The video feed was being broadcast by Fischer, who was parked closer, within a hundred yards, one of several sedans parked along the street. A small camera had been placed atop the car's dashboard.

Fischer watched the two stop at the street and look back and forth, orienting themselves.

"Where are they going?" Ottman's voice crackled over the phone's speaker.

It took only a block and a half to know exactly where the Americans were headed.

41

Caught up in the great rubber boom of the late 1800s, Puerto Maldonado resided less than forty miles from the Bolivian border and was one of the last of the outlying areas to finally be explored. The city was permanently established when Carlos Fermin Fitzcarrald, a rubber baron, found a passage over land between two Amazon River tributaries, allowing him to easily and more efficiently float his revolutionary new product downstream.

Now, situated between three large natural reserves, modern-day Puerto Maldonado's current role was the capital city of the entire region. It was small by most standards but bustled as one of the largest incorporated cities located within the actual boundaries of the Amazon jungle. An urban sprawl of dozens of short buildings made up over two and a half square miles of flattened jungle and waterways, with a small cluster of government offices located downtown.

"Peruvians are more formal than we are, so expect a lot of handshaking. And try to remember to greet people when entering a place. *Buenos días* or *buenos tardes*. And also when you leave."

Rickards nodded and moved out of the way of several passing locals, their rich, darkened skin contrasting perfectly against brightly colored and remarkably modern clothing.

"And also," she continued, "keep your wallet in your front pocket. Pickpocketing and purse snatching are common here."

"Charming."

She shot him a sarcastic glance as they neared the corner, where Angela peered up to study a street sign.

It was farther than they thought, especially in the heat, which was quickly turning Rickards' gray T-shirt dark with perspiration around the collar.

When they finally reached the street they were looking for, they didn't have to travel far before spotting the cluster of government buildings. Most were average-sized office buildings that looked to be modestly maintained.

They found the General Services entrance and entered through a white-painted metal door that clanged loudly when closing behind them.

As if calling everyone to attention, the door caused all three heads in the room to look up. All women, with the closest the first to speak.

"*Puedo ayudarte?*"

"*Perdonanos,*" Angela replied with a smile. "*Estamos buscando a alguien.*"

Upon detecting Angela's accent, the younger woman, dressed comfortably in a blue-green dress, switched to English. "Who are you looking for?"

"Andre Lopez, please."

The woman, still sitting, turned and looked at one of her colleagues, who abruptly stopped typing.

The typist, a heavyset older woman, stood up and approached the counter. "You are looking for Andre?" Her

English was also surprisingly good.

"Yes. Is he here?"

The woman placed both hands on the waist-high counter. "I'm sorry. I'm afraid he is not here."

"When will he be back?"

Rickards noticed a slight fidget in the woman's hands.

"I am sorry. But Andre Lopez is not here. He has not been seen for several days. He left."

Angela looked curiously at Rickards. "What does that mean?"

The woman leaned forward and lowered her voice, pausing slightly to make sure she used the correct wording.

"He has *run off*."

"Run off?"

"Yes," the woman said quietly. "With another woman." After a moment, seeing the confusion on Angela's face, she leaned in a little further, now whispering. "His fiancée came home to find another woman's clothes in their house. And their money at the bank, gone."

Angela continued staring, unsure of what to say.

"When did this happen?"

"Last week." The woman looked at Rickards. "Was he supposed to help you with something?"

Angela started blinking, before shaking her head and reaching into her bag. "Uh…we believe he mailed this letter a few weeks ago. From here. A special delivery. Something that had been lost for a long time."

The woman took the photocopy and studied the picture of the envelope before shaking her head. "It does not look familiar." She turned and called the third woman, who was short, with long, gray-streaked hair.

After a rapid exchange in Spanish, she, too, shook her head.

"None of you know anything about this?"

"No, I'm sorry."

"Nothing in your computers?"

The two women looked at each other.

"No notes, or anything?"

"I'm sorry," the woman repeated. "Perhaps his supervisor knows something. She works in another building."

"Can we get her name and address?" Rickards asked.

"*Sí.* Of course." The woman reached under the counter and retrieved a small piece of paper. Finding a pen, she jotted something down. The other two women watched without a word.

"Here is her name, address and phone number. She is in the large administration building about a half kilometer down this street."

When they stepped back outside into the heat, Angela immediately whirled around.

"Are you kidding me? He *ran off*?! Days before we get here?"

Rickards didn't speak, instead squinting and peering out over their surroundings.

"Doesn't that strike you as a little odd?"

"It does."

Angela suddenly stopped and grabbed Joe's arm. "Wait a minute! Do you think this Andre guy was the one who opened the letter?"

"Maybe."

"What if he did? What if he opened it and saw what was inside?"

"As in?"

"As in he saw what was written on the pages?!"

"And then what?"

"Maybe he figured something out!"

"Figured what out? We can't figure it out, and we know a lot more than him. That's why we're here."

"He would have seen the name of the village," she said. "Alerta! It's only a couple hours away. What if he knew something, or found out what this 'Almv10' means at the end of the message?"

Rickards mulled it over with a frown.

"Possible?" she asked.

"Possible maybe, but I doubt probable."

Angela turned and spotted the same three women through the window. All were speaking together and watching her and Rickards standing outside.

When they reached the street, Angela continued left for several feet before realizing Rickards had stopped.

"What is it?

"Something doesn't feel right here," he said.

"What do you mean?"

He shook his head. "I don't know. But I'm not sure we want to go marching into his boss's office just yet. Suppose this Lopez figured something out and ran off. With a woman. Frankly, those two don't seem to mesh," Rickards said, thinking as he spoke. "But let's just assume for the moment it does. Secondarily, the guy disappears for some other reason. Maybe just for the woman, and our letter has nothing to do with it. Regardless, I think either scenario may engender more than a little curiosity by the authorities as to why you and I are here asking questions."

She nodded. "Okay. But what if his boss knows something?"

"Such as?"

"I don't know. Where he is. Maybe he left a note. At the very least, I'm guessing someone in the department has been looking through his emails. Isn't that how you guys do it?"

Rickards nodded. "Yes, it is. But it also means that anyone even remotely connected would be a person of interest. And *we* are remotely connected."

"Okay. Then what do you suggest?"

"A phone."

42

The phone used was in a convenience store back the way they came and a few blocks from the hotel. After purchasing two bottles of cold water, Angela asked the owner, an old woman likely in her seventies, if she could use her *teléfono*.

As she dialed the number on the paper, Rickards edged closer to the small shop's front window and peered up and down the street.

"Hello," said Angela. "I'm calling for Maria Camila Sanchez." After a pause, she nodded. "Yes. Fine."

She said to Rickards, "They're getting her."

He nodded and noticed something curious outside. He gave a quick motion to Angela with his finger, signaling he'd be right back.

Even at five o'clock, the sun had not fallen near enough to provide any noticeable relief from the heat, inducing Rickards to shade his eyes with one hand while peering across the street.

In the shade on the other side, at the edge of a small park, were several boys not much older than nine or ten. All were walking in a group behind a smaller boy in the front.

At first glance, they appeared to be together. But after a few moments, it was clear they weren't. The group of boys was actually trailing the first, taunting the small boy in front, who appeared slightly darker skinned than the rest.

They were calling after the younger boy in words Rickards couldn't understand. But the sound was derogatory.

Finally, one of the kids in the lead reached out and knocked something from the small boy's hands and then snatched it away to show those behind him. It appeared to be a small bag of something.

Rickards watched the boy in front quickly twist around

in an effort to take his bag back, but the rest had spread out and began tossing it between them.

Rickards looked up and down the empty street and took a swig of cold water before stepping off the curb. He approached silently as the boys continued taunting and laughing and was less than twenty feet away when they noticed him.

The smallest boy did not see him. Instead, he turned away, trying to retrieve both his bag and now an item the others had taken out.

Silently, Rickards passed beneath the shade of several large trees and stopped a few feet from them. When the small boy noticed the expressions on the other faces, he turned and looked back with the rest.

"Give it back," Rickards said in English.

The group of boys slowed to a standstill, all wearing a look of uncertainty.

"Give it...back," he repeated and pointed at the bag.

When they didn't move, he moved closer, still pointing, and snapped his fingers.

The message was clear. And the boys responded—first, by looking back and forth at each other, then slowly reaching out and handing the items back.

The smaller boy grabbed them both and scurried away, glancing only briefly at Rickards as he did so. His face was dark, with a slightly wider-bridged nose and cheekbones. He resembled pictures of natives Rickards had seen in a magazine on the plane.

He watched the kid leave and turned back to find the other boys had suddenly scattered, resulting in a small grin—until he heard a loud voice.

Not one, but two voices. Deep and loud, from two men not more than a hundred feet away.

And were approaching.

Both were large and appeared young, perhaps in their twenties, dressed in casual clothing. And both appeared visibly upset.

One of the men pointed to the scattered boys as they marched toward him, shouting in Spanish, words that were completely unintelligible to Rickards.

He took a step back and checked behind him, then raised both hands in a nonconfrontational gesture.

"Take it easy. Take it easy."

But the two men didn't. If anything, they became more incensed, now spreading apart as they drew closer.

"I don't want any trouble. I was just—" Rickard shook his head and decided to stop talking. It didn't matter. They weren't listening and probably couldn't understand even if they were.

The men seemed to be growing increasingly irate, working themselves up into a frenzy. They were now on each side of him, yelling and pointing back to the group of boys, who had now regrouped to watch.

Not a positive development. It was Rickards' last thought before one of the men lunged forward with a hard right punch.

But the man wasn't expecting what Rickards did. Stepping calmly to the side, he forced the first man to instinctively lunge even further, drawing him off-balance. This allowed Rickards to grab a fist, twisting it up and around, then outward, momentarily lifting the man's entire body off the ground before falling hard onto the concrete with a powerful thud.

In a flash, Rickards was struck hard across the jaw, causing him to stumble backward along with the momentum of the second man. Long enough to work a foot between the man's legs and trip him up, following him down to the ground with a punch across the bridge of the guy's nose.

"Oh my God, what are you doing?!"

Rickards regained his footing and found Angela Reed standing behind him, staring in incredulity. Behind him, both men rose to their feet, wavering and yelling profusely, but clearly reluctant at a second attack.

"It wasn't my fault."

"What happened to not bothering anyone?!"

"Well, okay. There's that," he said. "But I was just helping some kid."

"What kid?"

Rickards turned, looking, but found the small boy nowhere in sight.

Of course.

She rushed to grab him before the two men regained their confidence. "We have to get out of here!"

Not far away, Fischer sat expressionless, watching the commotion with the same small camera perched on the dashboard in front of him.

Americans. Brash and clumsy.

They were all like that. Americans. Like bulls in a china shop. Never any tact or discretion. But to Fischer, the scuffle revealed something else. Something very important.

Regardless of whatever problems he had, Joe Rickards had some fight in him. And that meant he would not go easily.

43

"You've got to be kidding!"

Rickards trod behind Angela apologetically. "I'm sorry. It was an accident."

She turned and stared at him sarcastically. "Oh, really?! Those men just happened to fall on the ground by accident?"

Well, the first one, kind of.

He cleared his throat. "They approached me."

"Is that right? And *why* did they approach you?"

Rickards deliberated but decided to end it. "Never mind."

Angela started forward again, passing an elderly couple who slowed to observe them. "We've been here for *four* hours!"

Rickards shook his head. It didn't matter. He continued behind her, rubbing his jaw. *So much for people respecting the native indigenas.*

In her hotel room, she closed the door hard behind her and watched Rickards fall into an old vinyl chair next to a small desk.

"Did you get anything from Lopez's boss?" he asked.

She inhaled. "It didn't sound like she knew anything more. Or if she did, she wasn't about to tell me. I had to get off the phone when she started asking questions."

"What did you say?"

"That I had to go to the bathroom."

"What?"

"I got nervous. It was the only thing I could think of."

Rickards leaned back with a hand still on his jaw. "We're not exactly batting a thousand here."

"I don't understand it," Angela said, pacing. "Nothing is making sense. My grandfather. This thing with Lillian. And now our only link here to the letter is gone? We should have called him before we came."

"Probably," Rickards said, his gaze dropping as he pondered. "And you're right. It's not making sense." After a pause, he slowly squinted and spoke quietly to himself. "Are we out of the box?"

"Huh?"

He looked up, not realizing he'd spoken loud enough to be heard. "I said, are we outside the box?"

"What box?"

He sighed and dropped his hand over the arm of the chair. "It's not making sense. But it should be. Every investigation, no matter what it is, *should* make more sense as more details are uncovered. Sometimes it takes a while, but eventually, the more you learn, the more comes to light."

"That doesn't feel like that's what's happening," Angela replied.

"No, it doesn't," agreed Rickards. "Which doesn't make sense." He looked up at her. "Which means we need to step outside the box. When nothing feels right, you need to get outside of your presumptions and question them. Question what you assume is correct."

"Meaning what?"

"For starters, what if the story on Lopez is wrong?"

"As in he *didn't* run off?"

"Correct. A man engaged to be married, with some unknown woman?"

"It's possible."

"Possible, yes. But is it likely?"

"We don't even know him."

"That's right." Rickards nodded. "Or his relationship. So all things being equal while making no assumptions about his relationship...is it more likely to be true, or less?"

"You're the man. You tell me."

"All things being equal," Rickards said, "it's less likely. Most men don't run off with another woman when they're engaged."

"Some do."

He nodded. "Some do. But on average, most don't. We're talking overall."

"Okay, so..."

"So, what happens if we assume the story is *not* true?"

"Then I guess the question becomes what happened to him."

"Which then calls into question another assumption."

"And that is?"

"Your grandfather's girlfriend."

"Lillian?"

"Maybe she's at her sister's and maybe she's not. If she is, how likely would it be for the phones to go out again?"

"There could be a number of reasons."

"There could. But all things being equal…"

"It does seem coincidental."

Rickards stared ahead, blinking. "Most seasoned investigators don't believe in coincidences, Angela. Most believe that what has the appearance of coincidence…is just a string of events that haven't yet been identified."

"What are you saying? You think something happened to her?"

"I don't know."

She looked at her phone, sitting on the tall wooden dresser next to the TV. "I'm calling the nursing home."

But as she began dialing, Rickards suddenly rose from the chair and grabbed her arm. "Wait."

He moved quickly to the door, opened it and stepped out, pulling her with him.

"What are you doing?"

Rickards stared down at her. "There's a third assumption that we need to consider."

"Like what?"

"Exclusivity," he said. "This entire time we've been acting under the assumption that we're the only ones who know about this. The connection to your grandfather, his brother, and that letter."

"And your question is?"

"Are we really the only ones?"

Angela didn't answer. Nor did she move. She merely stared until gradually taking a small step back and curiously looking around. "Why are we in the hallway?"

44

Fernandez, the senior Peruvian intelligence officer, stood before Ottman with a stonelike expression. He was dressed in a pressed white uniform and perfectly polished black shoes, his rank of colonel, a black flap with six small gold bars, displayed prominently on each shoulder and giving a strong, formidable appearance. Very different from the thoughts that were silently running through his head.

The colonel was also beginning to perspire.

"He is a U.S. federal officer," he finally said.

"That is correct," replied Ottman, comfortably seated in one of the apartment's plush chairs.

"We cannot just make him disappear. He went through customs. He's now in the system."

"Only hours ago. Not too late to delete the records."

"It's not that easy." Fernandez shook his head. "I don't have any control—" The colonel stopped, visibly perturbed.

In the chair, Ottman remained calm. "I did not suggest it was easy."

"This is not what we talked about. Not part of our agreement. If my involvement is exposed, it won't matter what country I'm living in."

The elderly Ottman almost let a grin escape but didn't. It was something he had seen many times throughout his life. *Corruption* was an unforgiving mistress. Just a little was easy both to engage and hide. Eventually, though, events unraveled in unexpected ways, causing circumstances to change quickly. Allowing lies and deception to mount and slowly begin to spin out of control. Forcing the perpetrator to finally face and ultimately admit to themselves just how deep down the hole they had gone. And in Fernandez's case, just how committed he now was.

A single bead of sweat appeared on the colonel's

unblemished, olive-colored forehead. He couldn't back out. Not without attracting the attention of several other high-ranking officials in the government, and potentially the president himself. Let alone risking an international incident over the disappearance of a federal agent from the most powerful country in the world.

"What has he done?" Fernandez asked.

"It's not what he's done. It's what he knows. If one of them holds the key, it must be seized. At all costs."

"But you want to seize them without knowing."

"It's worth the risk."

For who? thought the colonel. "His flight information can be tracked from the States. They will know he landed here."

"But if they cannot verify he went through customs, it leaves many possibilities of what could have happened."

"What about credit card transactions?"

"We can take care of that," Ottman replied. If they could drain Lopez's bank account and plant evidence without anyone noticing, they could change Rickards' credit card transactions.

Fernandez continued staring at Ottman, or rather the man he still believed was named Bauer, quietly weighing his options.

He was in deep now. Perhaps too deep.

The call came barely fifteen minutes later. Ottman took it while Fernandez was still in the room--and listening.

"Go ahead."

Fischer's voice echoed over the tiny speaker. "They've left the hotel again. This time in their car."

"Which direction are they headed?"

"North."

Ottman peered at the colonel standing near the window. "Toward Alerta."

"Correct."

"Can you hear them?"

142

"Yes," said Fischer. "The transmitter is working, but it has a one-kilometer range. When we reach the road north, I will need to fall back to avoid detection."

"What are they saying?"

In his car, Fischer moved the phone from his ear and lowered it down to the small, portable speaker.

"—don't think so." It was Rickards' voice. "If your uncle's secret is somehow still in this town, why hasn't Lopez come back yet? It's only a two-hour drive. If he found something significant, at the very least he would have come back to get some help."

Angela's voice was quiet for a moment. "Maybe he's still looking for it."

"It feels like there's something you're not telling me."

"Me?"

"Yes," Rickards' voice said. "Starting with what that guy was really searching for."

"Lopez?"

"No."

"My uncle?"

"No. The first guy. That British explorer."

"Percy Fawcett?"

"What was Fawcett actually searching for?"

"I told you."

"No, you didn't. I read some of your grandfather's journals on the plane. His pursuit of trying to understand what happened to his brother. But there was nothing about Fawcett. No mention at all."

"Because my grandfather didn't know Fawcett had anything to do with my uncle."

"That's right. And when he did, he suddenly gets on an airplane in the middle of a snowstorm," Rickards said. "So he clearly knew something more about Fawcett."

"Everyone knows about Percy Fawcett."

"Then what does *everyone* think he was looking for?" He cut Angela off as she began to answer. "Not what the history books say. But what other people say."

There was a pause in the speaker. When Angela answered, her voice was in a lower tone. "They're just theories."

"I'm sure they are."

"Some are…pretty wild."

"How wild?"

"Like conspiracy theories."

"I've seen a lot of conspiracy theories that turned out to be true."

"I haven't. I'm an anthropologist. My job is to follow the facts, not what people wish was true. I've lived my life—"

"Spill it!"

The speaker went silent again before she finally answered. "Fawcett said he was looking for the remains of a lost civilization. A place he called 'Z.' A civilization most scholars think was too large to exist in such a harsh environment as the Amazon. But Fawcett was convinced it did. And he was looking for its remains." She paused again. "But some people, other people, think he was looking for Paititi."

"Excuse me?"

"Paititi," she repeated.

"And what is that?"

"The lost Incan city. Also known as the Lost City of Gold."

"Did you say *gold?*"

"Yes. A lost Incan city buried deep in the Amazon. The same one that was mentioned in Sir Arthur Conan Doyle's book *The Lost World*. But it's just a theory."

"*The* Sir Arthur Conan Doyle?"

"Yes," Angela said. "He lived around the turn of the nineteenth century."

There was another pause.

"Wait a minute," Rickards' voice sounded. "A writer wrote a book about this lost city over a hundred years ago?"

"A fictional book."

"And when was our explorer Percy Fawcett searching the jungles of South America?"

"Around the same time."

"And did these two guys know each other?"

"Yes. They were friends."

"Jesus," Rickards moaned. "Don't you think that was need-to-know information?"

"Everyone knows that Doyle's book was based on some of Fawcett's exploits. It's not particularly controversial."

"Why not?"

"Because Doyle's book was fiction," Angela said. "And because Fawcett was also known to embellish his stories. A lot."

"Including this Paititi?"

"It's assumed that Fawcett told Doyle about the legend and Doyle added it to his story. It's never been found. And believe me, hundreds, maybe thousands, of people have looked for it."

"You're sure it's not real."

"Believe me," she said. "It's not real. People have been searching for it for years. Now they're even scanning the jungle with things like radar and lidar. And they still haven't found it."

Rickards was quiet for a long time. "Okay. I told you I don't believe in coincidences. So let me ask you something for the sake of being thorough. With you as our resident historian—"

"Anthropologist."

"Fine. With you as our anthropologist, are you aware of any other historical books that were believed to be fiction but turned out to be fact?"

In his car, Fischer could almost hear Angela take a deep breath, prompting him to glance down at the speaker as he drove.

"Actually...yes." There was a small change in her voice.

145

"With *The Iliad*. Written by Homer, about the Trojan War. And the city of Troy. Everyone thought it was fiction until someone found Troy's remains using clues from the book. An Austrian archaeologist, I think. Or maybe German.

Rickards nodded. "Even I know that story."

"You're saying that you think Paititi is real. Like Troy was real?"

"No. I've known about Paititi for exactly one minute. But I am suggesting that maybe we shouldn't be ruling anything out."

"Doyle's book has been read thousands of times. Millions, probably. If there were real clues as to where Paititi might actually be, people would have discovered it by now."

Rickards didn't answer.

"Right?"

"The quote in your uncle's letter, the one written in German, was from Fawcett's book."

"Yes."

"And Fawcett's book was *not* fiction."

"Correct."

"Then what did the Germans think they'd found?"

Back in the suite, the two older men continued listening until Ottman ended the call--as soon as Paititi was mentioned. The colonel stood facing him.

He wished Fernandez hadn't heard that. He had leverage on the man, but people could still be unpredictable.

"We need them in custody," Ottman said flatly. He tapped a few buttons on his phone to bring up a video, sliding the device forward and pushing *Play* for Fernandez to watch as a small video clip began playing.

"In case you need another reason."

45

The drive took less than two hours, by precisely twelve minutes, allowing them to reach the town well before the southern hemisphere's sunset. A town still in full light and looking almost exactly as he had expected. Much like a small abandoned town in the U.S. would look.

Dozens of houses and shanties lined both sides of the single-lane road, which seemed to pass through without so much as a whisper, disappearing north into another dense canopy of the overhead jungle. On either side, the houses were shabby at best. Poorly painted, if at all, and most resting beneath red, rusted metal roofs made of corrugated sheet metal.

Scattered along the road, in front of several dwellings, were cars or small trucks. Most parked haphazardly along a thin strip of open dirt, hugging each side of the road's asphalt.

What struck Angela more than anything else, though, was the lack of even a single person in sight.

"This may not take long."

She ignored him and leaned forward, peering through the windshield. "There's supposed to be a town center around here."

With a hand still on the wheel, Rickards flicked his finger forward at a large outline as it appeared around a turn, standing alone past the houses.

"Looks new."

She nodded. "It is, judging from some satellite images."

He slowed the car and rolled it into the empty dirt lot in front of the building—two-storied, moderately built, and painted in a light tan color. There were two doors on the bottom and two more at the top of the stairs, though only the bottom offices appeared to be utilized so far. Both had large, hand-painted signs overhead. The first read *Oficina Postal.* The second *ELP.*

"I can guess the first one. Any idea what ELP is?" Rickards asked.

"I think it's the local utility company."

Rickards turned and peered around, checking his side mirrors before looking back over his shoulder. "Kind of dead. What do people in Peru do for fun on a Tuesday evening?"

"I've never been here before." She shrugged. "But generally speaking, pretty much what any developed culture does. Work, come home, eat dinner."

He grinned at her hint of reciprocated sarcasm and moved back to the building. "Well, they obviously don't sit around writing and mailing letters."

Angela laughed. "Like I said. Not that different."

Fischer knew he was getting close when the speaker next to him finally came back to life, picking up their transmitted voices again.

He slowed his car and pulled to the side of the road, edging just around a bend until he spotted the other car in the distance. It was parked in front of a two-story building.

He shifted into reverse and backed up by several feet until he could no longer see them. And they could no longer see him.

***

After trying both doors and finding them locked, Rickards turned around. "Any ideas?"

"I'm not sure." Angela scanned the area, the tiny town bordered entirely by distant green trees, before turning back across the road, where her eyes suddenly stopped on someone standing on the opposite side.

"Joe."

"Yeah?" He followed her gaze and spotted the girl standing between two rundown houses. Her dark head was shaved and she stood tall, wearing what appeared to be a faded pink dress. Angela couldn't make out what the spots on her clothing were. Maybe flowers.

The girl was gripping a walking stick in her left hand and a basket in her right. Unmoving, staring back at them.

Angela wasted no time. She immediately smiled and whispered to Joe.

"Stay here."

The girl did not move. Instead, she watched the white woman gently approach from the opposite side. After reaching the edge of the pavement, the woman stopped …and waved. A small, friendly gesture.

After a curious pause, the young girl waved back.

Angela kept her hand up as a neutral, non-threatening sign while she crossed over the asphalt. Stopping on the opposite side, she waved again.

The girl, now less than fifty feet away, took longer this time, but still repeated the gesture.

Angela remained still and grinned. *"Buenos días."*

The girl nodded. The spots on her dress were indeed flowers.

"Soy un visitante. Me puedes ayudar?"

The girl remained still, her eyes flicking briefly back across the street to Rickards, who was leaning calmly against the small car.

"Estoy buscando un amigo. Desde hace mucho tiempo," Angela said.

The girl ambled forward a few steps. *"Quien?"*

"Un hombre blanco."

The girl came a little closer, just moments before a door squeaked open, and they both glanced at the house, where a woman appeared on the porch. In her late thirties or early forties, she had dark, smooth skin that glistened from the evening humidity. Attractive brown eyes examined Angela curiously. Angela waved again from the road, sheepishly.

The woman, clearly the girl's mother, studied her for a long moment, listening while her daughter repeated what Angela had said.

When the girl finished, the mother became quiet, leaving all three in a tense and uncomfortable silence dotted only by the chirping of scattered crickets beginning their evening ritual.

After a full minute of stillness, the woman finally moved forward, stepping off her ramshackle porch, over two weather-worn steps and onto the grass, where she motioned to her daughter.

The girl trotted to her and wrapped an arm around her mother's waist.

"*De donde eres?*"

"*Los Estados Unidos,*" Angela answered.

The woman nodded with a tilt of her head. "You American?"

"Yes. I am."

The mother glanced at Joe, still waiting across the road near the car. "Why you here?"

"You speak English." Angela grinned. "Uh…we came to look for someone."

"You look?" the woman replied but tried the sentence again. "*Who* you look?"

"A friend. From a long time ago. Many years."

The woman blinked.

"Is Spanish easier?" asked Angela. "*Español?*"

"Engleesh," the woman replied. "I—"

She looked at her daughter, who grinned and said, "Practice."

"I practeece."

Angela grinned. "Of course."

"Me…Elena," she said.

Angela gently touched her chest. "Angela."

Looking across the street, Elena eyed Rickards again.

"He American?"

"Yes. We both are. American. And looking for a friend, who was also American. Many years ago."

"How...long?"

"Before you and I were born. Maybe sixty years?"

"What call you friend?" The woman looked down when her daughter began whispering something. "What name?"

"Roger Reed," Angela said. "I have a picture."

She inched forward while reaching into her back pocket, withdrawing a few pieces of paper. One she removed and held out to the woman.

Elena stepped forward and took it, not noticing the slight trembling in Angela's hand. She examined the old black-and-white photo until, grinning, she handed it back. "Me too young."

"I understand." Angela glanced up and down along the empty road. "Is there anyone else who might know?"

Again, the girl whispered up to her mother.

"Why you look him?"

"He disappeared. A long time ago. We want to know what happened to him."

"Why?"

Angela shrugged. "We think he may have left something."

The girl's mother looked up at the fading light, the cool color of the evening becoming dark blue with scattered wisps of pink clouds. The sun was already well below the jungled mountain behind them. She motioned back across the road to Rickards. "Call you friend."

Angela turned and waved Rickards over. She waited as he calmly walked across the asphalt and stopped next to her, allowing Elena to look him up and down.

"Who you name?"

"Joe," he replied. "Rickards."

Elena studied him, ending with a batted eyelash. "Why you come?"

"I haven't the slightest idea," he said and looked at

Angela sarcastically.

The woman didn't understand the words but seemed to understand the look he gave her and grinned, revealing an attractive set of white teeth between her two full lips. She turned to Angela, then once again to Rickards, before motioning them to follow.

Rickards guessed that the town was not more than a mile in circumference, making for a relatively short trek through and between several shanty homes before they reached one farther back from the road. This one was smaller and in seemingly worse condition than Elena's, if that were possible, leaving Rickards to duck beneath a sagging plywood awning before stepping up onto a very old porch step. Thick, waist-high bushes surrounded the entire structure as if the jungle were attempting to slowly reclaim its spot.

He felt the boards bow under his weight and stepped off again, back beside Angela.

Several feet in front of them, Elena reached out and knocked loudly against the front door, darkened from a thin film of gray mold. It was promptly opened by a young man barely in his twenties, with darker skin and dressed in shorts and a tank top, immediately smiling.

"Elena!"

The woman accepted a hug and motioned to the two Americans while speaking rapidly in a dialect Angela did not recognize.

The young man listened patiently, maintaining his smile and peering curiously at her, then Rickards. His expression became excited at the word *American*, causing him to smile even wider.

"You are American?" he asked.

"Yes. Do you speak English?"

"I speak English!" the young man said excitedly. "Me name Saturnin." He made a surfing gesture with his hands. "I love America! Brady Bunch! Chips!"

Rickards squinted and leaned to the side, where he spotted the corner of a television screen inside the tiny living room.

The young man looked back and forth between them and raised both thumbs. "Fonzie! Ayyyy."

"Great," Rickards mumbled.

"This is a good sign," whispered Angela, before extending a hand to shake Saturnin's as he rushed forward.

"Friends!"

"Is he talking about the show or the noun?"

"Quiet," she said and nodded with a big smile. "Yes, friends!"

"Why you here?"

"We're looking for someone."

He pointed to himself proudly. "Saturnin knows everyone!"

"Oh good. We—"

"Mayor!"

Angela stopped. "Excuse me?"

"I am mayor. Of Alerta!"

"You're the mayor?"

He grinned again, showing a wide set of teeth with one missing. "Yes. Saturnin is mayor and knows everyone!"

Rickards was becoming amused. "How old are you?"

"Twenty-one. Youthest mayor in Alerta!"

"Great." With that, Rickards motioned as if passing the conversation to Angela.

"Saturnin," she said and put a hand on his arm. "Um, congratulations! We…need help. Finding someone. From a long time ago."

The young mayor raised his dark eyebrows inquisitively. "Who you looking for?"

"Someone who was here a very long time ago. Sixty years."

His eyes opened wide. "Sixty?"

"About."

Saturnin turned and spoke again to Elena, this time in a

longer exchange. Then he turned back to Angela. "You have picture?"

"Yes." She reached back and retrieved it again. Allowing Rickards to notice the shaking in her hand.

Saturnin studied the small photo and pursed his lips. He looked up and studied both of them again before handing it back. "Come," he said. "Come with Saturnin."

The three Peruvians led the way into the darkness, toward another group of porch lights. Rickards followed, but paused when Angela didn't join him. "You coming?"

She stared at him, biting her lip.

"You okay?"

"Um." She turned and looked around. "Do you…know where we are? I mean, like where the car is?"

"I think so."

Angela nodded and, with a hint of reluctance, took a step forward, then another, until reaching Rickards. She took a breath and grabbed his shirt sleeve. "Let's go."

They caught up three houses later, where Elena and her daughter were waiting outside. The front door was open, allowing the interior light to shine out onto an even smaller porch.

Elena motioned them inside, prompting Rickards to take the lead, ducking as he stepped into a small, poorly lit room. Angela was close behind him, followed by Elena and her daughter.

From a small hallway, Saturnin emerged, moving slowly and leading a figure out from the back room. They watched as an old man, small and frail, shuffled forward while grasping Saturnin's left arm. Together, they moved into the cramped front room, where Saturnin lowered the old man into a torn, padded chair that looked just as old. Next to the chair was a small wooden table, marred and stained from years of use. A matching chair rested on the opposite side. A lamp in the corner tenuously leaned against the plywood wall and projected shadows over magazines and clothing stacked in small piles on the floor. A rusted, bent walker stood nearby, which Elena grabbed and pulled close.

"It's his grandfather," the young girl whispered, standing next to Angela.

Angela glanced down with surprise. "Saturnin's grandfather?"

The girl nodded. "My mother and Saturnin like you. More than the German."

"German?"

They were interrupted by Saturnin taking Angela's hand and motioning her to the open chair. "Talking is hard," the young mayor said, "but he hears good."

Angela lowered herself down nervously and glanced up at Rickards. She then smiled gently at the old man, who, with one clouded eye, appeared to be staring at her.

"Does he understand English?"

"Little much."

"Ah, okay." Angela scooted in and leaned forward, raising her voice. "H-hello there. Thank you for seeing us."

The old man barely moved.

She glanced back at Joe. "We are trying to find someone. Or something about someone. Who was here many years ago."

Angela turned and looked up at Rickards with an expression that said *help*.

The old man grunted and tried to speak but delivered something unintelligible. Saturnin moved in and spoke quietly in his grandfather's ear, using the same dialect he had with Elena.

The old man squinted and focused on Angela. With a slight waver, he studied her through his good eye and mumbled, his hand shaking in an attempt to motion something.

"What your friend's name?"

"Roger Reed. We think he was here in the fifties."

Saturnin repeated the words while Angela again retrieved her photograph. She placed it on the table in front of the old man and watched while Saturnin picked it up and

155

inserted it between his grandfather's crooked fingers, helping him hold it still.

His grandfather stared at the picture with a leathery expression that never changed. After a long silence, he turned and spoke to Saturnin in a low, garbled tone.

"Why your friend was here?"

"We don't know."

Saturnin repeated the message.

The man continued staring at the picture gripped between his dark, wrinkled fingers. His one good eye moved back and forth between the photo and Angela before he mumbled something else.

"My grandfather says he remembers you friend."

"Really?!" Angela looked at Rickards excitedly, just as his phone rang inside his pocket. He fumbled momentarily and pulled it out, examining the screen. He frowned apologetically to Angela and briskly exited the small room, moving out and down the porch, back onto the grass outside.

Inside, Angela turned back around. "He remembers him?"

Saturnin nodded and listened to his grandfather again. "He says he knew of him. A kind man." After listening more, he grinned at Angela. "He also says you look like him."

"He was my great-uncle."

In the darkness outside, Rickards quickly raised the phone to his ear, surprised it was even connecting. "Hello?"

"Joe? It's Ken Stives."

"Who?"

"Ken Stives. Can you hear me?"

"Yes, I can hear you."

"Can you hear me, Joe?"

"Yes! Can you hear me?"

"Barely, where are you?"

"In South America," Rickards answered.

"South America?"

"It's a long story. What's up?"

"Sorry, you're fading in and out."

"That's because I'm in the middle of nowhere." Rickards looked around and moved away from the small shanties. "That better?"

"A little."

"What's up, Ken?"

"I'm not really sure. But I think something weird is going on."

"What do you mean?"

"I mean with that letter of yours."

"What about it?"

There was a brief shuffling on the other end. "Remember when I told you I talked to the mail carrier who delivered it? To your friend's grandfather?"

"Yeah."

"Well, now I can't find him. Or even get a hold of him. And he hasn't shown up for work in three days."

"What?"

"No one can find him, man. They've tried calling him, and I've even gone to his house. He's nowhere to be found."

"You're kidding."

"Not kidding. The guy has vanished. His wife is freaking out. Apparently, someone called in to a local branch saying they were new and asked who their new mail carrier was. But that's it. The police are now involved and are interviewing people."

Rickards' expression grew still. He slowly raised his arm and looked at the date on his watch. "What day did he go missing?"

"Saturday. None of us can find him, so I wanted to see if you'd talked to him."

"How would I talk to him? I don't even know his name."

"Oh, I thought maybe I told you."

"You didn't."

Inside, Angela watched eagerly as Saturnin continued translating to his grandfather.

"Can you tell me why my uncle was here? Did he leave anything?"

After a moment, the young mayor frowned. "He say he does not know."

Angela retrieved the copy of the original letter from another pocket and unfolded it. She laid it on the table. "Does your grandfather understand what this means?"

The old man's shaking hand took the paper and held it up, reading, then finally lowering it again.

"I'm sorry. He say no."

"Does he know what this *Almv10* means?"

Saturnin asked and waited. This time, instead of mumbling, his grandfather struggled to lean forward, raising his shaking hand up and reaching out toward her. His crooked fingers trembled from side to side before he raised them up and down.

"What is he doing?"

Saturnin shrugged. "I don't know."

Suddenly, Rickards stormed forcefully back up the steps and into the house. He looked directly down at Angela. "We're leaving."

"What?"

"I said, we're leaving. Right now!"

With a firm grip on her arm, he pulled Angela from the tiny house and back into the darkness outside, where she finally yanked herself free.

"What are you doing?!"

"We have to get out of here."

"Why?"

"Because something weird is happening," Rickards said. "My friend from the post office, Ken Stives—you remember him—just called me. He said the mail carrier who delivered that letter is now missing."

"What?!"

"Yeah. And I just called the nursing home. They've issued a missing person's on Lillian Porter. She wasn't at her sister's house. Someone else knows about that letter!"

"Oh God."

"We're leaving," he repeated. "Now!"

She blinked and followed him down the set of creaking steps. Reaching the bottom, she gasped when the area suddenly exploded into a flood of blinding white light from headlights of what appeared to be four different cars hidden in the darkness and surrounding the front of the tiny home.

Angela seized Joe's arm as he instinctively stepped in front of her. Behind them, Elena and Saturnin both rushed onto the porch and instantly covered their eyes.

Beside one of the cars, Colonel Fernandez stepped forward, blocking part of a headlight as he studied the two Americans frozen in the white glare.

He hoped the old German Bauer—or whatever his name was—was right that they could keep a federal agent in custody without anyone knowing. Because if not, he'd better have enough money, or resources, to bribe one hell of a lot of people.

46

Gau Lower Silesia, Poland

January 23rd, 1962

The earthly pounding against solid brick was almost entirely muffled by vast surrounding fields of white snow, pristine and untouched, interrupted only by a single track of footprints winding through trees and stretching downhill to a dense patch of snow-covered ash and maple trees.

The pounding stopped and a lone figure stood up from a waist-deep hole, again scanning the low-lying forested hills. He was kilometers from the nearest farm, but one could never anticipate who might be wandering the hillsides in the dead of winter.

Still seeing nothing, twenty-five-year-old Karl Ottman readjusted the wool cloth covering his nose and mouth back into place and continued digging.

He'd found the first layer of brick resting several feet beneath the soil, precisely where his father told him it would be with the right calculations. He continued clearing away more dirt to widen the opening.

Once it was large enough, he raised the heavy pick over his head and brought the tip crashing down onto the thick red brick, barely scraping its surface. It would take several more impacts before even the faintest crack appeared.

Again and again, with each new blow, the crack began to widen and crumble around its edges, enough to allow the pick head to finally pierce the surface.

Ottman looked up again and scanned.

Still no one.

After several more swings, the first brick finally broke into multiple pieces, prompting Ottman to sink to his knees and begin pulling them apart.

One by one, he threw the chunks out of the hole, where they disappeared into the deep surrounding snow. Then he rose back to his feet to attack the next layer of brick.

It took two more hours to finally punch through the second tier. When he did, the heavy pick suddenly slipped from his gloved hands and nearly disappeared into blackness below.

Ottman wrestled it back up through the hole and continued swinging. Each strike widened the dark mouth, with chunk after chunk disappearing into the empty chasm. Each piece of brick echoed as it struck ground somewhere beneath him.

Twenty minutes later, the hole was wide enough to shine a light into. It was nearly nightfall before he had an opening large enough to allow a human body through.

Once he was inside, dangling from the ropes, it was just as he expected.

And exactly as described.

Of course, it wasn't the tunnel he had been searching for. That was another fifty meters further down, through solid earth and rock that would require digging equipment and dozens of men. No, what the young Ottman needed was something even more difficult to find—one of four access tunnels extending up from the main cavern. Those four small tunnels, spaced at 1,000 meters apart, led down into the hidden tunnel.

After sliding down the short rope, Ottman stepped onto the slick stone and inched downward, counting one step at a time with a bare hand carefully pressed against the wall. The smallest patch of ice could spell doom and cause a sudden slip or fall. Or, even worse, a serious injury, leaving Karl Ottman alone and stranded, unable to climb back out.

After the 187th step, the access tunnel opened into a wider, colder space, revealing a rusted handrail along an outer edge. But when Ottman carefully peered over the edge, he saw nothing. Until he pointed his torch downward.

From the oddly shaped stone walkway, the view was even more breathtaking than he had imagined. Hidden in utter darkness for years and illuminated now only by the beam of his wandering torch, the dark gray armored metal beast stretched as far as his light could reach. Perfectly preserved and frozen in time for nearly twenty years. An artifact of Nazi history that time had completely forgotten.

Hiding motionlessly inside a collapsed tunnel no one alive knew anything about.

Except Ottman.

The others who had known were now all dead. Two by natural causes, and three more from suicide before the Nuremberg trials. And finally, the last one, Ottman's own father, from fire.

Erhard Ottman, father, former S.S. officer, and founding member of the Ahnenerbe. Desperately trying to communicate to his only heir through a pair of half-melted, burnt lips and vocal cords that were barely functional. Using the last of his strength to explain not just what the Nazi Gold Train was, but where it was buried. Precisely.

The tunnel itself was too far from the surface for Ottman to reach. And any trace of railroad tracks would not be found within half a kilometer. They had been disassembled by laboring Jews who were simply told the materials were needed elsewhere.

The four access tunnels existed much closer to the surface yet were still sealed off. The one he had found was the same from which his father had exited when the train had been hidden, before making careful notes on its location.

If his son could find it, if he could find the train, it would give him all the resources he would ever need to help him locate one of two remaining copies of Fawcett's letter—the copies he had sent to Hitler and Himmler. And within them, the most important archaeological discovery in human history.

Before his father's death, Karl Ottman had not known any of this. Any of what his father had found during the war, anything about the train of Nazi gold, or anything about the three copies of documents, one of which his father had tried to save from the fire and failed.

In the final three hours of his life, Ottman's father struggled to explain everything he could through gasps and garbles, even refusing surgery that might have saved him. He could not risk it. Could not risk the chance of the secrets dying with him on an operating table.

But three hours was not long enough. The gargling, bubbling fluids only grew worse, making what few words he could manage increasingly unintelligible, leaving his son stunned and reeling with far more questions than answers.

And of course, his word.

His word to a dying father that he would find the train, the documents, and finally, the secret of which Fawcett had spoken.

An oath that would take him longer than ever imagined. The better part of his adult life.

47

Joe Rickards was awoken by an ache in his right arm. His shoulder, to be precise. A deep painful throbbing stemming from lack of circulation.

His eyes slowly opened under an overhead light—a bright glare which, after several long seconds, grew into the shape of a single light bulb high overhead.

Rickards blinked and looked at his right shoulder, pulsating with pain. That's when he discovered his hand was raised over his head and handcuffed to a rail affixed to the wall, causing his arm to hang limply.

He blinked again, this time longer, and tried to focus. He followed his arm up the wall to the railing, then down back to his body and finally, to the bed on which he was lying. Sheetless, with a badly stained mattress, and one foot hanging over the side.

He raised his leg. One *shoeless* foot.

With a painful wince, he turned and pushed himself back up in the bed, leaning against a cold, filthy wall to give some much-needed support to his dead shoulder.

It wasn't until he heard someone speaking that he looked up.

"What the hell did you do?"

Rickards' eyes struggled to focus and found a figure standing nearby, on the opposite side of a long set of steel bars.

He stared for a long time, blinking.

"Don't remember?"

Rickards licked his lips with some effort. "What?"

The figure pointed at him between the bars. "I said, what did you do?"

Rickards pushed further up and shook his head.

The other man grinned. "I've never seen someone handcuffed to the wall in a holding cell before."

Rickards squinted at the man. Large, both in inches and girth, and bald, with black skin and a long straight white goatee below his chin. "Who are you?"

The man laughed heartily. "I'm the one in the cell next to you. And suddenly feeling a hell of a lot better about my situation." He studied Rickards curiously. "Name's Mike Morton."

Rickards' lips were slow. "Joe."

"Pleased to meet you, Joe. I think. Judging by the look on your face, I'd say you're feeling about as bad as you look."

"Thanks."

"Anytime."

Rickards peered thoughtfully at the man. "You're American."

Mike displayed a wide grin between his white mustache and goatee. "Even better. Texan."

Rickards nodded with a dry grin and looked around the rest of his holding cell. The needles of intense pain now shooting through his arm were a sign his circulation was returning. He glanced up at the light again. "How long have I been here?"

"Few hours." Morton turned to look back at an argument behind him between two other prisoners in his larger group cell, before gradually turning back around. "You were pretty out of it when they brought you in. Heard the guards talking about a woman too."

Rickards didn't remember any of it. He struggled to recall his last memories. A call from Ken Stives, then rushing into the tiny house to grab Angela. And finally, some clouded memories that weren't crystalizing. *Bright lights and...a shadow. Maybe a human figure. Then pain in one of his legs.* He fought to hold onto the images.

Pain. In his leg. And the image of...a dart.

"So, what exactly did you do wrong?"

Rickards shook his head. "I got on a plane."

"I see. Well, it couldn't be too bad. Otherwise, you'd be on your way to the Palace of Justice for processing. You just get here?"

He nodded.

Was it yesterday? He wasn't sure how much time had passed.

He focused on Morton, only half visible between the bars but clearly in better spirits. "What are you here for?"

"Ah, I'm here all the time."

Rickards squinted. "What does that mean?"

"I'm in for trespassing. It's a long story."

"How often is *all the time?*"

"Once every couple weeks. Sometimes more. Law says they have to hold me for twelve hours, but then they just let me go." Morton gave a spirited gesture down his body. "I'm not exactly a threat at my age."

"How old are you?"

"Sixty-nine. But I've been told I don't look a day over seventy-three."

With a small, pained smile, Rickards looked up to see if there was a way to free his arm from the railing by working the cuffs back and forth. He couldn't.

"You with that girl?"

"Did you see her?"

"No, just heard some talking between the guards."

"Any idea where they took her?"

"Nope. But I'm guessing it was the same guys brought you in that took her. Almost dragging ya, by the way." He grinned again. "Figured you robbed a bank or something."

"Nope. No bank."

"Well, if getting on a plane was all you did, then you appear to have made a terrific first impression. On somebody."

"Apparently."

"And the guys that brought you in weren't cops. They looked like military."

"Wonderful."

"What do you do there, Joe?"

"Huh?"

"For a living. Your job."

After a pause, Rickards answered, "I'm a house painter."

Morton laughed. "Gotcha. I take it this is your first time in beautiful Puerto Maldonado."

He nodded. "You an ex-pat?"

"Good guess. Yep. Been down here a couple years since retiring."

"Congratulations."

Morton laughed. "Word of advice there, Joe. Be careful with the sarcasm down here. I think it's funny, but the Peruvians are a touchy bunch. They don't take a lot of lip. Especially from Americans. I stay polite and they always let me out."

"Thanks. But something tells me I'm not leaving anytime soon."

"Why's that?"

"Because they weren't after me. They wanted the girl."

48

It was true. And even in his weakened state, it took Rickards only minutes to realize it. Angela held all the cards. Literally. She had the copies. She had the pictures. And her grandfather's journals. She also had all the details about her grandfather, her uncle, their backgrounds, and the entire history behind it all.

But none of those were the reason Karl Ottman wanted her. It was much simpler than that.

She was the easy target.

Rickards was a risk on all fronts. A federal agent, prone to violence, and, according to Ottman's sources in the States, diagnosed as potentially unstable.

The Reed woman was none of those. At least not on paper. However, at the moment, she looked to Ottman as if she was about to come apart from some kind of *condition*, as he studied her through the one-way mirror.

Angela Reed, cuffed to a chair and visibly shaking, was related to both men, knew the Lillian Porter woman, and was the obvious beneficiary of anything her grandfather or uncle might have left behind. And therefore, would know a hell of a lot more than Rickards. She would also undoubtedly be easier to intimidate, which already appeared to be working.

When he entered the room, Angela's shaking grew even worse, her handcuff causing an audible rattling sound. Above her, the overhead lamp gave the room a Gestapo-like feeling and a special sense of irony for Ottman. Some interrogation techniques had stood the test of time for a reason.

He ambled quietly past her and around the edge of the

table. Lowering himself into the opposite chair, he opened his taut, wrinkled mouth to speak, only to be interrupted by Angela.

"Where's Joe?"

Ottman closed his mouth and examined her. This was far from ideal. He wanted a private location, not a Peruvian police department. People knew they were here. And certain things that happened here would be recorded by matter of procedure, requiring even more effort to have those traces erased. Damage control was quickly becoming a problem, not the least of which was Colonel Fernandez, who was growing into a considerable issue. The man was becoming increasingly paranoid, convinced that having Rickards in the facility for any length of time was a political fuse just waiting to be lit.

Fernandez was not as unshakable as Ottman had originally thought. *Duress was always the window into a person's true makeup.* If there was one common trait amongst people like Fernandez, it was that their dedication only went so far. And they would quickly turn desperate to avoid the risk of going down alone. Meaning that if Fernandez were backed into a corner, he would do whatever was necessary to survive. That, of course, was quickly making him less of an asset and more of a liability.

"I would be more concerned about yourself," Ottman finally replied to Angela, "than Mr. Rickards."

Angela's mental state had cascaded from nervousness, to frightened, to terrified. All her fears about traveling back to South America were being realized in spades. The *feel* of a third-world country was unique and distinct. Dark below the surface. A place where rules and procedures fell away the farther one traveled from highly populated areas. Reminding her just how quickly her naivete had eroded when living in Bolivia as a young archaeologist. And not just for her. Most of the other students were also shocked at the utter disregard for the law the further out they traveled.

Still, though, she and the others continued to believe their foreign status was enough to protect them. And it did for a while--until the attack, which was not from the authorities, but the local cartel.

The feeling of helplessness was returning. Quickly. The sick sensation of being trapped and utterly at the whim of someone else's mood or agenda.

And now it was happening all over again. Fear—exuding from within her chest wall, all the way down her arms and legs. Leaving her within a hair's breadth of outright panic.

She peered nervously at the large mirror, frightened at the thought of who might be waiting on the other side.

"I'm an American citizen," she said in a whisper.

"Yes," the old man replied. "I know."

"I would like a phone call."

At this, Ottman smiled. "And who might you call?"

Angela fell quiet.

"We both know why you're here, Ms. Reed. What you've come for." He reached into the breast pocket of his suit and pulled out her copies of the letter and envelope. He unfolded them and laid them down on the metal table.

The sick feeling inside her worsened.

"Shall we start again?" he asked.

She didn't reply, prompting Ottman to continue and lower another item onto the table. One of her grandfather's journals.

"I hope this *situation* is finally beginning to dawn on you."

She glanced silently at the small leather-bound book.

"I know more than you think, Ms. Reed. More than you do, in fact, about what this is all about. What I need from you are simply a few missing pieces."

"I don't know anything."

"Of course you do. Otherwise, you wouldn't be here."

"I'm a tourist."

Ottman glanced at his watch without expression. Then he shook his head. "I am many things, Ms. Reed, but a patient man is not one of them. Nor compassionate. I suggest you dispense with the games and reconsider your answers."

"I haven't done anything wrong."

"This isn't about doing something wrong," he said. "It's about being in the *wrong place*. And at the wrong time. But if you cooperate, there is no reason both you and Mr. Rickards cannot be on the next flight home, unharmed and nothing lost but a few short days. You can return to your lives just as they were. Back to your job at the university, as though nothing happened."

"And Lillian?"

Ottman shrugged. "To anyone *else*."

The affirmation in the old man's eyes made her stomach turn. "I'm going to be sick."

"Listen to me." Ottman slammed his palm down on the table. "Carefully. I need information. That is all. And I *will* have it. One way or another. The only question is whether I will allow both you and Mr. Rickards to walk out. It's up to you."

Angela swallowed her nausea, trying to shift her thoughts from Lillian to Joe. "What...kind of information?"

Ottman leaned forward, sensing a change. "Everything you know about the letter and the man who sent it. Your uncle."

"You mean great-uncle."

"Great-uncle."

Angela remained motionless, staring at him. Nervously, she mulled the question. Her uncle and grandfather had already died over this. Would they have wanted her to as well?

"He was a Monuments Man," she replied.

"Yes. I know."

"He died fifty years before I was born. So I don't know much."

"I doubt that." After a contemplative pause, he pushed the copy of the letter forward. "What is this?"

"A letter."

"No. At the bottom, where it says *Almv10*. What does it mean?"

"I don't know."

Something suddenly clicked for Angela, deep down, and her expression changed. Still staring at the man, she asked, "What nationality are you?"

"What?"

"I said, what nationality are you?"

"Who or what I am is irrelevant. What you should be worried about..."

There it was again. In his voice. Very distant, but there. A faint crispness in his words. And a slight inflection in his short *A*'s. Her attention moved to his face, his strong jawline and nose, leaving her wondering what color hair he used to have.

"You're Austrian. Or German."

Ottman studied the young woman's eyes.

"My background is the least of your concerns."

The mental distraction allowed Angela's trembling to momentarily subside. He was German! How had she not seen it before? she wondered. Because his English was near perfect. She blinked, thinking to herself. What had the little girl said in Alerta? They trusted her more than "the German."

It was him. Or someone like him. In Alerta searching for the same thing. Her eyes moved to the copy of the letter in front of her. And on it, the paragraph written by her uncle. The quote from Percy Fawcett's book translated into *German*.

The old man in front of her didn't ask what it said. He didn't have to. *He could already read it!*

Ottman watched silently as Angela's eyes turned back to the letter. She was beginning to put the pieces together, or she wouldn't have asked about his nationality.

"You do not seem very concerned about your

health…Angela."

The tone in his words made her look up again.

"We can sit here and traipse about for as long as you like," he lied. "But my patience will only endure for so long, before your chances of being on the next plane go to zero."

Ottman placed his phone on the table and tapped on the screen to begin playing a video. In a view from across the street, Joe Rickards could be seen fighting with two men in the park, just before Angela herself appeared in the frame.

Ottman watched the look on Angela's face as it grew from surprise to shock. He reached forward again and froze it.

"How difficult," Ottman said, "do you think it would be to turn this into a few weeks in jail? Or perhaps months? For both of you."

49

Mike Morton turned around again at the commotion behind him, this time louder. He suddenly yelled in Spanish at two men on the opposite side of the large cell before dangling his tongue out and shaking his head back and forth.

When he turned back, he grinned at Rickards. "They leave you alone if they think you're crazy."

Rickards grinned back.

"Works pretty much anywhere, too."

"I bet it does."

Rickards sat up and slid off the squeaking cot, managing to twist and stand in front of the wall. He was still dizzy, but at least he was able to eliminate the strain from his shoulder, rubbing it with his free hand.

"You all right?"

"Doesn't matter."

Morton glanced over his shoulder and put his face between the bars. In a lower voice, he asked, "So, what agency are you with?"

Rickards stared at him, then looked past at the others behind him, all watching the two Americans. "I don't know what you mean."

Morton nodded and gave him a wink. "Roger that." He then straightened and spoke again, loudly. "So, what did you come down here for? You don't look like you're here on business. Let me guess, Machu Picchu?"

"No."

"Mapinguari!"

"I don't know what that is."

"The Sasquatch of South America. No, wait, El Lobizon, the werewolf!"

"No."

"You here to see the pink dolphins?"

"Sorry."

A jovial Morton frowned. "*Are* you here on business?"

"I just came to help someone."

"The woman."

"Yeah. Not exactly sure why we're in here, though."

"I've got news for you, Joe. Down here, they don't need a reason."

"Well, I did sort of get in a fight. In the park."

"You got in a fight? With who, your lady friend?"

"No. Some locals."

"Oh geez. That's not good."

"Yeah, that was explained to me."

"So, you think that's why you're in here?"

"No idea. But it's my best guess. What about you?"

Morton grinned. "Ah, you know. Just an ex-pat living the dream. Single and carefree."

"You're wearing a wedding ring."

The large man glanced down.

"Your wife didn't want to come?"

Morton's grin faded. "She couldn't come. Unfortunately."

Rickards read the expression in Morton's brown eyes. "I'm sorry."

"It's okay," he said, straightening again. "I'm sure she wouldn't have wanted to see me in here."

"Especially over and over."

Morton laughed. "Right."

"So, why all the trespassing?"

"Because they don't always have roads where I need to go."

Rickards cocked his head. It wasn't really an answer, but then again, neither were his. There was something different about the man. Something Rickards couldn't quite put his finger on. Affable, but not bothersome, with a distinct feeling of understated intelligence.

"What did you retire from, Mike?"

"NASA."

Rickards looked at him, surprised. "The space agency?"

"That's the one."

"And what did you do for them?"

"What didn't I do?" he chuckled. "I was an engineer. Worked on propulsion systems and then later, satellites."

"No kidding."

"Nope." Morton puffed out his chest slightly for effect. "Was the youngest engineer to work on the Saturn V rockets back in the seventies."

"Really?"

"Really. Our last rocket put Skylab into orbit, which is how I got into the sats."

"So, you're a real-life rocket scientist."

Morton laughed. "That's right."

"You never know who you're going to meet in a Peruvian jail. An actual rocket scientist."

Morton winked back at him. "And a house painter."

174

50

When Ottman stepped back into the observation room behind the one-way mirror, Colonel Fernandez was waiting with arms folded across his decorated chest. His face and posture were both heated.

"She doesn't know anything," he growled in a thick accent. "Not a damn thing!"

Ottman turned and looked at the Reed woman through the glass. "She knows more."

"She knows nothing!"

Ottman ignored the colonel's outburst and looked at two of his men standing behind him. One of them, Fischer, raised an eyebrow.

Fernandez continued, barking, "I cannot keep them for nothing! Especially *him*."

"Of course you can. You have the video."

"Of a fight," Fernandez almost spat. "It's barely more than an argument."

Now the old man looked directly at the colonel, irritation visible in his cold blue eyes. "You will keep them until you are instructed to let them go."

The officer shook his head bitterly but said nothing. Instead, he stepped within inches of Ottman as he passed on his way to the door. He yanked it open, glared at the old man and stepped out, slamming the door shut behind him.

Ottman turned back to the window, where Angela had suddenly looked in his direction after hearing the slamming door.

"Now what?" Fischer asked, stepping forward.

51

One of the guards yelled something in Spanish, causing Mike Morton to turn. He then grinned back at Rickards. "That's me. Not even twelve hours this time."

He reached a hand through the bars attempting to shake, prompting Rickards to do the same, only to find they couldn't reach each other. Both men smiled and shrugged.

"Nice to meet you, Joe."

"Pleasure."

Morton turned and walked to the front of the cell, meeting the young guard at the door, waiting until it slid sideways to allow him to exit. After a short exchange in Spanish, the guard grinned and reached past Morton, slamming the cage closed again.

Together, the two left the room, passing Rickards' cell on the way out. "Go Texas."

Morton winked. "Hope you get to see your pink dolphins."

***

The colonel was fuming. The situation was quickly becoming untenable. Something about which the German didn't show the slightest concern.

Fernandez made it to the door leading into the offices before one of his soldiers suddenly threw it open from the other side, relieved to find him.

"Sir, you have an urgent call!"

"From who?"

The soldier gulped. "The United States. From their State Department."

The colonel's face went white.

✝✝✝

Rickards couldn't tell how long it was before the guard came back for him. Maybe forty-five minutes. The guard hurried to his cell door and spoke quickly in Spanish, with Rickards unable to understand a word. All he could do was stand up and calmly wait next to the railing.

The guard gave him several commands until finally concluding the American wasn't comprehending anything. Irritated, he slid the door open, stepped forward into the cell and rushed to unlock the handcuff from the railing. He pushed Rickards toward the door, where another guard was waiting, this one larger and taller.

The waiting guard wrapped a hand around Rickards' arm and pulled him out and down the short hall until they reached a locked door. The guard tapped on its narrow glass window.

The door opened from the other side, allowing Rickards and his guard through. They passed two more guards and then went through a second door.

As he was pulled forward, Rickards looked down at the other end of the handcuffs dangling below his hand. Their procedures couldn't be this lax.

They continued forward and turned left down another, longer hallway painted in a bland off-white with a long, polished speckled floor. They made it only halfway to the end before someone yelled behind them.

The guard halted and turned, as did Rickards, to find another man hurrying to catch them. This one wearing a military uniform.

The man spoke authoritatively to the guard before turning and motioning to yet another person approaching from around the corner. This man, older than the others, walked briskly toward them. Judging from the decorations on his chest, he was a high-ranking officer. Rickards guessed a major or colonel.

The stone-faced officer approached until within just a few feet, where he surprised Rickards by speaking English.

"Mr. Rickards, I am Colonel Fernandez." He motioned the guard to remove Rickards' remaining handcuff. "We are sorry to have detained you. It appears there has been a mistake. We would like to extend our sincerest apologies."

A puzzled Rickards watched while the handcuff was unlocked and slipped from his wrist. His eyes returned to Fernandez. "This was an accident?"

"A misunderstanding. I assure you our officers will be reprimanded. Please accept my apology."

Rickards stared at him apprehensively. "What about Angela Reed?"

"She too is being released. Also with our apology. This man," he said, looking at the guard, "will take you to where you can reclaim your things."

Rickards looked back and forth between them. "Okayyy."

"I hope you can forgive us, and we can, as you say, put this to bed."

"Fine."

Fernandez produced an uncomfortable smile and waved the guard forward, watching the two now as they turned and walked in the opposite direction. Near the end of the hall, as they approached a wide, windowed door, Rickards glanced back to see Fernandez still standing in the hallway.

What the colonel did not realize was the position he was standing in. Relaxed, with hands at his sides, dressed in pressed fatigues.

Something Rickards knew from his years as an investigator was that everyone had a unique posture, especially when standing or walking. Almost like a visual fingerprint to someone who noticed such details.

It was the same stance Rickards had seen the night before of a silhouette standing in front of the automobile headlights.

Just before they were taken.

52

Rickards was quickly escorted to the front office, where he spotted Angela. She was alone, sitting on a blue plastic bench against the wall. Above her head, a wide bulletin board was covered with papers and flyers momentarily reminding him of the tiny frozen Tri-County airport he and Dana Gutierrez had visited in Colorado, where the whole thing had started.

When Angela saw him, she jumped to her feet and rushed across the room, tearfully hugging him. After several seconds, she released and stepped back. "Sorry."

"It's okay. Been a strange couple of days."

She sniffed and wiped her nose with a tissue. "That's putting it mildly."

"What say we get out of here?"

"Yes," she said with a hearty nod. "Please!"

Ignoring the feeble smiles from the officers at the desk, Rickards opened the door and followed Angela outside, finding himself relieved to be back in the warm, humid air. In front of them, several concrete steps led down to the sidewalk, where parked cars lined the street in front of them. Beyond, on the opposite side, a small grassy area sat between two downtown buildings, where a few locals were relaxing.

They made it halfway down the steps before Rickards noticed, across the street, two people standing under a small tree watching him and Angela. A boy and what looked like his grandfather.

Rickards blinked and looked closer. It was the same boy he had tried to help the day before. In the park. And who had subsequently disappeared.

Suddenly, the roar of an engine rounded the corner, followed immediately by an old yellow Toyota pickup truck, scratched and dented everywhere. It screeched to an abrupt halt near the bottom of the steps.

Rickards took a cautionary step back and squinted through the front window of the truck. He watched as the reflective window was manually rolled down from the inside, revealing a large, dark figure behind the wheel.

The figure was Mike Morton, and he was staring out at both of them. "Get in!"

Rickards leaned forward. "What?"

"I said get in. Now!"

Rickards blinked twice before glancing up and down the street. Then pulled Angela forward.

"W-what's going on?"

"I don't know."

Rickards rushed down the last few steps and across the sidewalk while Mike pushed the passenger door open. In one motion, Rickards shoved Angela into the front seat, clambering in behind her.

A stomp on the gas caused the small truck to lurch forward and simultaneously slam the passenger door shut.

The small engine roared and the truck took off like a bat out of hell, streaking forward past the line of cars until Morton yanked hard on the wheel and careened around the first corner. He reaccelerated and turned again, this time left, causing several people on the street to stop and stare.

Angela's eyes bulged, and she searched for something to grab onto. "*What* is going on?!"

"In a second," Morton said. "We have to get some distance between us."

After a few more blocks and another turn, Morton slowed the vehicle and checked his rearview mirror. Satisfied, he calmly turned into a narrow alley behind a small building, trash cans and stacked boxes scattered every several feet.

"Who are you?!" Angela screamed.

Rickards laid a calming hand on her leg. "It's okay. Angela, meet Mike Morton. A rocket scientist from Texas."

Morton grinned. "We go way back. And sorry about all that. I didn't want them seeing you getting into my car."

Her eyes went wide. "Why?"

"Because if they saw you with me," he said, "they might put two and two together."

"What does that mean?"

"They'd know I was the one who called."

Rickards leaned forward, looking past Angela. "What are you talking about?"

Crammed in behind the steering wheel, Morton glanced back and forth between them and the road. "I was the one who got you out."

"How the hell did you do that?"

"Well, this part you might not like so much. So try to remember that it actually worked."

"What call?"

Morton grinned sheepishly. "I phoned in and said I was calling from the U.S. State Department."

"What?"

"I demanded to know why you were being detained. And that the State Department was launching a full investigation through Peru's Ministry of Foreign Affairs."

Rickards stared at him, speechless.

Morton shrugged again and eased to a stop at a traffic light. "I had a hunch you were some kind of law enforcement. I didn't know which agency, but I figured the guys holding you probably knew."

Rickards blinked, his mouth wide open, and then abruptly...laughed.

Morton gave a wide smile. "I was afraid if they spotted you getting into my car, they'd know it was me who called."

Still laughing, Rickards leaned back and looked out the front window. "Yeah. I'm guessing they might."

Between them, Angela was utterly confused, looking back and forth between the two. "So then you two know each other."

"We go way back. At least an hour."

53

Ottman was growing impatient, still waiting with two of his men and peering intently through the one-way glass into an empty room.

Was dauert so lange?

When the door finally opened behind them, he knew something was wrong the moment he saw Fernandez.

The colonel looked directly into the old man's eyes. "They are gone."

"What?!"

"I warned you," Fernandez said. "They would find out."

Ottman became incensed. "No!"

"The Americans called!" Fernandez growled. "From their State Department. They found out he was here and threatened to go through our ministry. I told you we should not have taken them!"

"What have you—" Ottman was livid. "*Scheisse!*" He

immediately turned to Fischer and his second man, Becker. No words were necessary. The panic on Ottman's face was evident and all it took for both men to bolt out of the room, headed for the front door of the building.

"How could you be so stupid?!" Ottman screamed. "They are the only link—" He stopped and rushed to the door, bumping the colonel and sending him back several steps.

Through the lobby and then out the front doors, Fischer and Becker came to a stop outside in the bright sun,

searching from side to side, the entire entrance and street in front of the Puerto Maldonado Police Station.

There was nothing.

The Americans were gone.

54

Reaching the hotel, Rickards and Angela got new keys from the desk and rushed down the hall to their rooms, followed by a lumbering Mike Morton.

When Angela reached her door, she inserted the card and pushed the door open, immediately stopping in her tracks.

Rickards, only one step behind, nearly ran into her, barely stopping in time to stare over her shoulder.

The room was a mess. Sheets pulled off the bed and were strewn across the floor, the only chair in the room overturned and ripped open from the bottom. All the drawers still partially open and her bags emptied all over the stripped bed.

"My God," she cried. "This is like a bad dream."

Rickards said nothing.

"Whoa," an out-of-breath Morton said when he arrived and saw the room. "What the hell have you two gotten yourselves into?"

Angela walked forward and picked through pieces of her clothing. "It's true," she said. "He knows a lot more."

"Who knows more?"

Angela looked at him and frowned. "The man in the room. The German."

"What German?"

She gave Rickards a puzzled look. "Didn't he talk to you?"

"No one talked to me."

Behind him, Mike Morton made a face. "Oh, thanks a lot, man."

"No one *outside* of that cell," he said, rolling his eyes at Mike and then squinting at Angela. "What...German?"

"An old man. The one who questioned me."

"Did he give you a name?"

"No."

"But he said he was German?"

"No. I picked up on it. And it made him very uncomfortable."

"What did he ask you?"

"He wanted to know everything I knew about the letter. My uncle. My grandfather."

"And what did you tell him?"

She stared at Rickards. Then took a breath and pursed her lips. The anxiety was returning.

"I told him the truth," she blurted. "Whatever he wanted to know. Okay?! I was scared! I didn't know what they had done with you, and he said we could go home if I just told him everything!"

"And you believed him?"

"Yes!" she cried. "Yes, I believed him. What possible threat are we to him if we tell him what he wants? We don't *know* anything!"

Rickards remained quiet.

"We don't!" she insisted.

"We know *enough*," he said. "Enough to be kidnapped."

"He doesn't know either."

"What do you mean?"

"He was fishing. And I don't think he knows what for."

Rickards finally turned and glanced back again at Morton. "You probably don't want to be part of this."

Mike shrugged. "I don't know. Sounds kind of interesting."

Rickards shook his head and returned to Angela. "What do you want to do?"

"I don't know. What do *you* think we should do?"

"I think we should get on a plane and get out of here. We're dealing with something bad. And if it hadn't been for this guy," he motioned his head toward Mike Morton, "we'd still be at the station. And I don't know if you noticed, but the guys who took us were military, not small-town police."

She looked at him, still trembling. "I think they did something to Lillian. That German guy knew who she was."

Rickards sighed. "All the more reason to leave."

She nodded and looked into his eyes. "But what if we do and they still don't find what they're after? Would they come back?"

Again, Rickards didn't answer.

She looked at her shaking hands. "Look at me. I'm scared to death. All I can think of is what happened before." She glanced uncomfortably at Morton against the wall, then looked back at Rickards. "I didn't tell you what happened before."

"Yes, you did."

"No, I didn't!" She sniffed. *Her whole body was shaking.* "I told you some of the other women were raped in that attack.

But not me." She paused. "But…I lied. I was one of them."

Standing in front of her, Rickards suddenly deflated.

"I was raped," she said through tear-filled eyes. "By men like that. Monsters that take whatever they want. When they want it. Men who make up their own rules with no one to stop them." She stared at them. "What kind of world do we live in, when we're too afraid of the monsters to do anything? Even when there's more of us. We still cower. For what? So we can live a terrible life?"

"It's not your fault," Rickards said.

"I know it's not my fault. You don't have to tell me that. I've known for a long time. What you need to tell me is how I run back home now and spend the rest of my life cowering. With the fear of them coming back. Tell me why I have to suffer my whole life…because of them!"

She glanced briefly at Morton, who remained frozen.

"When I'm old and on my deathbed, will I still remember? The cowering?"

Rickards looked at her through pained but honest eyes and nodded. "You will."

55

The voice on the phone confirmed it. The same voice that had assisted Fischer in Colorado. Sharp and precise.

"They bought tickets. Leaving Puerto Maldonado in thirty minutes. To Lima, then back to Los Angeles."

"Both of them?"

"Yes."

"How long ago?"

"Seven minutes."

Fischer checked his watch and stared at Ottman, who was glaring back from the middle of Angela's ransacked hotel room. They had barely missed them. "Get Fischer a ticket on that flight."

The voice paused. "It's full."

A fuming Ottman tried to think. Even Fischer and Becker could not reach them in time. They could get past security but would have to find a way to get two others bumped from the flight. Which would take time. And even then, Fischer could not do anything until Colorado. Not until they were far from the airports and out of the city.

Ottman couldn't believe it. He literally could not believe it.

Fernandez was a dead man.

***

"So let me get this straight," Morton said, shifting the truck into third gear and accelerating. Trees and houses now speeding by on both sides. "Your great-uncle shows up here after the war, sends his brother, your grandfather, a letter that somehow gets lost for sixty years, which is tied to some British explorer back in the twenties?"

"More or less."

"And what do you think it was that this guy found?"

"We're not sure."

"But you have an idea."

Next to Morton, scrunched into the middle seat, Angela frowned. "It's more like a theory."

"Well, lay it on me."

Angela hesitated, glancing first at Rickards. "Maybe...Paititi?"

Morton's eyes widened, and he looked at her before turning back to the road and letting out a long whistle.

"You've heard of it?"

He nodded. "Everyone down here has heard of it. But

no one believes it. Because it's never been found. And believe me, it ain't for lack of trying."

He gripped both sides of the wheel and shook his bald head. "The old lost city of gold, huh? Now that's one thing a bunch of Nazis do *not* need to find."

"We don't know exactly what they're looking for," Angela reiterated.

"I have to think that anything made out of gold would have either been found by now or shown up on someone's lidar like a giant Christmas tree."

"That's what I was thinking. Records say the conquistadors who went from city to city murdering Incas for their gold supposedly drove them into hiding. To a secret Incan location so deep and remote that the Spaniards were never able to find it."

"Taking the rest of their gold with them."

"Correct. So, the last thing the Incas would want was someplace that lights up under a bright sun."

"So, you don't believe the city made of gold thing."

"I think it makes more sense that it would be a city of gold, rather than a city made of gold."

Morton looked at her. "You mean as in the gold being hidden inside. Or buried."

"Somewhere below ground and out of sight. That's what I would do. In fact, maybe it's not in a city at all."

"Then in what?"

"I don't know." She shrugged. "Tunnels maybe? Caves? A lot of ancient civilizations created vast tunneling systems all over the world. We're finding new ones all the time. Would it be all that strange for the Incas to do the same thing?"

Morton raised his eyebrows at the thought and looked across to Rickards. "Oh, I like her."

Rickards nodded and shifted in his seat. "Look, Mike, this is all conjecture. The truth is we have no idea what we're looking for."

"Yeah. I know," he said, checking a side mirror before

188

passing a slow motorized scooter carrying three passengers. "You're here to find out what spooked her grandfather. And his brother."

"More or less."

Morton nodded. "I get it."

Angela turned when Mike reached into his shirt pocket and retrieved a small bottle. He removed the lid and popped a tiny pill into his mouth.

"Nitroglycerin," he said. "For my heart."

She nodded and looked forward, out at the jungle view before them and the narrow winding road, which had left the city miles behind. They were now surrounded on both sides by walls of thick green vegetation and dark trees, many growing up and out over the road, with branches hanging down almost low enough to scrape the roof of the truck as they sped beneath them.

"So, where exactly are we headed?"

"Bolivia," Morton replied. "You said those goons gave you back your wallets and passports, right?"

"Yes. And phones."

"Yeah? Do you have a signal way out here?"

They both checked.

"No."

"Let me see them."

Angela took Joe's and showed them to Morton, who promptly grabbed them in his thick paw and threw both phones out through his open window. He looked at them and grinned.

"Just in case."

56

They turned off onto a small, much rougher road littered

with potholes, causing the truck to shake and bounce wildly from side to side. Unnerving for Angela and Rickards but did not seem to bother Mike Morton in the slightest. Instead, he merely rolled the steering wheel back and forth like an Indy driver.

Just much, much slower.

The wild vegetation almost completely enveloped them now, with long thin strands of wild grass stretching nearly as tall as the trees making it impossible to see in any direction except forward and backward. Though even backward was difficult, obscured by a thick trailing cloud of dust.

And now, all of it, even the dust, glowed brilliantly beneath the gleam of late afternoon sun, blazing down between clouds upon a darkening azure sky. All the while, behind them, a rumbling in the bed of the truck told them their bags were still there.

Angela's trembling had stopped, witnessed by her hands now calmly resting atop raised knees, squeezed to one side of the truck's gear shift.

It was a welcome feeling over the last two hours. One that left her wondering why. Perhaps it was the revelation and emotional release to Joe and Mike in her hotel room when she'd been struggling so hard to maintain her composure. It was a secret she had never fully revealed to anyone except her grandmother.

Angela had tried to sleep, but due to her seated position, as well as the constant rocking of the vehicle, she couldn't, until finally, late in the day, exhaustion finally won out, taking her slowly as she lowered her wavering chin and leaned softly against Rickards' shoulder.

***

Angela awoke to the sound of screeching birds,

promptly followed by the rolling and abrupt stop of the truck, then a short screech of metal as Morton pulled up and engaged the parking brake.

"We're here."

Rickards was the first to straighten, blinking and looking around through a dirtier windshield than when they'd dropped off to sleep. "Where is here?"

"I think you're going to like this," Morton said and threw open his door.

Angela followed Rickards out and rose, stretching her arms over her head and yawning. A gratifying feeling after being cooped up for so long. Next to her, Rickards blinked several times, clearly having fallen asleep himself. Together, they watched Morton flip the driver's seat forward to retrieve an odd-looking pole from behind it. Several feet long and bound with wires repeatedly circling over several pieces of electronics.

"What's that?"

"The reason I get arrested."

She looked at Rickards, who shrugged, before both followed the larger Morton as he ambled forward to what appeared to be the end of the dirt road where a wall of tall grass and vegetation blocked most of their way, save for one smaller opening to one side.

Once through, the path extended perhaps fifty feet until widening into an open patch where the grass had been sheared down to knee height. Resting in the middle, sat an old and rather dirty camper trailer, perhaps twenty-five feet long.

The area was peaceful. Angela noted a soft light shining out through the trailer's small windows.

"Home sweet home. Don't let it fool you, things are hard to keep clean out here."

With that, he continued forward and put his hands to his mouth, calling out something in a language that wasn't English.

"I think that's Quechuan," Angela said.

"Of course." Rickards nodded. "Quechuan."

"It's one of the languages spoken by descendants of the Inca," she said. "At least I think so."

Ahead of them, Morton leaned the pole against the rear of the trailer, waiting when something was suddenly heard rustling in the bushes to the right. Moments later, a male figure appeared, emerging smoothly out of the tall grass carrying an armful of firewood. He was dressed in a bright T-shirt over long, dark shorts with modern sandals on his feet.

He shouted something short back to Morton, who answered with several words.

"You understand any of that?" Rickards asked.

Angela nodded. "Mike is telling him that I'm awesome. And you're not."

"Funny."

"I have no idea what they're saying."

A third voice was heard from within the trailer and the screen door opened from the inside, moments before a dark woman's head appeared, looking around, first spotting the other man approaching, then Morton, and finally, Angela and Rickards.

Mike Morton waved them forward. "I'd like you two to meet Anku and his wife, Killa." He spoke again in Quechuan, introducing both Americans.

Both Anku and Killa smiled welcomingly as they eagerly approached. Both were young, dark-skinned and attractive. Killa, dressed in a multicolored dress and matching headdress with a blue bow just above her forehead, continued smiling and reached for Angela's hand.

"Halo," Anku said and enthusiastically shook Joe's.

Killa made an attempt at hello that sounded closer to *mellow*, causing her husband to laugh.

Morton put a hand on the younger man's lean shoulder. "Anku and his wife are my business partners."

"Business partners?"

He nodded. "He is my CNO and Killa is the CCO."

"I can't wait to hear this."

"Chief Navigational Officer and Chief Culinary Officer."

Angela laughed and smiled at both of them. "Make sure you ask for stock options."

Neither understood a word, but they continued smiling graciously.

"Come on," Morton chuckled and ruffled Anku's long black hair. "You must be even hungrier than I am by now."

57

Angela peered into her bowl curiously, pleasantly surprised. "What is this?"

Nearby, Morton sat on an old folding chair which squeaked every time he moved his heavy frame. "It's a special of Killa's. Made with corn, potatoes, spices and pig."

Angela took another bite. "It's delicious."

Morton nodded in agreement and scooped another bite. "Guinea pig is very popular around here."

A few feet away, in the glow of a small lamp, Rickards calmly lowered his bowl and put it on the ground.

"Did you say guinea pig?"

"Mmm-hmm."

Angela nodded, smiling politely as her chewing slowed to a crawl. "Great."

Morton winked and continued eating. "Don't worry, you'll get used to it."

"I'll bet."

"At least they're not into human sacrifices anymore,"

Rickards offered.

Morton chuckled. "Truth be told, even during the Incan empire, human sacrifices were not as common as a lot of people think. More often than not, it was done when a king died, and his servants were sacrificed so they could serve him in death."

Angela grinned at Rickards. "Enchanting, isn't it?"

Morton finished and lowered his own bowl to the ground. "A lot of the Incan culture is misunderstood. Even by experts. Anku and Killa are both descendants and think it's quite funny, especially when I ask about some of them. But I suppose it's human nature. The more time that goes by, the more we rely on hearsay and supposition. Especially with things so different from our own traditions."

"How long have you been traveling with them?"

"About a year. I met them during one of my excursions."

"Would these be illegal excursions?" asked Rickards.

"Illegal is a little vague out here. You have to remember; this is their land. We may have forgotten that, but they haven't."

"Hence the trespassing."

"A lot of *indigenas* in the area think our laws of possession are funny. After all, how do you own something that will be here long after you're gone? And everyone you know. Even your entire bloodline. It's illogical to them."

"I can see that."

"The longer you're out here, the harder it is to continue seeing things from our old point of view, let alone defend them. Because for us, it's all about the here and now."

"True," acknowledged Angela. "But there's an argument to be made on both sides. For example, much of the here and now *dictates* the future."

"Agreed. It's definitely a tradeoff, but the *indigenas* see things very differently on many levels. Nevertheless, there's still quite a bit of commonality if you step back a bit. A lot like with our Native American Indians."

"Didn't seem to turn out too well for them," replied

Rickards.

"Can't argue that. But fighting and taking over land has been going on for thousands of years in every corner of the world. Animals do the same thing. It's part of who we are as a species. As inhabitants of the Earth. And ironically, the *indigenas* also understand that."

"Doesn't seem to make things any better."

Morton nodded at Angela. "Very true. I'm just saying that history and cultures are a lot more complicated than many of us want to believe or acknowledge. It's easier just to have one belief and stick to it."

"Especially when everyone believes they're in the right," said Angela.

Morton squinted slightly and studied her in the light. "Why, aren't you turning out to be an interesting gal?"

"You don't know the half of it," replied Rickards.

She ignored the joke and studied Mike in return. "So, tell us about these *excursions*."

"Not yet. I want to hear more about that letter of yours. Do you still have it?"

"No, the German man took it. But if you have a piece of paper, I can write it down."

"Write it down?"

She nodded. "I obsessed about it enough that I have it memorized."

Morton immediately got up and walked the twenty feet back to the trailer, calling Killa inside. After a brief exchange at the door, he returned with a piece of paper and a pencil, along with a book to write on.

Angela took them, glancing at the title of the textbook. "*Energy Defined?*"

"Mmm-hmm."

She shrugged and placed the paper on top, scribbling for several minutes. When she was done, Morton examined it thoughtfully.

"What's this second paragraph here?"

"A quote from Percy Fawcett's writings. In the original

letter it was written in German."

"*In* German?"

"Yes."

"And Fawcett was that English chap?"

She laughed. "He was."

"And what is this here? Written below your uncle's message: ALMV10?"

"We don't know. Nothing I found by searching made any sense."

"Hmm." Morton nodded and stepped back, lowering himself back into his chair with a loud squeak. "And you don't know why the Fawcett quote was included?"

"Only speculation."

"Which is what the German was probing about this morning."

"Yes."

"And you said you're not sure if even he knows exactly what he's looking for."

"It doesn't feel like it. But I could be wrong."

Morton nodded again and stared at the paper. "Interesting..."

After a few minutes, he spoke again. "And how do you know this was sent in the fifties?"

"The stamp on the original envelope. Fifties or very early sixties, at most."

"And that old German guy now has this stamp?"

"A picture of it. Yes."

"Hmm."

Several more minutes passed, leaving Angela to glance quizzically at Joe in the darkness. Who had been quietly sitting and listening.

"As I think about this," Morton said, "I keep coming back to the same question—if this letter was so precious and so urgent, why was only one sent?" He looked at Angela. "I mean, surely your uncle must have wondered why he hadn't heard back from his brother."

"It's something we've considered."

"And?"

Angela gave a helpless shrug. "We don't know."

Several more minutes passed before Mike Morton finally took the letter, folded it and placed it into a small shirt pocket. "I need to think on this."

"Okaaay."

With that, the older man leaned forward, closer to the lamp, and placed both elbows on his knees. "My turn."

They both watched him expectantly.

"What I'm going to tell you," he started, "may seem a bit odd. And it's something I haven't shared with anyone except Anku and Killa. But my Quechuan is not very good, so who knows what they understood." Morton paused to collect his thoughts. "When I was nineteen years old, I went to work for NASA. Recruited in college, and of all people, by my college physics professor."

"Wow."

"I mentioned to Joe that I was one of the youngest to work on the *Saturn V* program. Which is true. And our last *Saturn* rocket was the one that put *Skylab* into orbit. Also true. But for me, that was just the beginning. In the midseventies, when the program ended, I was drafted again, or rather transferred, to the *Skylab* team and then eventually to the *Landsat* program."

"What's *Landsat?*" asked Rickards.

"The *Landsat* program was a series of programs of increasingly more sensitive and sophisticated satellites used for studying the Earth, primarily imaging in the visible spectrums for geography and surface mapping. But over time, our satellites and other sats expanded into other areas of study. Things like meteorological, thermal and sea surfaces, using things like the *Jason* satellites. Eventually, we paved the way for *GRACE*."

"And Grace is?"

Morton grinned. "*GRACE* stands for Gravity Recovery And Climate Experiment. Twin satellites that were so sensitive we were able to map, in detail, the Earth's gravitational fields--which, incidentally, solved a number of physics issues for us. But aside from that, before *GRACE* was another program called *CERES: Clouds and the Earth's Radiant Energy System.*

"And as you can guess from the name, *CERES* was designed to measure energy levels, both in the atmosphere and on the planet's surface. And while its purpose was primarily to measure solar energy, the instruments designed were strong enough to measure other forms of energy too. Thermal, electromagnetic, chemical, kinetic and probably a few more, to varying degrees."

Angela nodded. "Okay, this is interesting, but I should probably warn you that I was never that great at science."

"Don't worry, there's no quiz. The reason I'm telling you this is that before the first official *CERES* instruments were launched in 1997, a prototype was first created."

Morton stopped and looked at both of them. "You still with me?"

Angela squinted and Rickards held up his thumb and index finger, leaving only a tiny space between them.

"Okay. Here's the gist. *CERES* was designed to measure energy on the Earth, but the prototype designed to provide a working model was launched two years before that. And it worked for several months, until it reentered our atmosphere and died, as expected. But not before it did something very surprising."

58

"What was so surprising?" asked Rickards.

Morton remained still, staring at both of them. "It

measured something it wasn't supposed to measure."

They looked at each other. "Like what?"

"Perhaps instead, I should say, something it wasn't *designed* to measure."

"What was it designed to measure?"

Morton paused. "You have to understand, there are a lot of different forms of energy, and even each of those contains different types. For example, just within electromagnetism, you have radio waves, microwaves, ultraviolet, X-rays, Gamma rays and more, all different types of energy swirling around us, over the planet, as well as through outer space, depending on a few things. And like I said, those instruments on the *CERES* prototype were designed for just a few. But what that prototype recorded before falling to Earth was something no one was expecting. And it did so because we never gave it a lot of rules on what it should be looking for."

"And what did it record?"

"Let me clarify one more thing--that the *shapes* of these energies can vary quite a lot. But if you were able to see them, most would look rounded or donut-shaped as they travel out from the source. And as we would later find with the gravity waves, what our *CERES* prototype detected was that a lot of these energies moved not just around the planet but actually *through* it."

"Is that...unusual?"

"Not really. Not in theory. But we weren't necessarily expecting it, either. Primarily because the core of our planet is very dense, which is why we experience a lot of energy waves like radios and cell phones, that don't work well underground."

Rickards turned and looked at the back of the trailer, mostly hidden in the dark except for the brightly lit windows. "I'm guessing this has something to do with that pole you had in the truck."

"Very good," said Morton. "It wasn't all that strange for the prototype to reveal all these energy patterns. But what was strange was that it revealed things subsequent satellite launches never did."

"Why is that?"

"Most people think it was faulty data or a faulty hardware design and therefore, it wasn't valid."

"So, the prototype thought it saw something the others didn't?"

"Correct."

"And what was that?"

"Imagine," Morton said, "that you could see all the different types of energy, all those waves swirling about in slow motion, up and down and in and out of each other." For effect, he interlocked his fingers and moved them around. "That is all normal. But what is not normal, and what the prototype saw only briefly—was a single location where all of those energies appeared to converge into a single point. And actually *touch* the surface of our planet."

Angela tilted her head. "They did what?"

"They converged."

"Why?"

"I have no idea," Morton said. "But that's what I'm trying to find out."

Rickards motioned back to the trailer. "With that pole."

Morton nodded. "It's a bit more than just a pole, but yes."

"Huh," said Rickards. "So that's what you're looking for."

"Yes."

"With Anku and Killa."

"Yes."

"And that's why you keep getting arrested for trespassing?"

Morton nodded. "That's why I keep getting arrested for trespassing."

"So, Anku is your guide."

"One of the best there is."

Rickards nodded from his own chair. "Explains why you

mentioned their concept of property rights. I'm guessing that getting caught with someone of Incan descent buys you a little extra compassion with the authorities."

"It helps," he acknowledged.

"So basically, you're out here looking for a mystery energy source," said Angela.

Mike Morton shook his head. "Not exactly a source. But yes, something like that."

She glanced at the trailer when the door opened and Anku stepped out. Turning back to Morton, she asked, "So why isn't anyone else from NASA out here looking for...whatever it is?"

"Because they think I'm crazy." He grinned. "Everyone thinks the prototype was faulty and reported bad data."

"And you don't?"

"No," Morton said.

"Why not?"

"Because I was one of the guys who designed it."

They both stopped and stared at Anku, who stepped into the glow of the light with a wide smile. He handed something to Morton, who took it and then crossed to Angela and Joe, holding out his hand. In his palm were two short green shafts or sticks. Each taking one, Rickards noticed the sticks felt soft and fibrous. They both watched as Mike inserted one end into his mouth and began chewing it.

"What is this?"

"A favorite Incan dessert. Called *sweet tube*. Try it."

Angela glanced at Joe, who was clearly waiting for her.

"Does this come from anything I'm not used to eating?"

"You mean like guinea pig?"

"Yes, like that."

"No," Morton snickered. "This is a root. Sweet, like a sweet potato."

Angela eyed him suspiciously and slowly inserted it between her lips, nibbling the tip. Then, surprised, she chewed a little harder.

"It's not bad," she said. "Tastes like…red licorice. But not as sweet."

Rickards looked up at Anku, who was waiting. He took a small bite and chewed slowly, nodding politely at him.

The young man smiled approvingly and went back to the trailer, where he retrieved a short mug. One end of a sweet tube could be seen protruding from the top of the cup as Anku sat down on a nearby log and began stirring.

"What is that?"

Morton winked. "Anku and I are compatriots. Fellow Catholics, if you can believe it. He introduced me to sweet tubes, and I introduced him to iced tea."

Angela chuckled. "Seems like a fair trade." She took the tube out of her mouth and briefly studied it before continuing to chew. "It's actually really good."

Mike Morton eased back in his chair. "It's also medicinal. Twenty-five percent of western pharmaceuticals are derived from rainforest ingredients."

"Is that right?"

"Yep."

Rickards withdrew the stick. "This is a drug?"

"No, not this. It's more similar to an herb. It stimulates your circulation and helps increase blood flow."

Angela looked around and blinked several times. "I feel a little weird."

"It also gives you a small dopamine kick," Morton said. "About the same as half a glass of wine."

"Wow," she said, grinning. "They should market these in the states."

"Nah, too mild for most people."

Angela settled back into her chair. "So, Mike, how close are you to finding what you're looking for?"

"Pretty close," he said. "Based on the measurements I've been picking up, possibly within a hundred to two hundred square kilometers."

Next to her, Rickards looked around their small camp, into the nearby darkness. "Where exactly are we?"

"About ten miles from the mountains, where the Amazon ends, and the Andes begin."

"What do you suppose you're going to find?"

"I don't know," he replied. "But you two have got me thinking."

"About what?"

"About that letter of yours."

He stared thoughtfully into the glowing light of the lantern. "I'll be honest. I never really believed in Paititi. But this story with your uncle has me thinking about some of the local legends around here. Over the years, Inca beliefs have gradually been mixed with Catholicism. But they still believe in things like the *mallkus*, guardian spirits who reside in nature. Especially up in the mountains. And shamans, of which Anku's father is one, called *yatiri*, still make ritual payments to these spirits in exchange for prosperity and protection. But even more, one site very sacred for the Quechuan people is Machu Picchu, a place in the Andes where the very forces of nature are believed to dwell."

Angela was staring at Morton in the darkness, blinking repeatedly. "And?"

"The forces of nature would include all the forces of energy," he concluded. "And I'll tell you this, when it comes to energy, especially things like electromagnetism, few things on this planet are better conductors of electrical energy...than *gold*."

59

"You are certain?"

"Yes," confirmed the voice on the phone. "They were not on the flight, neither getting on nor disembarking in

Lima."

Ottman leaned back in his chair, looking up at Fischer and Becker. *Just as they thought.*

He had to wait for the plane to land in Lima to be sure. But now there was no doubt. Neither the Reed woman nor Rickards had taken the opportunity to flee.

But why?

With as frightened as the woman was, why would she not leave?

In Ottman's mind, there was only one answer. The woman knew something. Just as he originally suspected. And she clearly believed she could deceive him long enough to locate Paititi.

But she was wrong. She had no idea how long he had been planning for this very moment. Ottman knew far more than she did and had vast resources at his disposal, more than she could possibly imagine, not only from the Nazi Train, but all he had leveraged from it. Vast resources that were limited only by his need to keep things quiet. But if it came to it, if Ottman felt the secret was somehow slipping away, eluding him when he was so close, he would unleash it all. Release every resource, every option he had at his disposal, to find it.

No matter what the consequences.

He snapped from his thoughts when the voice continued.

"They are likely still in the same vehicle that picked them up outside the station," the voice said. "A yellow, older-model truck."

"Can you see who was driving?"

"Not from satellite. But I can see that it traveled to the hotel, then out of Puerto Maldonado."

"They got back into the same vehicle after the hotel."

"Correct."

"Where is it now?" asked Ottman.

"I cannot be sure. Still in the jungle somewhere, beneath the trees. Based on distance, terrain and available roads, it should lie within an eighty-kilometer diameter of the last sighting. Further analysis should give us a smaller target range."

"How long?"

"Hours."

Ottman turned his attention to Fischer. "Call the trucks."

"Yes, sir."

A helicopter was faster, but impractical for the Amazon's terrain. But unlike the chopper, military trucks—sourced straight from the Peruvian army—could follow them anywhere, though commandeering them required time, no matter how much money Ottman had.

The old man pressed his lips together in an effort to remain calm. He lowered his hands onto the padded arms of the chair and inhaled quietly. *Patience*, he said to himself. *Nothing done quickly is done well.*

On the other end of the phone, the eyes belonging to Ottman's cyber expert flitted back and forth between several brightly illuminated computer screens.

It would take time, but with thermal imaging, he should be able to reveal all available roads in the area beneath the dense canopy, and perhaps whether some still bore any lingering signs of recent activity. But it would have to be done before the next sunrise, when all differences in heat signatures were erased.

To his right, on another monitor, was a screen of constantly scrolling text. Numbers and letters all rotating in and out of dozens of open character slots, trying to find the right combination, copied too quickly to follow, while in the top frame was listed the complete wording from Roger Reed's original letter. The note to his brother, as well as the paragraph copied from Fawcett's book.

It was clear the letters ALMV10 at the bottom of the note was a code, meaning somewhere within the rest of the letters, either in the note or Fawcett's transcription, had to be the primer. The key to cracking what ALMV10 meant.

His eyes briefly glanced at the progress on the scrolling screen, rotating an innumerable number of combinations at blinding speed. Too fast, in fact, to discern anything within the constant blur of letter changes.

Much faster than any human brain could do it.

60

It was seventeen minutes after five a.m. when the door to the trailer opened and swung outward with a squeak, allowing in the earliest rays of morning. Glowing through open patches of overhead canopy, it was enough to dimly light the surrounding area and the three metal chairs still positioned in the tall grass, now covered in thin clear beads of morning dew.

Adding another shirt and setting her hair in a quick bun, Angela was only mildly surprised to see Mike Morton already waiting outside when she opened the door, sipping a steaming cup of tea.

She looked around for Joe, whose frame could still be glimpsed in the back of the truck bed beneath a dark blanket.

"How long have you been up?"

"Couple hours," he replied.

Angela briefly glanced around and came back to Morton, who was still staring at her. "Is something wrong?"

"Nope."

"Thank you for making room in here for me with Killa."

He laughed. "You're welcome."

When he didn't look away, Angela began to wonder if

she had something on her face. Fighting the urge to check, she asked, "Everything okay?"

"Better than okay."

"Better?"

"Mmm-hmm."

Curious, she descended the trailer's three metal steps and jumped down onto the thick grass next to him. "Why is that?"

Morton calmly sipped his tea. "I may have something on that letter of yours."

Angela's eyes widened. "Like what?"

Morton looked at the truck to see Rickards slowly rising. "I think your uncle used a code."

"You mean the letters at the end?"

"Yes. ALMV10." Morton withdrew the copy she made for him the night before and showed it to her. All over the page were mathematical scribblings.

"What is this?"

"Doodling," he said. "Searching for different possibilities."

"And?"

He raised his mug to welcome Rickards, who was now approaching while yawning beneath a head of messy hair.

"It's not what I thought," Morton said, finishing his tea. "It's simpler."

Angela glanced at Rickards, who cleared his throat. "Simpler than what?"

"Simpler than what I was expecting. Given the age of the letter, I assumed this was a cipher and not a code. So I started looking at some of the most common ciphers out there. Ciphers that were well-known fifty or sixty years ago. There are dozens of classics--substitutional, transpositional, algorithmic. All used pretty effectively and over long periods of time. Caesar's cipher, for example, lasted over eight hundred years before someone cracked it."

"What's the difference between a cipher and a code?"

"There's some overlap, but often a code uses a primer,

where ciphers generally don't. It really depends on how complicated you're expecting the encryption to be. I ran through several possible scenarios and assumed the primer was somewhere either in the letter or disguised within the paragraph from Fawcett's book.

"A lot of those would take a while to crack, even with computers, so eventually I had to step back and rethink things."

Angela grinned at Rickards. "Outside the box."

"Encryption is often thought of too linearly," Morton said. "Too often it's from the encoder's perspective, which is the process of hiding something. But an encrypter, believe it or not, has to not only focus on how well he can encode something, but he *also* has to consider things from the opposite direction, or the decrypter's perspective. Meaning a secret code is not just about how well you can scramble something, but how problematic it will then be to *unscramble*. After all, who wants to encrypt a message no one can ever decrypt, even its intended recipient? It makes the whole thing a wasted effort. Kind of like the Voynich manuscript, which is a long text from the fifteenth century written with illustrations and symbols no one understands, not even today. So, whatever message someone was trying to convey through their cipher, it doesn't really matter anymore."

Morton looked at Angela. "Clearly, your uncle would not have done that. So I stepped back and reasoned that whatever he inscribed would have been something he could be sure his brother could figure out. The long and short is that it's a normal human reaction to assume a code is more complicated than it really is, and assuming so makes the job of unscrambling infinitely harder.

"One mistake I made was assuming all six characters were part of the cipher, which I eventually had to concede might not be the case. A-L-M-V, sure. But not necessarily one-zero. I've worked with a lot of mathematical patterns and formulas over the years, and something about the one and zero didn't feel right." He looked at Angela. "In the original letter, do you remember whether there was a space between the V and the one?"

Angela closed her eyes, thinking. "Sorry, I don't remember."

After a momentary thought, Morton shrugged. "That's okay. It doesn't matter. Anyway, at that point, I was thinking, what were the chances of your uncle, a history professor, also being a math expert? Possible? Yes. Probable? No. So regardless of whether it was a cipher or a code, it was likely more basic. Something applied only to the first four characters and not the one and zero. And, if those assumptions were correct, then it made the next one that much easier. Because the first four characters are alpha only. Not numbers. And one of the easiest and fastest alpha-only ciphers...is Atbash."

"Atbash?"

Morton nodded. "It wasn't until I thought the two numbers might not be part of it that I was able to figure it out. Otherwise, I'm not sure I would have. Alphanumeric ciphers are much more complicated."

"So, you assumed it was a simple cipher in the first place," Angela said.

"Eventually. I tried to put myself in your uncle's place and think of something simple, fast and still relatively effective."

"Which was Atbash," Rickards said.

"Yep. And you want to know the funniest part? Atbash is also a commonly used cipher for kids' puzzles. When I was growing up in the fifties, they were even used with prizes in cereal boxes. So I'll bet a lot of American kids are familiar with Atbash and don't even realize it."

"So, what does it say?!" Angela pressed.

Morton reached out and folded the paper over while she was still holding it. On the back were two lines of letters. The first read "A-L-M-V 1-0." And directly below it the second line: "Z-O-N-E 1-0."

"Zone Ten?"

Mike Morton nodded. "Yep."

"What is Zone Ten?"

The large man standing in front of her grinned from ear to ear and twirled his empty mug around his index finger.

"That's the easy part. Zone Ten…is La Paz."

"La Paz?"

"As in La Paz, Bolivia. Just over the border."

"How do you know that?"

"Because I've been there. It's in the center of town. Kind of an urban plaza and one of the largest open spaces in the city. Also called Plaza San Francisco."

Angela turned and immediately looked at Rickards. "La Paz!"

"Okay?"

"La Paz," she said again, excitedly, "was the very first place in South America Percy Fawcett traveled to." Angela whirled toward Morton. "You said you thought a primer was hidden in the paragraph transcribed from Fawcett's book."

"Originally," he nodded, "but—"

"Don't you see?!" she said back to Rickards. "The primer to A-L-M-V was not *in* the quote from Fawcett's book. It was Fawcett himself! Personally! The place he first visited!"

61

Ottman glanced out of his side window. Wide and steel-framed, it gave him a clear view down the side of a shallow valley colored in rich, dark green, then up the opposite side, to a ridgeline just as green below a fiery sunrise overhead.

Its golden rays lit up the entire canopy as far as the eye could see.

It was stunning, if only for a minute, before a long line of dense trees passed between them, once again obscuring the view—an amazing view that Ottman barely acknowledged.

Instead, he silently sat preoccupied in the back seat of the olive-colored Humvee, running through a multitude of scenarios in his mind.

Next to him, Fischer lowered a bulky satellite phone and signaled the driver on the shoulder. "There's a reservoir about twenty kilometers ahead. You know it?"

The uniformed driver nodded without speaking.

"Turn off there."

The soldier behind the wheel barely acknowledged him, instead keeping his eyes glued to the road in front of him. The vehicle bounced constantly from the holes in the asphalt, gradually growing worse the deeper they pushed into the jungle.

Fischer checked his watch and looked at Ottman. "About thirty minutes."

***

Both Humvees sped over the narrow dirt road with giant rumbling tires, glancing over rocks and dips with minimal effect. Charging like racing beasts over a path now barely wide enough to hold them. Trees brushing heavily against both sides. Ottman couldn't see anything except walls of grass and towering trees, blanketing each side and casting most of the road in morning shadows.

When they arrived, the giant trucks slowed at the end of the path. A small opening could be seen at the end of a grass wall, accentuated by two narrow rows of bent grass. They traveled perhaps thirty meters before the men found a large open area, with grass cut to knee-height.

In the middle was an old, dingy travel trailer, parked by

itself with two-by-fours stacked beneath the front hitch and back tires for support. Behind each muddy tire sat an oversized rock, wedged into position to prevent it from moving.

Ottman, the only one not carrying a rifle, walked carefully behind Becker, half waiting for something unexpected in the morning stillness. But the only sounds he heard were from cicadas in the surrounding trees.

Leading, Fischer reached the trailer first and carefully peered through the lower corner of one of the windows before lowering himself beneath it. Behind him, a Peruvian soldier did the same, while two more circled to the opposite side.

Fischer waited several seconds, listening for sounds inside. Hearing nothing, he looked to Ottman standing farther away, behind Becker.

The old man nodded and Fischer moved. He rose quickly to the trailer's door, spinning past it to the other side while simultaneously checking the latch.

Locked.

With a shake of his head, he waited for Ottman's nod, then immediately stepped back and fired three rounds into the door latch, sending chunks of metal and fiberglass exploding and falling to the ground with several pieces bouncing off or sticking to Fischer. Who immediately grabbed the hole near the door handle with his gloved hand and yanked it open.

The operation was smooth and fast, allowing Fischer and one of the soldiers to gain entrance to the trailer in mere seconds. Showcasing an exercise in efficiency and bone-chilling accuracy.

The scene was witnessed quietly by Killa from a nearby tree. Sitting comfortably atop a wide branch, wrapped in a dark blanket, blending in against the tree trunk. Where she nibbled on small berries and watched the soldiers below with intense curiosity.

62

Squeezed back into the center of the small truck's cab, Angela twisted her head around and peered through the tiny rear window to see Anku's two bare legs standing up in the back of the truck, towering over the top of the cab as they drove with wind blowing through his hair.

"Is he okay back there?"

"It's where he always rides," Morton said, reaching forward to pop a small cassette tape into the vehicle's stereo. Instantly, the imperial death march from *Star Wars* played, and Morton turned it up loudly and slid the back window open. "He loves it," he said with a shrug. "Something about being surrounded by ancestral spirits."

"We're on a mission," she smiled.

"Yeah. But he does it no matter where we go."

Morton drove aggressively down the tiny road, now reduced to little more than two-foot paths side by side, winding through tall, brightly glowing green grass.

"How far is La Paz?" Rickards asked.

"Not far. But on this road, about an hour and a half."

Angela suddenly reached for the dash to steady herself as Morton swerved around a large hole. "You're sure about that cipher?"

"It ain't rocket science. Like I said, your uncle wanted his brother to figure it out. I just had to think it through."

"So, what do you think is in La Paz?"

"Beats the hell out of me." Morton shrugged. "But if there's a connection between your letter and what I'm looking for, I want to know what it is."

"Have you tried just asking Anku and Killa about

213

Paititi?"

Morton nodded. "Multiple times."

"And?"

"To them, Paititi is not a treasure. It's spiritual," he said, touching his chest. "Inside here. Which reminds me."

He reached into his shirt pocket, popped the lid, and tossed another pill into his mouth.

Angela looked up when she heard Anku howl into the wind above the cab. "Does he know where we're going?"

Morton kept his eyes on the road. "I don't think he cares."

63

"They're moving," said the voice. "I can spot glimpses of the truck beneath the trees. Headed south."

"Where to?" asked Ottman.

"La Paz."

"How long until they arrive?"

"Judging by their speed and the terrain, perhaps forty-five minutes."

"Can we catch them?"

"Doubtful. But you will be close."

"Do they know we're behind them?"

"Unclear. But they do not appear particularly rushed."

Ottman nodded and turned to Fischer, sitting beside him. "Call Fernandez. Tell him to get to La Paz with some men. Immediately. And to take them, as soon as he has the chance."

64

By the time they'd emerged from beneath the trees and began a slow, winding climb up the mountainside, Angela was on the verge of losing what was left in her stomach. Her nausea was made most noticeably worse by the continuous switchbacks, requiring Morton to slow down to a near crawl.

With gritted teeth, she closed her eyes and tried to maintain a hold over her system.

"Try to look forward," Rickards offered, rolling down his window.

"Great idea. I'll try that when we're no longer *moving*."

After what felt like hours, they crested the last incline, where the road finally widened and aligned into a relatively straight two-lane paved road. Angela was now able to carefully raise her head and maintain a forward line of sight through the front windshield.

Minutes later, the first hints of houses appeared in the distance, then more, eventually forming the outskirts of Bolivia's third-largest city.

Known as Nuestra Señora de La Paz, or Our Lady of Peace, the city had a population that topped 700,000 and rose two miles above sea level, resting in a wide canyon carved by the Choqueyapu River. A modern, gleaming cityscape set against the backdrop of Bolivia's second-largest mountain, Illimani, distant and visible in colored hues of blue and purple beneath layers of white clouds. Below, every nook and cranny of the valley was filled with sprawling tentacles of the city, including dozens of tall buildings and skyscrapers at its heart.

"Wow," marveled Angela.

Mike Morton slowed and gradually began to descend the other side of the ridge. "You should see it at night."

"I can imagine."

"It's *big*," said Rickards

"The de facto capital of Bolivia," explained Morton. "Technically, the capital is Sucre, but this is where the government seat is." He winked at Angela. "And it looks a lot different I'm sure than sixty years ago."

It took thirty-five more minutes to reach the center, through narrow streets and crowded sidewalks filled with thousands of locals. It resembled any other modern city in the world at 8:30 a.m. on a workday, leaving Angela with an odd mix of both familiarity and uniqueness, even in the middle of old town, where Plaza San Francisco bordered Perez Velasco Street, a main artery of the city, carrying a thick flow of workers just a block away.

Beneath their feet, the massive concrete plaza was still slick from overnight rain, with patches of steam beginning to rise with the help of the sun overhead. Angela did a full three-hundred-and-sixty-degree turn before stopping on Morton and Anku. The latter peered around as if with an air of satisfaction.

"I present," Morton said, gesturing around the plaza, "Zone Ten."

Next to Angela, Rickards waited patiently as she blinked and scanned the area again.

"Any ideas?"

Angela shook her head. "I don't—" She stopped while scanning the plaza, freezing on the enormous building positioned directly behind Morton. "What's that?"

"A church."

"Really?" she said sarcastically. "I *know* it's a church. It's the biggest thing here."

"It's the Basilica of San Francisco," Morton said, nodding. "Rebuilt from the original Catholic church that founded La Paz. I took a tour last year."

She stared at it intently, then twisted slowly toward

Rickards. "Am I hallucinating?"

"The old man in Alerta."

She nodded without taking her eyes away.

Morton looked back and forth between them. "Need to know, people."

"We were looking for my uncle in Alerta," Angela explained. "Before we were abducted by those men. Two of the residents didn't know my uncle. They were too young. But the young man's grandfather did."

"The mayor."

She grinned. "The *mayor's* grandfather."

"What did he say?" asked Morton.

"He couldn't speak much. But right before the Germans showed up, he gave me a sign."

"What kind of sign?"

"I didn't understand at the time," Angela confessed. "I thought he was trying to spell something. Until just now, standing here." She looked away from the church and back at Mike Morton. Then, raising her hand in front of him, she traced the same motion that old man had made. Up and down, then left and right. "It was a cross."

65

"A cross," Morton said with an air of skepticism. "And he knew your uncle?"

"He seemed to," said Rickards. "Or at least knew *of* him."

"He remarked how much I looked like his picture."

"Your uncle's picture?" Morton asked as if studying her

more closely. "Do you?"

Rickards nodded. "She does."

"And the woman's daughter," said Angela, "the little girl whispered something about the Germans having been there before us."

Mike Morton remained silent, pondering and looking up at the giant church and its tower. All constructed from light brown brick covered in dark roofing and rising high overhead. Beneath the tower, the rest of the three-story church sprawled in both directions, easily a hundred feet on either end. It was dotted with dozens of small, antiquated doors and windows.

"Well," Morton finally said, shrugging. "It beats the hell out of anything I have. Let's take a look."

They made it nearly a hundred yards across the plaza before Angela noticed someone was missing and glanced back to find Rickards. He was standing still, halfway to the church entrance, wearing a solemn expression.

"Joe?"

His gaze fell from the large tower onto her.

"You go ahead. I think I'll stay here."

Angela glanced at Morton, with Anku next to him watching. "What?"

"I'll wait here," he repeated, before adding, "You guys take your time."

"What are you talking about?"

"This is as far as I go."

Angela couldn't hide her surprise. "You don't want to come inside?"

Rickards calmly and quietly shook his head.

She left Morton and walked back to him, lowering her voice. "What's wrong?"

With some hesitation, he said, "I'm not a believer."

"Neither am I. But we're not going to mass. We're just asking questions."

"And I think you should."

"But you don't want to go."

"No."

Angela raised her hands in a helpless gesture. "What gives? You don't have to be Catholic."

"It's not about faith, Angela."

"Then what's it about?"

His answer was not one she was expecting.

"Blame."

***

It felt instantly cooler inside. Sheltered from the sun and heat, the church entrance seemed to almost glow with rays of light streaming in from multiple angles, including from the open tower directly above them. Below, thick stones reflected brightly from the floor, adding to the effect with an almost polished appearance.

Nearby, several people were milling around the large entrance, examining its walls with pictures and inscriptions before continuing farther into the church through one of many side doors.

Around them, large statues were positioned in each of the room's four corners--one of Christ, one of Mary, and two others Angela did not recognize. On the far wall, between Christ and Mary, a wide mosaic of stained glass colored the floor beneath it with a rainbow of colors.

Still distracted from her conversation with Joe, Angela stood next to Anku and watched as Mike Morton plodded toward a large reception area against the south wall where a small patch of dark hair could be seen poking over the top of the counter. Angela realized it was a young woman intently staring down at her phone.

After a few minutes, Morton returned. "She's going to find someone we can talk to."

"What did you say?"

"That we need someone to tell us where Paititi is."

"Are you serious?"

Morton frowned sarcastically. "Is everyone in Colorado as gullible as you are?"

"Then what exactly are we *going* to say?"

"I dunno. Depends on who it is, I guess. If we get someone who's part of the clergy, best to just be honest. Believe me, they've heard it all and will know if we're lying."

"I'm not talking about lying. I'm talking about trying not to sound insane."

"At this point, that may be impossible."

***

Deacon Velez was short, with olive skin and, like Mike Morton, bald and somewhat rotund. Somewhere in his forties, he was comfortably dressed in a black, full-length cassock and approached them with a welcoming smile.

"Good morning. I was told you wanted to speak with someone."

Morton bowed respectfully. "Good morning, Deacon Velez. Yes, we do. We have something of importance to discuss."

"Of course." Velez's English was surprisingly good. "What can I do for you?"

"This is my friend Angela," he said. "And this is Anku."

"Very nice to meet you, Angela." Velez smiled. He turned to Anku. *"Allillachu, Anku."*

The Quechuan grinned broadly and bowed.

Morton took a step forward and spoke in a lower tone. "Deacon, is there a place we can talk in private?"

66

The deacon's office was down a long hallway, toward the north end of the church and sparsely decorated as one might expect, with a desk, two cloth chairs and a large crucifix hanging on the wall above. On the opposite wall, a very old and very heavy bookshelf was packed with books, giving Angela the impression it had been there for multiple generations. A few feet away, an equally aged wrought iron lamp stood tall in the corner atop the room's red carpet.

After entering, Angela glanced back. "Where's Anku?"

Morton checked back down the hall and shrugged. "Don't know."

Both took a seat and waited for Velez to close the door and move behind his desk, where he calmly sat down. "Now then," he said, "what is it you would like to discuss?"

Morton cleared his throat. "Deacon, this is probably going to sound a little loco, but we can assure you it's not."

Velez gave an amused smile and placed both hands together atop his desk. "Okay."

With that, Morton turned to Angela. "Go ahead, Professor."

***

Velez remained completely silent, listening patiently until Angela had finished. When she did, he remained quiet, digesting what she had said. Gradually, he leaned back in his chair.

"That is an interesting story," the deacon said, dropping each hand onto an arm of his chair. He inhaled, thinking.

"Do you have a picture of your uncle?" he finally asked.

Angela shook her head. "It was taken."

"I see." Velez nodded. "Do you have *any* identification?"

"Yes!"

Angela quickly leaned to the side and reached into her right front pocket, pulling out her passport. She held it out to the deacon, who opened the small booklet and examined it.

"And where is this friend of yours, Joe?"

"He's...outside. He didn't want to come in."

"Why not?" Velez asked, returning her passport.

She paused, trying to think how to explain. "It's complicated."

"Hmm." The deacon nodded and took another moment to think, briefly scratching his cheek. "I have been a deacon at this church for a long time. Fourteen years. Clearly not long enough to have met or known your great-uncle. But the head priest I arrived under, Father Mamani, had been here for many years before I."

"May we speak with him?"

"I'm afraid not. He passed several years ago. A wonderful man from whom I learned a great deal, and I'm sure would have been very interested in hearing your story."

Velez grew thoughtful again, looking at both of them before suddenly standing up. "Please come with me."

Out of his office, he led them down the same hall until they reached the end. He stopped at a large wooden door, closed and secured with a heavy black latch.

With some effort, Velez slid the long latch to the left with a loud clunk and pulled the door toward them. It swung outward with a loud, piercing squeak.

He reached in and flipped on a light, then motioned for them to follow as he stepped through. Around a corner, the hall descended down over dozens of stairs. At the bottom, he turned on another light, a single bulb affixed to the stone ceiling, weakly illuminating several rows of large boxes and cabinets. All were locked with individual combination locks of varying sizes.

The deacon carefully walked through them and stopped at one of the many wooden cabinets before lifting its lock and spinning the dial. Moments later, he yanked it down to release it.

Velez calmly pulled one side of the cabinet open and peered inside, searching before reaching in. He retrieved a small handheld box and turned back to face them.

"What was your grandfather's name?"

"My grandfather? Gerald Reed."

"And the relation again?"

"My uncle's younger brother."

Velez nodded and handed the item to her. "Then I believe this belongs to you."

Angela took it into her hands. Another box, but small, almost cubed and bound tightly inside a thick strand of brown twine. On top of the lightly sanded wood were two words carved carefully into the lid: *Gerald Reed.*

A stunned Angela looked at Velez.

"Father Mamani told me the brother might still come for it someday. Or, in your case, a granddaughter."

Her hands were trembling. She rotated the object with fumbling fingers. "Oh my G—" she whispered and suddenly caught herself. "Sorry."

Velez smiled. "That's all right. Something tells me He had a hand in this."

She glanced at a fascinated Mike Morton before looking back down and tracing the twine, still tightly wound on all four sides and knotted. She began trying to get a fingernail under a piece of the knot but couldn't. She was startled when Morton immediately produced a small knife.

She took the knife and wriggled the tip of the blade under one strand, then twisted back and forth repeatedly until it finally broke. Then she unwound the rest from around the box.

Angela nervously glanced from one man to the other and suddenly thought of Joe, wishing he was standing next to her. With a deep breath, she pushed the thought from her mind and firmly gripped both sides of the box, pulling the two pieces apart.

To her surprise, it was empty. Or nearly empty. It held only the tiniest piece of folded paper.

When unfolded, she could immediately see the handwriting was not her uncle's. She guessed probably Father Mamani's. It was a simple, two-word sentence.

Open it.

A puzzled Angela looked at Velez, who examined the message.

"I don't understand."

The deacon took a deep breath. "It means I need to take you to him."

"To who? Mamani?"

"Your uncle. I said I never met him. Not that I didn't know where he was."

67

Most older Catholic churches contain small crypts, often located beneath the altar, for bishops and other important clergy and occasionally notable laypeople. Basilica San Francisco was no exception. Something Morton was aware of but still utterly fascinated to see in person.

As was Angela.

The long, wide underground passage was lined with the same light-colored brick, faded over centuries, with deep, jagged cracks in the mortar. Their footsteps eerily echoed with every stride.

Dozens and dozens of bronze plaques lined the walls,

where many of the church's former priests and clergy lay permanently entombed. It was a long, surreal walk until they reached the end, where Velez approached a wall of smaller squares made from smooth black iron with small round holes in each.

The deacon withdrew something from his cassock--a long, black key Angela didn't remember him picking up and inserted it into one of several unmarked doors. But instead of turning the key, he stepped back.

"Your uncle was cremated, something we are reluctant to do, but Father Mamani seemed to condone in this case. He never told me why."

Angela wordlessly stared at the small door.

"I've never opened it," said Velez. "And don't know what's inside. I think that's something for you to do." With that, he stepped further back. "I'll be waiting upstairs."

The two watched Velez calmly retreat the way they had come, disappearing back up the stone steps. The sound of his footsteps faded into silence.

Angela blinked at Morton and then looked back at the long, black key protruding from the hole.

"You want me to leave?" asked Morton.

"No. I don't."

With a deep breath, she inched forward until directly in front of the key. Still trembling, she raised her right hand and grasped the end of it...and turned.

The door swung open without a sound, revealing a dark rectangular cavity approximately three feet deep.

The first object she withdrew was a wallet of brown marred leather which held several items inside. Her great-uncle's wallet. It contained small folded pieces of paper that appeared to be letters with faded scribbling, as well as several black-and-white photos. All the pictures were of people she did not recognize--except one. A woman sitting in a chair with her head turned toward the camera. She had long dark wavy hair, youthful eyes and only a hint of a smile.

Morton looked at it over her shoulder. "Who's that?"

"My great-grandmother."

She exhaled and reached up again, this time pulling out a long silver chain with two flat tabs with etchings on each. Her uncle's dog tags. Next was his passport. Old and just as faded with a thin band wrapped around it.

Angela unwrapped it and carefully opened the booklet, catching just in time a small card that fell out. It was made of thick paper and was covered in strange writing.

Unable to read it, she handed it to Mike, who shook his head.

Next was a leather-bound book, also wrapped. And then the last item, waiting patiently in the dark cavity behind the rest, was a square wooden urn with the name Roger Reed carved neatly across the front.

Angela handed the book to Morton and reached up with both hands to carefully retrieve the urn, quietly staring at it for a very long time.

"You okay?"

She nodded.

She then carefully turned the box, examining it. She had found her uncle where no one would have ever expected. In South America. In the basement of an ancient church, cremated in a plain wooden box, where he would have been lost forever if not for his letter.

Angela remained still as she contemplated, before exhaling and lowering the box to the floor.

"I'm glad you found him," Morton said.

She smiled. "Me too. For him *and* my grandfather."

"A man who never gave up on his older brother."

"No, he didn't."

Angela took the book and untied the leather band around it. It contained what appeared to be about a hundred thin sheets of paper. Some spotted, some with stains, but each covered in meticulous handwriting.

Page by page, she flipped through it, scanning. Occasionally stopping to read more, slowing more and more often toward the end of the book.

"It's his journal," she finally whispered.

"Does it say what happened?"

She flipped to the back and read without a sound, before finally shaking her head. "But it does say what he found."

Morton's eyes narrowed. "Like what?"

Slowly, Angela's face changed to a subtle grin. "Like *IT.*"

68

Alerta, Peru

September 7th, 1956

It was getting harder to breathe. The symptoms were progressing faster than predicted and he was vomiting almost daily now.

It was malaria. The ancient virus birthed from the remains of mosquitos trapped for centuries in amber to become one of man's deadliest infectious diseases, especially in warm tropical climates.

Roger Reed wiped the sweat from his forehead, unable to tell anymore how much of the perspiration was from the jungle heat and how much from the sickness. He had no idea where he'd gotten it. Sandia? Caican? There was no way to know, but he couldn't stop wondering. Maybe it was true. Maybe the area *was* cursed. And his discovery was the ultimate punishment.

His head was pounding as it had been for days, made

worse by lack of food. Reed hadn't eaten in…

He wasn't sure anymore. Three days?

It was a curse. It had to be. No amount of coincidence would allow him to search for all these years, only to kill him upon finally finding it. No thanks to the bastard Percy Fawcett. Or the Nazis.

Fawcett's secret letter had been a ruse. Vague hints at what he had found laced with half-truths and misdirection carefully woven throughout to prevent anyone else from finding it until Fawcett was ready. A letter only his family possessed and that was later stolen by Nazi researchers during the war.

But Reed had slowly pieced it all together, meticulously studying Fawcett's writings as if they were a bible. Over and over. Just like Heinrich Schliemann had sifted word by word through Homer's *Iliad*. But the *Iliad* wasn't intentionally filled with misleading details.

Over the years, Roger Reed had come to despise Fawcett. He would have given up entirely had he not finally located Fawcett's first major landmark in Tangara de Serra, barely a year after Reed had disappeared from the Army.

How could he have known it would take so long? That his ambition would turn to obsession, and that he would have to live his lie far longer than he ever thought? Hiding. Unable to contact anyone, even his own family, if for nothing else but to let them know he was alive, for fear the Army would find out where he'd disappeared to.

He knew they were looking for him. They had to be. Even now. Because someone else must have known. Someone had to have also seen the documents Reed found in the caves. Soldiers were crawling all over the place. The notion that he was the only one was impossible.

It was a find of unimaginable proportions. Virtually every project the Nazis had worked on—all documented, filed, boxed and stowed away in an underground cave deep in the mountains of central Germany to ensure the rise again of the Nazi party.

Reed's thoughts returned to his family. What had the Army told them about their son? Missing in action? AWOL? No, they would have to claim he was a traitor. Of course, they would. Brand him a traitor to get him to surface and clear his name. But they were wrong. It wouldn't work. Reed wouldn't bite. He wasn't stupid or weak. He wouldn't surface. He couldn't. Not until he found what he was after. Only then would he have the power to clear his name.

But Fawcett had ruined it. Ruined it all. Fawcett and his goddamn antics had slowly destroyed Reed's life, causing him to spend a decade just to prove he was right.

Another wave of nausea washed over him and Reed closed his eyes, waiting it out. He opened them again to see the faint outline of the jungle rising before him, foreboding and motionless in the darkness, waiting to take him one last time.

For good this time. He could feel it.

He reached in and withdrew the small envelope from his pocket. Wrinkled, but still securely sealed. Written several days before, before his symptoms had gotten so bad. A letter to his brother, who would be more than old enough now.

Roger Reed stared at the letter, squinting in the darkness, barely able to make out the lettering in those predawn hours. Why did it have to be sent from Alerta again? He couldn't remember. Then it came back. That's right. In case the Army intercepted it. Alerta was far enough away to keep them from discovering the secret. Father Mamani had a brother there, and Roger could stay with him while waiting for Gerald, unless he had to retreat back to La Paz for more medication.

Gerald would know how to decode the last letters. He would remember that Fawcett's first trip was to La Paz. Then he could find the church, if need be.

Reed closed his eyes again, trying to relax. The malaria was making it hard to concentrate. But he would fight through it. He had to. He needed help. Someone he could truly trust, and someone who would understand just how important all of this was.

Someone who could tell his mother and father he was still alive. That the pain they had endured was not in vain. And that what he did, he did not for himself but for the world. Because something had to be done to keep it from the Nazis.

Thousands of them had left Germany and were now crawling all over South America. God forbid there was another copy of Percy Fawcett's letter floating around somewhere.

He would give his brother Gerald three weeks before sending another letter. This one to his father.

Unfortunately, the disease had taken a stronger hold on Reed's system than he knew. And just like the thousands of American lives already claimed by malaria throughout the South Pacific, Reed's would be yet another. His symptoms were about to worsen dramatically.

There would be no second letter.

69

Angela waited patiently for Mike, who was sitting quietly in a pew before the basilica's stunning and somewhat intimidating altar. Where a massive crucifix, Christ on the cross made of solid white marble, stared down at him with mournful eyes.

She quietly approached and sat next to him just as

Morton slipped another pill into his mouth.

"Are you all right?"

He nodded. "It's been getting worse."

"Your heart?"

He nodded.

She slid closer and stared up at the statue. "How long ago did you lose her?"

"Who?"

"Your wife."

Morton lowered his head. "A long time. Seven years. Seven long years."

"You miss her."

"Very much."

"I bet she was a wonderful woman."

"She was," he said without looking up. "Truly wonderful. And perfect. At least for me."

Angela gently placed a hand on his heavy shoulder.

Morton's voice wavered slightly. "I...miss her...so much. Sometimes I don't know why—" When he looked up, tears glistened in his eyes. "Every memory I have has her in it. I can't even remember living without her. Until now." He frowned. "I can still smell her. Hear the way she laughed. And sometimes, if I really try, I can still feel how soft her hands were. On my face."

Angela slid closer. "I'm sorry, Mike."

He blinked and both tears fell, hitting his dark cheeks. "It's funny. When you lose someone you really love, you forget all the things you didn't like. Things that irritated you." He looked at Angela. "Now I can't remember a single one. Nothing that I didn't love."

"I'm starting to feel some of that with my grandfather. Even the differences I do remember just feel stupid now."

He looked up at the altar. "Nothing else matters, Angela. Nothing. Take it from me, an old man who's seen a hell of a lot in his day. Too much. Of how the world really is. And I'm here to tell you none of it matters. None of it. Just love. It's our only real protection against the world out there.

Everything else is just some veiled disguise of meaninglessness. You just have to realize it in time."

"I believe you."

Morton reached over and patted her knee. "I'm glad you were strong enough to come here. And I'm sorry for everything that's happened to you. Truly."

She leaned closer and hugged his arm. "Thank you. I guess some of us just end up traveling a rougher road."

"It's true. But then again, not everyone can make it. Even on an easier path. You must come from a strong family. And strong parents."

Angela grinned.

"Come to think of it, I don't recall you mentioning anything about your parents."

She stared straight ahead and shrugged. "I didn't have any."

"What do you mean?"

"I never knew my father. And my mother died. During childbirth."

"I'm sorry."

"It's okay. I never met my mother, but I knew a lot about her. She liked peanut butter and banana sandwiches," Angela said, smiling. "She *was* strong though. Abandoned by my birth father, she never looked back. Held down a job and went to school at night while getting ready to raise a daughter. She was really something."

"I'll bet she was."

"While I was being delivered, she began hemorrhaging. Badly. And they couldn't stop it in time. It was a freak thing, especially these days, but they were able to save me. We only knew each other for a few minutes."

Morton sighed. "Hence being raised by your grandparents."

"Right."

"Well, for what it's worth, I'm sure she would have been proud of you. Really proud. You're quite a young woman."

Angela chuckled. "Believe me, I have a lot of flaws."

"We all do. Doesn't make you any less impressive," he said. "I even looked you up."

"Huh?"

"On the internet. I looked you up."

Angela gave him a perplexed look. "How? When?"

"My trailer has a satellite dish with a data connection. You have a pretty impressive bio."

"I don't remember seeing a dish on your trailer."

"It was dark," he shrugged. "But you're still a very impressive young woman. With or without the flaws. I think you're going to do great things."

"Thank you. I think I can speak for both me *and* Joe when I say we're lucky to have met you down here."

"Likewise."

Angela thought of something and looked around. "Where is Anku?"

"I don't know. He wanders off a lot, which is really annoying in the jungle," he said, grinning.

She laughed and looked at Morton. "So, tell me, Mike, what is it that you think you'll find out there?"

"I'm not sure," he answered. "Could be anything. And I mean that literally."

"What do you mean?"

He tilted his head, thinking. "You remember what I said about that old satellite?"

Angela nodded. "You said it detected all the different types of energy converging on one spot."

"That's right. The truth is, I really don't know what it is," he said. "Energy is a very strange thing."

"Energy is strange?"

"Very. At the most fundamental level, energy is a bunch of electrons and protons, just like everything else, including us. But the *way* it behaves in the real world is very different from anything else.

"When it comes to physics, energy and mass are so tightly related that in some situations they can become one another. Energy can become mass, and mass can become

233

energy. In fact, another kind of energy, called kinetic energy, or what we call pressure, can actually change the very nature of other molecules."

"How so?"

"For example, if you put the metal mercury under enough intense pressure, that mercury will actually start to defy gravity and climb right out of the container."

"What?!"

"Yep. Or if you apply enough energy to an oxygen molecule, it becomes a solid and turns blood red."

"I had no idea."

He nodded. "Even Einstein knew there was something very unique about energy, which is why he believed in reincarnation. Because energy, like what we have inside of us, cannot just disappear. Energy has to *go* somewhere. So the question is, where does it go? Or even better, *what* does it become?"

"That's starting to sound a little spooky."

"I agree. Energy *is* spooky. In fact, if you really want spooky, look at dark energy."

"What's dark energy?"

"That's the big question. Astronomers don't even know. But they do know, without a doubt, that everything we see in the universe—all the stars, all the planets, all the galaxies—*everything* that is visible even with our giant telescopes, only comprises ten percent of all the matter in the universe."

"How is that possible?"

"I don't know. But we can see it and we can measure it. This also means that ninety percent of all the matter, or mass, in the universe *cannot* be seen. In fact, it can barely be detected. But we know it's there because we can measure the mass that we *can* see and its effects on things. And ninety percent is missing."

"So what does that mean?"

"What it means," said Morton, "is that most of our universe cannot currently be seen, let alone understood. But what we have figured out is that of the missing ninety percent, approximately thirty percent of that is what we call dark matter—matter we cannot see. Likely huge amounts of mass that does not reflect or produce light.

"But what's *really* weird," Morton said, "or rather *spooky*, is the rest of the universe. The remaining sixty percent, which is made up of energy itself. Energy we cannot see or measure, or even understand. But we already know from our own limited capabilities and experiments that energy, especially intense levels of energy, can and does do very strange things. Like I said, matter and energy turning into one another, theories of something after, and even the ability to change behaviors of certain fundamental elements. So, what happens if different forms of energy were to all converge in one place and even amplify each other?"

Angela had no answer.

"Those are just a few examples, but the bottom line is that when it comes to energy, all bets are off. Energy is hugely strange and unpredictable. Especially in very large or intense concentrations, where it can actually affect time and space, making it as close to mystical as anything we've observed in the known universe. And the closest thing to magic as the laws of physics will allow."

70

"Waiting for the tour?"

Outside, sitting on a circular concrete bench, Joe Rickards looked up at the voice to see a figure standing over him, silhouetted by the morning sun.

"Excuse me?"

The figure stepped forward and closer to the bench,

where he became more visible. He was tall and slender, with a lean jawline and full head of neatly combed gray hair.

"Are you waiting for the tour? Of the church?"

Rickards studied the man. His long black cassock descended just a few inches from the ground. "Uh, no. I'm not."

"I'm sorry," apologized the priest with a slight accent. "I do recommend it if you have time. It's quite good."

Rickards looked back to the church. "Thanks. But I'm just waiting for someone."

"I see." After looking about the plaza, he peered down again. "Mind if I sit down?"

Rickards gave him a sidelong glance and shrugged.

The man sat and smiled. "You're American?"

"I am." Rickards nodded. "But don't hold it against me."

The man laughed. "I take it you're here visiting."

"Briefly."

"And how are you enjoying La Paz?"

"Hurriedly, I'm afraid."

The man laughed again.

Both men watched people mingle about the church's entrance, where after a few moments, a child was seen staring up and pointing, prompting two other children to do the same. Then several adults.

Both Rickards and the priest followed the boy's raised hand up the face of the church tower, where they spotted a figure standing above them looking down from a small iron walkway.

It was Anku. His arms were raised above his head and he was calling out in Quechuan.

"That's not good."

"Probably not," nodded the priest beside him. "But then again, the Quechua live by a different set of rules."

"So I've heard." Rickards squinted, trying to make out Anku's face. "Can you tell what he's saying?"

The priest paused, listening. "Something about his ancestors and their spirits. That they speak to us and…" He paused again. "I'm afraid the rest I don't understand."

"Pay attention to your elders." Rickards shrugged. "Not the worst message, I guess."

"Certainly not." The man extended his hand to Rickards. "I'm Father Pataki."

"Joe Rickards," he answered, shaking the priest's hand.

"Pleased to meet you, Joe. I was just out on my morning stroll around the grounds and noticed you sitting here alone. Thought something might be troubling you."

"And why is that?"

"Just a hunch."

"Well, I'm fine. But thanks."

"Did your friends go inside?"

"Yes."

"How long ago?"

Rickards glanced at his watch. "Half hour."

Pataki nodded thoughtfully. "You chose not to join them?"

"That's right."

"I see," the father acknowledged. Then after another short pause, he asked, "What line of work are you in, Joe?"

"Law enforcement."

"Ah. A police officer."

"Not quite. An investigator."

"A detective, then."

Rickards didn't bother correcting him. "Yes. A detective."

"A very noble profession."

Internally, he smirked. Rickards was probably as far from noble as one could be.

"And where in America are you from?"

"Colorado."

"The Rocky Mountain State."

Rickards turned. "You know where Colorado is?"

"Indeed. I've been to your country twice. Once when I was a young man and once as an old man. I appreciated it more as an old man."

"Understandable," Rickards said, turning back to the church.

"It's funny," Pataki said, "to think of all the things I failed to appreciate as a young man. Traveling. Health. Wisdom." The priest grinned. "Being able to go up and down stairs."

"Don't feel bad. It's universal."

"I suppose it is. The excitement of youth eventually gives way to the patience and wisdom of age. It's the natural cycle of things, but sometimes difficult to accept. Both then and now."

Anku had stopped yelling and was now silently standing atop the tower, eyes closed with the wind on his face.

"You sound more like a philosopher than a priest."

Pataki chuckled. "I wasn't always a priest. But it is a job that requires different skills. And different outlooks."

"Like helping people who sit by themselves looking troubled?"

The father chuckled. "That is one, yes."

"Well, prepare to be disappointed."

"Why would I be disappointed?"

"Because I'm not that interesting."

"I disagree."

Rickards gave him another look.

"You're obviously intelligent, a visitor from Colorado who appears to be making a very rapid appearance to our city and who doesn't like churches. There's more than enough intrigue there."

Rickards couldn't help but grin.

"Why don't you like churches, Joe?"

The grin disappeared, and he turned away. "It doesn't matter."

"No?"

"Let's just say I'm not a religious man."

"A lot of atheists still enjoy seeing churches, if for nothing more than appreciating our rich history. Even if you think we're wrong, the stories are quite interesting."

238

"I'm not an atheist."

"I didn't say you were."

"You implied that I was."

Pataki smiled playfully. "And you inferred."

Rickards didn't respond.

The father looked up at a group of birds passing overhead. "Do you know why I became a priest, Joe?"

"No idea."

"Because I was troubled. I was a troubled young man who, as I became older, struggled to make sense out of this world."

Rickards turned back again to look at him.

"After we become adults, I'm afraid we begin to see the world for what it really is. A constant struggle. Not just to survive or prosper, but to actually find meaning in all of it. To find reason."

"I thought that's what the Bible was for."

Pataki nodded. "To many, it is. But for others, it's more explanation than meaning. Some people are content with explanations, but others need reason. To know that we're not all just wasting our time. That what we do actually matters."

Rickards stared at him, a hardness returning to his face. "I have news for them. Sometimes it really doesn't matter."

"No?"

"No," said Rickards coldly. "Maybe, just maybe, life is simply the pain we have to endure to finally realize in the long run, that nothing really matters."

Father Pataki thought about his words, surprising him when he said, "It's possible."

"What?"

"It's possible," he repeated. "I'm open enough to know I don't have all the answers. But what I do know is that we are not the first. Regardless of my own beliefs, I think it's safe to say that virtually every human being who has lived and died before us on this planet has suffered."

Rickards remained silent.

"Yes, our suffering is real. But our minds also want to convince ourselves that our own suffering is somehow special. Or unique. But it's not. Because every person who has lived and died has also suffered. Often in much worse ways than we have. Billions. Billions have lived before us. Many of them struggled just to survive. Struggled to feed themselves or their children. Fought wars, fought oppression, torture, genocide, plagues. And often far less able to do anything about it."

"Not exactly a rosy picture you're painting."

"I'm not trying to paint a picture, Joe. I'm merely applying context. Rationalization that helped me through my own struggles for meaning. I finally realized that regardless of knowing why or how, being here is still worthwhile. Even important."

"And why is that, to help another generation be thankful when we're gone?"

"No. Because being here provides meaning...for others who are not."

Rickards stared at him before shaking his head. "No, it doesn't. It provides nothing but an empty sense of hope. Until eventually, you realize that not even hope is real. And as for suffering, have other people suffered? Yes. Have they suffered more? Probably. But another person's pain doesn't do anything to lessen your own. No matter how much easier we may have it."

Father Pataki nodded thoughtfully. "That may be true. But if we cannot see tomorrow as a little better, as a little brighter, even by a small amount, what point is there?"

"That's exactly what I'm saying. At a certain point, there is no hope. When you realize the fruitlessness of it all. And there is nothing left to face...but your own blame."

Neither man spoke for several minutes, instead sitting next to each other, silently contemplating one another's words. Finally, Father Pataki looked and saw that Joe's eyes were closed and his chin was trembling.

"What happened, Joe?"

Rickards merely shook his head.

Pataki put a hand on his shoulder and could feel the trembling there, too.

"Let it out," he said. "Let it out before it eats you."

Rickards' lips barely moved. "It's too late. For me."

"Why?"

He sniffed. "Because they're already gone."

"Who is gone?"

Rickards suddenly turned to him, eyes open and filled with tears. "How many, Father?"

"How many what?"

"Of all those billions," Rickards said, "who have suffered. How many did it to themselves? How many committed the worst crime possible and were left alive as punishment? How many of those people do you think killed their *own* families?"

Pataki's eyes froze just as Rickards began to weep.

71

Father Pataki gripped Rickards' hand with both of his, clamping them firmly as the weeping turned to sobbing. Deep gut-wrenching sobs from a man convinced he had no place in this world. No worth. And no reason even to be remembered, let alone forgiven.

He was the lowest of all humans. The lowest among all the billions who had ever lived. Someone who contributed nothing. Allowed to live by sheer circumstance and nothing more.

But Father Pataki never let go. And when the sobs became uncontrollable, he immediately wrapped both of his arms around Rickards, holding him to his chest as if he would never let go.

Letting him know that even in his deepest grief...he was not alone.

72

It would take several long minutes before Rickards could speak. Eventually, he wiped the tears away with his hands, speaking through a voice still wavering.

It was his fault. It was all his fault. An accident he could have prevented, resulting in the death of his wife and daughter. Something that never should have happened, if it was not for him. If not for his own stupidity.

He was the one who'd known the brakes on the car were failing. He was the one who could have done something about it that night. He was the one who should have been awake to stop his wife from taking his car the next morning instead of hers.

One single horrific decision. One she had no way of knowing she was even making. Taking their daughter, Shannon, to school, sitting happily in the back seat. Innocent. Until the accident. An accident she could have avoided, or at least survived, if only he had done something about the brakes.

Only made worse with Joe not knowing. Having no idea, while following behind in her car. First filling the gas tank and then getting onto the freeway to see the stopped traffic. Inching forward for forty-five minutes before finally spotting his own car. Crumpled and destroyed.

It was a picture he would never forget, the horrific image of him finally reaching the vehicle.

He had killed his own family through nothing but

stupidity. Utter stupidity had taken the lives of his wife and daughter forever. Something that no amount of grief, no amount of pain and no amount of consolation would ever change.

And no amount of rationalization would ever convince him that he deserved to be alive while they were gone.

Father Pataki had no words. After thirty years as a priest, he thought he had seen it all. Strife. Misery. Torment. Enough to last a lifetime.

But guilt. Guilt was worst of all. Especially when it came to a child. There were simply no words that could ever make a difference. No words to help heal those permanent wounds in a parent's heart.

All he could do was keep his arm around Joe.

When it was over, there were no words spoken, just silence as the heaving subsided and tears began to dry.

Nothing to be said.

But one thing.

"Joe," Pataki finally whispered.

"Yeah."

"I can't begin to know what you're going through," he said. "No one can. And even if they could, it wouldn't matter. Not now. But I want you to try to remember something."

"What?"

"If you remember only one thing from our encounter, I want it to be this. That with everything I've been through, and everything I've seen, all of the darkness and all of the hopelessness. All the questions over meaning and purpose in this world. There is one thing that I believe to be emphatically and categorically true, regardless of your spiritual beliefs. And that is...that *responsibility* is purpose."

He grinned gently at Joe. "I know it doesn't sound like

much. But in time, when you can finally see through the darkness, look for it. Look for something. Some level of responsibility that you can commit to. Because it *is purpose*. And purpose alone will eventually pull you out."

73

Rickards had only minutes to digest the priest's words before he heard it.

Shouting from above.

He looked up and spotted Anku, gripping the railing with one hand and pointing with the other. Shouting unintelligibly in Quechuan.

Rickards followed Anku's arm and slowly turned around to see a small black dot in the sky.

When he looked back, Anku was gone—just before he heard the beating sound of helicopter rotors.

***

Inside the church, Anku's yelling continued, echoing downward as he scrambled down a long, sealed-off set of stairs. His shouts reverberated through the stone hallways and all the way to the church's sanctuary and altar, where Angela and Mike Morton suddenly turned around.

"Is that Anku?"

Morton nodded, trying to listen, taking only a second before frowning. "It's the Quechuan word for *trouble*!"

The two jumped from their seats and raced out of the sanctuary. Running down the hallway, back to the main entrance and then outside, where they stopped and looked up.

Above them, just a few hundred feet from the ground, was a large military helicopter.

"Mi-17," breathed Morton. "Russian made."

Angela spotted the single white stripe sandwiched between two red, painted on the aircraft's fuselage, before it arched and disappeared over to the top of the church. Reemerging several seconds later, it continued a tight circle over the Plaza.

"Is that Peruvian?"

"Yep." Morton grabbed her hand and looked around, noticing just as the helicopter swept around, a reflection within the dark interior of its open doorway. A telescopic lens.

Morton spun to find Deacon Velez standing in the wide entrance behind them, yelling above the noise and urgently motioning them back inside.

74

Pressing the small earphone further into his ear, Fischer turned to Karl Ottman inside the lead Humvee.

"They've spotted Reed."

"Where?"

"At the entrance to the church. They've just gone inside."

Ottman leaned quickly toward the driver. "How much longer?"

"We're here," the man said, suddenly veering around several cars. He then cut sharply back across the lane and accelerated up and over the sidewalk.

"Hold on!" he yelled and roared up the sharp incline of two dozen steps, briefly leaving the ground before bouncing down again on the paved northeast corner of Plaza San Francisco.

***

Angela and Morton followed Velez through the church, running at full speed, quickly winding in and out of rooms while dozens of visitors turned to watch.

Halfway down the hall, Velez turned to the left and headed down a short, tight hallway that ended at a heavy wooden door. He quickly unlatched it and threw it open with the weight of his body.

"This way!"

They exited, reentering the bright sunlight, making for a large garden in one corner of the church's courtyard.

Darting beneath several trees, they loosely followed a winding path until they reached a wide double set of descending concrete stairs leading down a level toward one of the giant plaza's two underground parking garages.

Velez continued downward before Angela stopped. "Wait!" She whirled around, frantically searching. "Where's Joe?"

No sooner had she spoken than a loud squeal sounded and a truck appeared around the church's southmost wing. It smashed through a barrier of small, stone-potted plants, causing the front bumper of Morton's yellow Toyota pickup to rip clean off and go twirling several times in the air before tumbling across the concrete.

Unfazed, the truck roared forward at full speed, Anku holding onto the top of the cab for dear life. They saw Rickards inside, behind the wheel, steering directly for them.

They covered the distance in seconds and careened to a

stop beneath the trees, tearing through a thick row of bushes.

Both men jumped from the vehicle as the sounds of the helicopter approached again, making another pass.

Morton was stunned. "How'd you know where we were?"

"Ask Anku."

Without another word, all four followed Velez hurriedly down the steps, disappearing into the parking garage.

***

High above, the Mi-17 circled over the top of the church, looking for the truck.

In front of the church, Ottman's Humvee screeched to a halt, allowing Fischer and Becker to leap out and sprint inside, where several people were frozen in place, watching.

Fischer spotted the young woman behind the desk and shouted, "Where did they go?!"

She stammered. "Uh…I don't—"

Becker was closer and on her in seconds, grabbing the girl by the shirt and forcefully hauling her up and over the counter. "Where?!" he screamed.

The panicking girl pointed to the hallway on the far side.

"Show us!" yelled Becker and threw her forward, sending her stumbling to the ground. "Now!"

***

Reaching the bottom of the stairs, Velez ran along the wall of the garage's first level, passing several cars before stopping and pointing his key ring at a small maroon Nissan.

When the others reached him, he handed the keys to Morton and Angela. "Take it!"

Out of breath, Angela stared at him. "Are you—"

Velez put a hand up to stop her, then grinned. "The Lord provides."

247

Morton needed no convincing. "Thanks, Father," he said and snatched the keys from his hand. But upon reaching the driver's side door, he frowned at the amount of room inside. Looking up, he immediately threw the keys to Rickards. "You're driving."

Rickards circled and passed him, glancing at the empty back seat. "Looks pretty tight in the back too."

"Just get in, I'll fit!"

Angela stared at Velez one last time before tightly wrapping her arms around him. "Thank you!"

"Out through the exit," he said. "Then keep to the right."

Rickards squeezed into the driver's seat and looked around. Finding the ignition, he inserted the key and searched for the brake release.

He found it and released before dropping the car into *Reverse* and backing them out of the spot. Then he stopped.

"Let's go!"

Rickards shook his head, slowly putting both hands on the wheel.

"What are you waiting for?!" yelled Morton. "Punch it!"

"We can't."

"Why not?!"

"They have a helicopter. They'll notice a car speeding out of the garage. We have to blend in."

Morton fell quiet and reached into his pocket for another pill. "Right. Good. That's a good idea."

Rickards finished his thought and calmly pulled the gearshift back into *Drive*. He turned to Angela, who was staring at him from the passenger's seat.

"Tell us where we're going, Professor."

***

Fischer and Becker threw the young girl to the side and burst out through the side door. Scanning the open

248

courtyard, they immediately spotted Morton's yellow truck parked idly beneath the trees with the driver's door still ajar.

When they reached it, Becker checked the cab while Fischer rushed forward across the garden to the edge of the steps. Unsure, he looked around, examining the rest of the courtyard, dotted with dozens of visitors, all strolling along the causeway atop the giant garage that connected to a strip of restaurants and shops on the opposite side.

Spotting no one, Fischer continued down the stairs to the top level of the garage.

Nothing.

75

Once they were out of the garage, Angela pulled out and opened her uncle's journal, prompting Morton, in the back seat, to look at her curiously.

"Where's the rest?"

She looked back. "In my pocket. But I left my uncle where he was. In the church."

Rickards briefly glanced at her from behind the wheel. "What did you find?"

"Him and his things," she said. She quickly unwrapped the journal and once again began flipping through the pages. "And this."

"What is that, a journal?"

"Yes."

"For the love of God, please tell me there's a map in it."

"There is," she said, finally stopping near the end of the book. "Not in the traditional sense, but definitely a drawing with a location. Just north of Lake Titicaca. A place called…" she squinted, "Ur…cag…uary."

"What?"

"Urcaguary," she repeated.

"What does that mean?" asked Morton.

"I don't know. It doesn't say."

The car fell silent while Angela continued studying the pages, until Anku, sitting quietly in the back with Morton, spoke.

"Urcaguary," he said with a different pronunciation.

"Yes, Urcaguary." Morton nodded.

Anku turned to look at him and smiled, saying something much longer in Quechuan.

Morton raised his eyebrows and replied.

When Anku spoke again, Angela twisted her head. "Does he know where it is?"

"Yes," Morton said, nodding. "But he says it's not a place. It's a name."

"A name? As in the name of a place?"

"No. As in the name of a person."

76

Karl Ottman watched as the thundering Russian Mi-17 helicopter approached and slowed to hover several meters from the ground, allowing the pilot to check for cross breeze before finally descending again and bouncing onto the grass field just outside of La Paz.

It had taken Ottman's cyber expert forty-five minutes to find them. One at a time, isolating each of the two dozen cars emerging from both sides of the parking garage. Painstakingly tracking each car as it made its way through the city, all on different routes until enough had stopped to allow the live satellite images to confirm they were not Reed and Rickards. Through a painstaking process of elimination, he finally concluded that one of two remaining cars was their target.

When one of the two finally stopped in a small suburb outside of La Paz, full attention was turned to the maroon-colored sedan heading northeast, passing the northern end of Lake Titicaca and the national reserve, before reaching a wide dirt road and turning east.

A fragile Ottman was hauled up into the body of the helicopter by the hand of Fischer, blades still beating the air, where he was then lowered into the middle of three leather-bound seats.

Harnesses were pulled across his body and tightened before both Fischer and Becker took their seats on either side. Both reached out to pull up heavy M16A2 rifles into their laps. Combat weapons known more simply as M16s.

Doors on both sides closed with a loud thud and headsets were pulled down from above onto each head, including Ottman's, who promptly raised a hand to move his microphone into place.

Reed and Rickards would now be outside of the city and away from populated areas, exactly what he had been waiting for.

Ottman had had enough of the games. They were close now. He could feel it. He was sure the Reed woman had found in the church what Ottman himself had been searching for all these years.

He could not have been more right.

77

"Whoa."

Navigating around potholes in the dirt road, Rickards glanced at Angela. "What?"

She looked up at him with a frozen expression. In her hands, also frozen, was something that had just slid out from between two pages of her uncle's journal.

"What's that?"

Angela slowly opened the small, folded paper. After a moment of reading, she gasped. "Oh…my…God."

Morton leaned forward from the back seat. "What?"

She didn't answer until Rickards abruptly pulled over, allowing the trail of billowing dust to envelop them.

When she did answer, it was as if a light had just gone off.

"It's a letter."

"Not another letter," groaned Rickards.

"No," she said. "Not a letter. *The* letter. It's what the Germans are looking for."

"What do you mean?"

"They already knew everything else," she said, "or at least they appeared to. Not a surprise, since Percy Fawcett's writings are all public information." She paused, raising the paper. "But not this one."

"And what is that?"

"It's a letter written by Fawcett to his wife. And dated 1923. Telling her to keep this one secret."

She turned back to search the journal more closely and found another paper. This one was larger and also folded and carefully stuffed inside. When she opened it, she stared at both Rickards and Morton. "And *this one* is in German."

Rickards glanced over his right shoulder. "*Sprechen sie Deutsch*, Mike?"

"Afraid not."

"I don't think you need to, this time," said Angela, turning the large paper around so they could both see it. "Look who it's addressed to."

Rickards squinted at it and his expression turned to a look of surprise. "You've got to be kidding."

Angela shook her head.

"What does it say?" Morton reached out to take it, studying it for a moment before his own eyes widened. "Heinrich Himmler!"

Angela looked at Rickards. "This is what my uncle found in Germany as a Monuments Man. *This* is why he disappeared!"

"This is what they don't have?"

She nodded, turning back to Fawcett's letter. "This is what they needed. It's the missing piece--a secret letter to his wife explaining where it is. Including descriptions and landmarks. Everything someone would need—"

"If something should happen to him," finished Rickards.

"That's right," Angela added. "Which means that Fawcett's final expedition was not to find it. Because he already had. It was to *excavate* it."

Rickards sat staring at her. "So, your uncle found these papers in Germany and came here to search for it."

"I think that's exactly what happened."

"And he found it?"

"Apparently."

"So, if he had Fawcett's secret instructions and landmarks, why did it take him a decade to do it?"

Angela was reading the journal. "I'm not sure. It looks like there may have been some misinformation in Fawcett's letter. Intentional misdirection, perhaps in case it fell into the wrong hands. Which obviously it did since the Nazis ended up with it."

"And what if your uncle is doing the same thing?"

Angela returned to the final handwritten pages of the

journal and considered the question. "No. He sounds angry in here. He is specifically telling us where it is."

She looked up from the leather-bound book and peered through the car's windshield. "It's this way."

78

The road continued east, steadily dropping in elevation with every turn as it wound deeper and deeper into the mouth of a large canyon. Walls on each side were lined in various layers and hues of strata beneath an afternoon haze that gave it a somewhat copperish tint.

The road became increasingly narrower over the several miles until it finally appeared little more than two parallel footpaths, prompting Rickards to continually look at Anku in his rearview mirror, wondering if they were still even on the correct road.

For his part, Anku remained calm and quiet, riding along with very little movement beyond the normal rocking of the car through dips and holes. He peered out through the dusty window at the canyon walls slowly crawling by, a relaxed smile on his face.

Morton tried to talk to him multiple times, but Anku's replies were brief. After yet another attempt, Rickards spoke up.

"Anything new?"

Morton shook his head. "Nope. Just keeps saying he hasn't been here in a long time. Since he was a boy."

"You sure he still knows the way?"

"He doesn't seem the least bit concerned."

When they finally arrived, it appeared to be just as Morton had expected, as well as Angela. Dozens of adobe-like houses made from large mud bricks lined the narrow road. Each sported thin metal roofs, with some structures open and entirely without doors, like sheds. Farther up the slope were actual huts made from materials resembling thin trees with brown grass tops.

Rickards brought the car to a stop just as several Quechuan gathered around the road to investigate. All were dressed in remarkably bright and colorful clothing, presenting a stark contrast against the drabness of the barren hills behind them.

In the back seat, Anku spoke briefly to Morton before studying the door to open it. Then he slammed the door shut behind him.

"He says to wait here."

"Are we unwelcome?"

"No. But the Quechua have customs for welcoming people, even their own."

"I see."

Together, the three remained inside, watching Anku approach and exchange several long gestures, followed by conversation and reaching out to embrace another man with a handshake that looked more like grasping each other's forearms.

Anku then disappeared around the corner of a building without even a glance back to the car.

"Would be nice to get out and stretch," Rickards muttered.

Morton shook his head at Rickards while adjusting himself in the back seat. "Don't. It's a sign of disrespect."

"Stretching?"

Morton inhaled and popped another tiny pill. "Standing on their ground uninvited."

Angela looked over her shoulder. "How many of those

are you allowed to take?"

"All of them, if I have to."

Morton returned the tiny bottle to a pocket and glanced at his watch. He paused, blinking, continuing to stare at it. After a short silence, he looked at the others. "My watch is no longer working."

Rickards looked at him in the mirror and checked his own, puzzled. "Neither is mine."

"Where's your stick?" Angela asked.

"It's not a stick. It's a highly sensitive piece of equipment. Made up of sensors that—"

"It's called a pole," said Rickards.

She laughed.

"Fine. It's a pole. And was left in my truck by Mario Andretti here." Morton grabbed the headrest of Rickards' seat and pulled himself forward. "Wait a minute. Turn on the radio."

"Huh?"

"I said, turn on the radio."

Rickards complied, reaching forward to press the knob. When the radio came on, it shocked all three by blaring something unrecognizable at full volume with all lights illuminated on the panel. They covered their ears until Rickards could turn it back off.

"Who the hell set it like that?"

"I don't think anyone did," Morton said slowly, before making a full scan through all of the windows. "I think we're *here*."

***

After a dozen or so minutes, Anku returned with several other Quechua, who gave the others permission to leave their vehicle. The Quechua then led them back the way they'd come, past several structures and up a steep trail, winding toward a dense grove of southern beech trees that provided cover to dozens more huts.

On the way up, they stopped several times for Morton, who struggled against the steep incline, sweating profusely and having to sit or kneel multiple times. Though he was heaving with deep breaths, he brushed off offers to help him back up.

Upon making it to flatter ground, they were then all led to the largest hut, situated deep beneath the trees and close to one of the canyon's cliff walls.

Inside, sitting on mats upon a dirt floor, were several waiting Quechua positioned in a semicircle as if by rank. Angela wondered how long they had been there.

In front, Anku bowed deeply and the others echoed the gesture, motioning respectfully to the very old woman sitting in the middle. She was dressed in similarly colored clothing. Her face was deeply wrinkled and she met their gazes with dark, beaming eyes.

"Urcaguary," Anku stated in a formal and elevated tone.

The three looked at each other and then down again to the old woman. "Urcaguary?"

The woman's only movement was a smile. She sat with her legs crossed, hands resting calmly on top of them.

"Hello…" Angela stammered.

There was no reaction, prompting Morton to translate. When she replied with something longer, he stared at her curiously before turning to the others. "She says, 'You are the first in a long time.'"

Angela and Rickards looked at each other.

"The first what?"

"I haven't the slightest idea."

Angela smiled shyly at the woman and then at the others on either side before lowering her head and kneeling onto the dirt. All nine of the Quechua silently watched.

Angela then turned to stare up at Rickards and Morton, waiting until they suddenly fell in beside her on the ground.

The old woman, Urcaguary, spoke again, and Morton turned to Angela and Joe. "She wants to know why we're here."

Angela blinked. "How good is your Quechuan?"

"Not good enough to recite the entire story."

"Tell her we're here for answers?"

Morton turned and translated.

Some of the men and women on either side, also elderly, whispered to each other. But Urcaguary remained steadfast. Studying them. She continued staring at the three for an uncomfortably long time before slowly leaning forward and taking a fistful of dirt from the ground. Then, in one swift movement, she threw it up into the air to create a dust cloud.

Through the wisps of dust, Urcaguary studied Angela closely until it slowly drifted down and settled again upon the ground.

"What was that?" Angela whispered.

The old woman spoke again and waited for Morton to translate, her eyes still on Angela.

"She says you're not here for answers. What you're looking for is peace."

Angela nervously peered at Urcaguary and watched as the woman reached out and threw another handful of dirt, this time studying Morton, and once again for Rickards.

"She says most people that come are looking for wealth. For gold."

"Paititi," Angela whispered, but was cut off when Urcaguary spoke again.

"She says Paititi is a myth. Created by the white man. People who trade their souls for riches and have grown in numbers like the stars."

"Tell her we're not here for riches."

Morton translated, and the old woman's expression seemed to change into a look of bemusement.

"She says today, everyone seeks riches except the Quechua. That's why they are here." Morton then paused, unsure of the last sentence. "As the symbol. Or maybe *for* the symbol. I'm not sure."

"Symbol of what?"

Morton repeated the question. When Urcaguary replied, he shook his head. "Symbol might not be the right word. It's something like statue, or shrine. Tribute, maybe." Morton continued listening. "Paititi, she says, is not what people think. Not what they want."

Angela reached behind herself and retrieved the journal, placing it on the ground. She then rose up and pulled some of her uncle's other items from her pocket, including his wallet and dog tags, placing them on top of the journal.

"Tell her I'm not looking for riches. I'm looking for a person."

The old woman remained still, listening, while eyeing the items on the ground. When Morton was done, she raised a hand and pointed to them.

"She's asking to see it."

Angela picked up the journal and leaned forward, extending it to her, but Urcaguary shook her head and pointed again.

To the wallet.

"Oh." Angela switched the items, offering the leather billfold.

The old woman took the wallet in her old hands and studied the outside before slowly rotating and unfolding the two halves. She examined its length, and then from the top, saw what was inside. With her fingertips, she pulled the slits open and pulled the items out one at a time.

The first several were small, hard pieces of paper with writing on them. Some bits she seemed to recognize, but most she didn't. She ignored them and moved on to a set of small photos, each displaying various people and settings. One of which she held out and moved from side to side, viewing from different angles. She had seen photographs before and had always been fascinated that the people in them always appeared to be looking directly at her.

Continuing through the small pouch, Urcaguary paused and pulled out a larger piece of paper from one of the larger slits. This one was thin, folded multiple times to allow it to fit into the wallet. She unfolded it and spread it out to reveal another photograph, also black-and-white, and larger, so as to include several people sitting outside together. All had dark brown skin like hers except for the white man in the middle. The same man in many of the other images.

But what caught Urcaguary's eye was not the white man in the picture but the other dark faces. Quechuans. Some of whom she recognized from long ago--including one of the younger faces.

Her own.

Urcaguary now recognized the white man in the picture and went back to reexamine the rest.

When finished, she again peered at Angela, now with a different expression.

"She wants to know who the man is," Morton said.

"He is my great-uncle."

Morton paused, realizing he didn't know the word for uncle. What he translated was *her grandfather to brother*.

Urcaguary held up the picture and compared it to Angela's face. Then she lowered the picture and spoke.

His eyes widened and he looked to Angela. "She says...she knows your uncle."

"What?"

"She says—"

"I heard you. Is she sure?"

"Do you seriously want me to ask her if *she's sure*?"

Flustered, Angela looked back at Urcaguary, trying to form a question. But instead, the old woman said something as close to English as she knew.

"Riiiiid."

Angela smiled broadly. "Reed."

"Reeeed," the woman corrected.

Angela turned excitedly to Rickards. To her surprise,

even he was grinning.

"How   When   " she stumbled. "Ask her...just ask her about him!"

Morton turned to Urcaguary and asked *how did you know him?*

The woman began speaking, and Morton nodded as he tried to keep up. "She said he was here many years ago. Over two generations. When she was young. A girl. A young girl. And he became friends with their elders." Morton then looked at Angela. "He was searching for Paititi."

Urcaguary continued.

"She says...he didn't find what he was searching for. The truth was something more. And he told the elders it needed to be protected. From the white man."

Angela looked puzzled. "This is *not* Paititi."

Morton asked and listened. "She says this is not the Paititi sought by the selfish. Paititi is not a place." He corrected himself. "No, wait, *more* than a place. I think."

"What does that mean?"

"No idea."

"What does she mean by more?"

Morton asked again. "Mmm, I'm not quite following now. More about a statue, or symbol...symbolism maybe. I can't be sure."

Suddenly, Urcaguary said something that caused Morton to abruptly stop speaking and raise his eyebrows. "And something about *great energy*."

79

"She says your uncle was a spiritual man. No," Morton

said, correcting himself again. "An honorable man." He sighed. "I think they use that word interchangeably."

"Does she know what happened to my uncle?"

Morton asked. "No." He continued listening. "But she said he was afraid."

"Afraid of what?"

After pausing, he answered, "Afraid of his own people."

"Americans?"

"I think she means white men, in general. Non-Quechuan." Listening more, he continued, "Paititi, she says, is for everyone. But not everyone is ready for Paititi. Not worthy, maybe." Morton suddenly stopped again and shook his head. "Not sure on that one."

When Urcaguary finally finished, Morton shrugged. "So, full disclosure here, I'm not exactly sure how much of this I'm getting right. I'm having to guess with some of the context here."

Angela nodded. "I think we get the gist. Whatever it is, it's dangerous."

"Apparently," added Rickards. "And they've been guarding it."

"But it's not made out of gold."

Morton thought for a moment. "I don't know. I think she's using gold and riches interchangeably as well. All I know for sure is that whatever it is, it's not to be taken."

"Do you think this is the place you've been looking for? With your energy theory?"

"It's not a theory. But yes. I do. But like I said, I still don't know what the hell it is."

"Because energy is weird."

He nodded. "It could even be something so powerful that the Quechua, and even your uncle, were afraid it could be harnessed."

"And the part about not being ready?'"

"Dunno. A test maybe. Like as in power corrupts?"

"Which could be why my uncle was so afraid the Nazis would find it. He probably thought they would try to use it."

"Makes sense."

After a long silence and several of the elders speaking quietly amongst themselves, Urcaguary spoke to Morton, who listened with a growing look of surprise on this face.

"Uh…"

"What?"

"It seems they agree that you are Reed's relative. And I *think* they've agreed to show it to us."

Now Urcaguary spoke directly to Angela. "She says Paititi can be seen only once." He paused, trying to understand. "For one soul."

"What does that mean?"

"I think by one soul, she means one individual."

"At a time?"

"That's not clear." Morton asked a question to clarify. "One time, she says, and never for the same."

"The same what?"

"Same age. No, time. Same amount of time."

Angela shook her head. "I don't understand."

"That makes two of us."

"What are we supposed to see?"

Morton waited until Urcaguary finished. "She just says *we'll know.*"

80

The climb into the canyon was almost straight up, or at least felt that way to Angela. The barely visible path wound up and over clumps of dirt and rock, between boulders, and occasionally over fallen tree trunks that were long and gangly, petrified with surfaces worn smooth by decades of erosion.

The path proved extremely difficult for the older and heavier Mike Morton to traverse. Nearly hyperventilating, he was drenched in sweat after just a few hundred yards.

Stopping to rest several times, he finally held up his hand when it was time to continue again, prompting Angela and Rickards to both lower him back down to a sitting position.

"I…can't do it," he said, heaving. "It's too much."

Angela kept his hand in hers. "That's okay, we can wait."

"No…." Morton said weakly. "This…will kill me. Trust me."

Beside them a few Quechua stood nearby, waiting patiently, joined by Urcaguary and another of the elders, none of whom appeared even slightly winded.

"We'll go slower," Rickards said.

"It's not…my strength," he said. "It's…my heart. If I push…any further…"

"How much farther is it?"

With several deep breaths, Morton asked them in Quechuan. When they replied, he seemed to slump. "Too far…for me."

Angela knelt down in front of him, still holding his hand. "What would you like to do, Mike?"

"Something tells me…" he said, still fighting for breath. "That whoever's following us…won't be far behind." He grinned and put his other hand on top of hers. "You go. Both of you. Before they get here."

Angela looked at Rickards before Morton pushed her back up onto her feet.

"Hurry," he panted. "And tell me what's up there."

The rest of the climb was even worse. Up large stretches of rock, in some cases requiring the help of dangling tree limbs to pull themselves up. Higher and higher into the canyon, feeling increasingly more mysterious with every step. The copper tint of its cliff walls slowly darkened the farther in they pushed. Finally, the ground began to level off into a plateau, where it then declined modestly into the heart of the canyon.

After several hundred more feet, Urcaguary and her small troop stopped. When Angela and Joe turned around, the old woman stared at them and leaned gently on her walking stick.

The two looked at each other, confused, before Urcaguary raised her arm and pointed into the canyon.

"What are we looking for?" Angela asked. But Morton was not there to translate. The question went unanswered. Urcaguary simply motioned again and then raised two fingers to her eyes, as if to say *look*.

Rickards turned back and followed the trail winding forward and disappearing into the distance. Then he grinned. "For Mike."

Once they were inside the canyon, things began to feel eerie. With less sunlight, the walls continued darkening until from certain angles, they almost appeared to shimmer briefly.

"Are you nervous?"

Rickards, walking ahead, nodded. "Does a bear— never mind."

Zigzagging in and out of the walls, they approached an area where the two sides almost touched one another, forcing them to turn sideways to squeeze through. Angela went first before Rickards' larger frame.

"Joe."

"Yeah?" he answered, pushing through to see Angela staring at him with her mouth open. The hair on top of her head was standing straight up.

"Whoa."

He raised his hand over his own head and felt hair several inches above his scalp.

Angela reached out and examined the tiny blonde hairs along her forearms. All standing up in unison.

"Mike said energy could get weird."

"I believe him."

She nodded. "He also said energy and mass could even become one another."

The two continued forward, much slower, until rounding an outcropping of orange rock that resembled a falling curtain or drape, where they stopped cold.

Angela gasped.

Directly before them, the canyon walls widened into a larger, open area. It was circular in appearance and in the middle rose something truly extraordinary.

81

Both were utterly speechless.

Standing in the middle of the open space, towering high above them and flanked by canyon walls on all sides, was perhaps the last thing they were expecting.

A tall, single narrow spire rising upward almost two hundred feet. It was made of what appeared to be solid, clear crystal.

"Hoooly cow."

Rickards stood motionless beside her, transfixed, as Angela eased forward and gently walked toward it, tilting her head back as it became taller with every step.

She stopped and turned back to Rickards, her voice hushed. "I've never seen anything like this."

"Me either."

She then spun back, staring in awe, recounting what Morton had told them. "Mike said symbol or statue. But he didn't think he had the right word."

"I can see why."

"This isn't a statue, Joe," she breathed. "This is something much more than that. I think the word Mike didn't know how to translate was *monument*."

Rickards continued forward until he'd passed Angela and was within several steps of the base. He peered intently at the crystal, perfectly clear on all sides, and entirely unblemished. *Almost,* he thought, stepping around and viewing from another angle, *translucent.*

He reached out to touch it, slowly and cautiously easing forward, until suddenly he yanked back when his fingers failed to detect the surface.

He turned and looked incredulously at Angela.

"Where mass could become energy," she murmured.

Rickards backed away, staring up at the spire. That's when he noticed something else.

Next to the monument, higher up in the canyon's colored walls, was a brief sparkle of light. Then another...and another, until dozens began appearing.

Then something else. Something higher above the strange spire and the cliff walls. In the air itself.

"What is that?" asked Angela.

He shook his head.

The air slowly began to change and sounds reverberated off the walls, increasing in volume as the air displayed strange wisps of light. The wisps became streaks, long and swirling, in different colors, faint hues of whites and blues and yellows, until a dozen colors were visible. Then two dozen, and then three. Each streak became longer and longer as it moved faster and faster.

Rickards continued stepping back. "What the hell?"

"Different kinds of energies. All coming together," she said, watching the tip of the crystal spire as it changed colors. "Through *this.*"

It was the last thing she said before everything changed. In seconds, the swirling wisps of lights suddenly accelerated, instantly becoming one, and the reverberating along the walls became a deafening roar.

Then came the trembling, beginning in the air and moving down through the rock beneath their feet. And then—an exploding flash of brilliant white light.

82

Two thousand feet above the canyon, a brilliant flash of light lit up the interior of the Mi-17 helicopter, briefly blinding everyone aboard, including the pilot, who instinctively raised his left hand in an effort to see his instruments, letting go of the collective and causing a sudden dip.

"What was that?!" Ottman cried.

Ignoring the Germans behind him, the pilot desperately seized the lever again next to his leg, searching through the glare for the outlines of his controls.

When it finally faded, what he saw was impossible.

Every mechanical component in front of him was pegged out. And every electronic instrument and screen lit up like a Christmas tree.

83

Angela and Joe had fallen to the ground, unable to stay on their feet, only to find the shaking subside as quickly as it had come. Overhead, the streaks were still swirling, wrapped tightly together in a brilliant braid of energy and light, funneling down and through the crystal, which was now refracting light in all directions, dotting the canyon walls with every conceivable color.

She stared at Joe, whose hair, like hers, was still standing on end. Suddenly, it fell back down and the roaring around them instantly disappeared, leaving an echoing emptiness, along with a multitude of wavelengths swirling down through the crystal monument.

"What just happened?"

Rickards rose to his feet, pulling her up next to him.

"That was...incredible," Angela said and heard her own words echoing as if in a bubble. "Do you hear that?"

"I do."

"What did we just witness?"

"I have no idea." Rickards raised both hands and stared at them. "But I can still feel it. Like it went through us."

She peered at her own two hands. "Me too." She lowered them and stared back at the giant spire. "Mike also said that enough energy could affect time—"

She stopped talking when she noticed Rickards' eyes staring curiously past and behind her.

When Angela turned, she was startled to see a figure on the opposite side of the monument, quietly walking toward them.

"Who is that?"

"I don't know."

At first glance, they both thought it was one of Urcaguary's group. But the figure had white skin and was dressed in normal clothing. Long blond hair hung down around the person's shoulders, and as the figure grew closer, they could see it was a woman. Younger with clear, youthful skin, probably in her thirties. Perhaps even her twenties.

She continued forward, one smooth step at a time, until stopping to examine the giant spire between them. It was not until after several seconds that the woman looked up and finally seemed to notice them.

When the woman faced them directly, Angela suddenly gasped aloud and stiffened.

Joe turned to see her with eyes wide open.

"You okay?"

She didn't answer.

"Angela?"

She didn't move. Not even a slight twitch. Instead, she remained frozen, staring at the woman with her mouth open.

"Angela?" Rickards looked back and forth between them. "Who is it?"

She grasped Rickards' arm as she spoke.

"It's…my mother."

84

"What?!"

"It…is…my…mother."

A dumbfounded Rickards blinked at her, trying to process what he thought he just heard. He looked back at the other woman, who had now stopped and was peering at Angela with a slow-forming curiosity. It took several long seconds for the look in her eyes to change from curiosity to recognition. Until her own eyes widened.

Angela's breathing became short and erratic. Her eyes filled with tears. "It's…not…possible."

Rickards didn't have time to reply. The woman was now walking toward them faster, her face just as shocked as Angela's. When she reached them, she stopped.

"A-Angela?" she whispered slowly.

The woman's entire face began to tremble and Angela broke into tears. "Mom?"

They both inched forward in disbelief, reaching out breathlessly, stunned when they touched each other's skin. They stood that way for several seconds until they suddenly lunged into each other's arms.

It was a long, astonishing embrace, before Angela pulled back to look again, crying just as her mother was. "H-how is this possible?"

"I don't know," she said, looking around the canyon walls. "What is this place?"

Angela didn't know how to respond. "Bolivia?"

Her mother stepped back, allowing her hands to slide down into Angela's. "I don't understand it."

Angela could only shake her head. "Neither do I…"

She didn't have to finish. Her mother let it go and merely stared at her daughter. At her eyes. Her hair. Her mouth. She reached and traced Angela's cheek. "I don't understand this…but I knew it was you. When I saw you…I just knew."

"I'm…sorry," Angela cried, sobbing. "I am so sorry."

Her mother, still dazed, looked at her as if puzzled. "For what?"

Angela tried to speak. "For causing you to…"

Her mother cut her off. "Oh my child! You didn't do anything."

"But I…"

Her mother frowned and pulled Angela into her, pressing her cheek against her daughter's. "You didn't *cause* anything. At all. It was not your fault. We just lost each other. That's all." She leaned back to look at her. "My God, is that what you thought?"

Unable to speak, Angela simply nodded.

"You blamed yourself when I was the one who left *you*." She reached up and stroked Angela's hair. "It wasn't your fault. Believe me. Sometimes that's just how things happen. And I'm so sorry you blamed yourself." Her mother began crying again. "I thought you would understand."

Angela wiped tears from her eyes.

"I am so very sorry," her mother wept. "I left you alone. I left you all alone and blaming yourself for me."

"I didn't know what to think," Angela stuttered. "I was only a child."

"Look at me," her mother said and stared into her eyes. "It was not you. It was *not* you. It was just a condition. An illness I didn't even know I had. And something that would have happened anyway."

"But—"

"Believe me," her mother said. "Believe me. It would have happened anyway. Besides, it doesn't matter. Not now. What matters is that we're here. We have each other. I don't know how…but we're together."

Her statement pried Rickards from his state of shock like a crowbar—a truly incomprehensible shock, leaving him speechless from head to toe at what he was witnessing. Unable to believe what was taking place, as though it were some extraordinary illusion.

Until Angela's mother spoke those words. *All that matters is that we have each other.* Rickards blinked and remembered what Mike Morton had said. Something he had translated from Urcaguary. *Never for the same amount of time.*

Rickards had no idea what was happening or what Mike Morton's bizarre entangled energy was doing. But something in Angela's mother's words caused a sudden churn in his stomach that told him it would not last.

Again, Angela wiped her streaming tears away.

"It's...*real*."

Her mother smiled in awe. "It is."

"I can touch you," she said, gripping both hands. "And hold you. But how?"

"I don't know."

"There are so many things I want to tell you. So many things—"

"Then tell me. Tell me everything. Because I have missed you so much, from that very first moment."

Angela beamed through her tears. "I'm an archaeologist. Like Grandpa. And a teacher."

Her mother beamed. "I love that."

"They raised me. Grandma and Grandpa. And it was..." she said, pausing. "It was *good*."

"I am so glad."

"And Uncle Roger! Uncle Roger was alive! After the war. Grandpa was right."

"What?"

"Grandpa was right all along. It's true!"

A hint of regret appeared in her mother's eyes as she tried to make sense out of it. "I didn't believe him."

"Neither did I. But he was right. Uncle Roger was alive. It's why we're here."

Her mother looked around, still enthralled. "But I still don't understand where we are."

"I don't either," said Angela. "And I don't want to understand it. I'm here, with you. It's all that matters. And I'm never leaving!"

At that, Rickards suddenly cleared his throat. "Uh, Angela."

When neither seemed to hear him, he repeated, louder. "Angela?"

She turned, finally, almost startled. "Oh my God, Mom, this is Joe! Joe Rickards. He helped me find this place."

She smiled warmly. "Hello, Joe."

He smiled politely. "Listen, Angela. I don't know what's

happening here. At all. But…I don't think it's *permanent.*"

"What are you talking about?"

"Remember what the woman said. It happens once, and you don't know for how long."

Angela's eyes shifted, gradually, from exhilaration to nervousness. She turned back to her mother. "No. No. It *is* permanent. And I'm not leaving." She shook her head fervently. "I've wished my whole life for this. I've dreamt of it so many times."

She stopped listening to her own words as they faded and she turned back to Joe.

He spoke reluctantly. "It's already impossible as it is."

"No," she repeated defiantly. "It's real. As long as I don't leave." She gripped her mother's hands tighter. But this time something didn't feel the same. Her mother's hands felt softer. It was slight, but noticeable.

"Mom?"

Her mother's eyes softened in front of her. "Something's changing."

"No. NO! Grab tighter!"

"Angela."

"Tighter!"

"Angela," her mother whispered again.

"What?"

"Listen to me…"

"No. No. Don't say it. Don't say anything!"

"Angela," her mother whispered. "Look at me."

Angela's eyes began filling with tears again. "Mom, no!"

"Listen to me. Listen carefully," she said, looking deeply into her daughter's eyes. "I…am proud of you."

Angela began sobbing uncontrollably.

"I am SO proud of you," her mother said. "For becoming the woman you are. And," Her mother paused, looking around. "For giving me *this.* I don't know how…but I could not have asked for anything more than to hold you again. To hold my one and only daughter and tell her how much I love her."

"Mom, please!" wept Angela. Her mother's hands were getting even softer. "Please just hold on!"

"I would if I could. Believe me. But being apart is not the worst thing. It's losing someone without being sure they know how you feel. How much you *really* love them. More than your words can describe. And how much they are *part* of you."

"Mom!"

"I love you, Angela." Her mother grinned. "I always have and always will. *That* you can keep with you, permanently. I'm proud of you, and I love you. Forever."

Angela covered her mouth with her hand, unable to control her crying. Tears flowed down her face. "I love you, Mom. I love you *so* much."

"Now I know how beautiful you are. Inside and out. And we will always be bound to one another." Her face grew faint as she looked back at the monument. "This is proof." She reached up and brushed the tears from Angela's cheek, only to find her hand pass through her daughter's skin. "Don't be afraid of the future, sweetheart. Be afraid of missing the present."

"I love you!"

"I know, my baby girl."

Angela's body was still shaking when her mother blew her a kiss and gently, gradually, faded away, leaving her standing and sobbing with Joe behind her, his arm beneath hers, helping to hold her up.

There were no words. No words at all. Nothing that could convey any of it. Finally feeling the arms of a mother she had never known. Had never felt or even smelled.

Angela stood there silently staring at the spire before finally turning to hug Joe. Not just for this. But for everything. And in the end, just being there next to her to support her. She was moved on levels that were simply unimaginable. Indescribable. And always would be.

They made it less than a hundred feet when something else happened. Something that stopped Joe Rickards in his tracks.

A sound he had not heard in a long time.

A voice. And a single word.

"Daddy?"

85

Rickards did not turn around.

He couldn't.

Petrified, he froze where he stood. Wordlessly and without movement, unable to let himself turn.

Until he heard it again.

"Daddy?"

He slowly twisted and looked behind him. The tall crystal spire was still glowing brightly, illuminating the area, including the small figure standing in front of him.

His daughter.

His six-year-old daughter.

Dressed in her favorite pink and red dress with black shoes. And his wife calmly standing behind her.

Joe's eyes and face suddenly crumpled and tears burst from his eyes, his mouth open and shaking as he collapsed onto his knees.

His daughter broke into a run.

She covered the distance and jumped into his arms, wrapping her hands behind his neck and squeezing tight, as though she would never let go.

Joe closed his eyes and prayed he was not hallucinating.

He opened them again to see his wife still before him with her long dark hair and beaming green eyes. Smiling broadly.

Without loosening the grip on his daughter, Joe rose to his feet and rushed forward, meeting her just as she began running herself and taking her into his free arm, crying harder than he ever had. He kissed them both, quickly and desperately, as though he would never stop.

When he finally did, he couldn't form words without sobbing.

His wife smiled and put a finger to his lips. "We're here, Joe. We're here."

No matter how hard he tried, he simply couldn't speak. Every attempt turned into more tears, his mouth trembling uncontrollably.

His wife looked past him to Angela, who was standing alone, also crying, this time out of sheer happiness, watching all three of them. It all made sense now. All of it.

"I..." he cried. "I...am...so...sorry! I am...so goddamned SORRY!"

With tears of her own, his wife put a hand on both sides of his face. "No," she said. "Don't."

Joe's daughter pulled her head back to look at him. "Daddy! Where have you been?"

"I...I..."

"I've missed you so much."

He nodded his head, peering at her through a wave of tears.

"She doesn't understand," said his wife, stroking their daughter's hair. "And it's okay. It's all okay."

"I'm so sorry!"

"Look at me," she said to him. "It's okay. It was an accident. It was just an accident."

"But it was my fault."

He tried to speak, but she quieted him again. "It didn't happen the way you think, Joe. The car. The accident. It wasn't because of you." She smiled and looked deeply into his eyes. "It wasn't the brakes."

"What?"

"It wasn't the brakes. It was something else. It was *someone* else."

He shook his head. "But I was there."

"You're an investigator," she said, shaking her head. "And you found a reason. A reason that made sense. But it was the wrong reason and you blamed yourself."

"No. I was there. I saw—" Joe suddenly stopped when he felt a hand on his back.

It was Angela.

"Joe," she said softly. "I don't think you want to use your time for this."

He stared at her, blinking, without words, then turned back around.

"I miss you so much!" he said, his tears returning.

His wife put her face against his. "I miss you too, baby. We both do." After a long moment, she leaned back and smiled again. "But being apart is not the worst thing."

"It is," he said, shaking his head. "It is. Without both of you, I am nothing. There's no reason for anything." He looked at his daughter and kissed her again. "I just want to be with you."

"You are," she smiled. "Right now."

"There's no reason for me to be here. Not without you."

"Sweetheart, living is not about missing those who have left. It's about caring for those who are still there."

"There…is no one here for me," he wept. "No one."

She leaned forward and kissed him. "But you need to stay for *me*. Someone is still there who I care about."

He looked at her, confused.

"My mother," she said softly, "is all alone. She's in a dark place and hurting."

"She blames me."

"How could she not when you blamed yourself?"

After a pause, Joe reached out and pulled her in close again. All three of their faces were touching. "God, I love you so much."

His daughter grinned and snuggled into his neck and chest. "I love you more."

His wife looked at them, then up at the sky where strange streaks of light could be seen, swirling above the strange spire and twisting downward.

"What is this place?"

"I don't know."

"How long has it been?"

Joe's mouth was still trembling. "Two years."

She nodded and looked at him. "You need to let go."

"I…can't."

"Joseph," she said. "Listen to me. You *need* to let go."

"But—"

"It was not your fault," she said. "And I need you there for me. Don't let my mother live her final years like this."

"But *you're* alone."

She continued stroking her daughter's hair. "I don't know where we are. Or what this is. But we're not alone. We came together. And that's more comforting than you can imagine."

Joe smiled at his daughter when she wiped the tears from his eyes with her tiny hand. "Does my room still look the same, Daddy?"

"Yes. Exactly the same."

She nodded her head. "You can use my animals if you want. To keep you company."

He kissed her and began crying again. He looked at his wife. "I don't want to be here."

"I know," she said, stroking the side of his face. "But you have to stay. For me and for you. But you have to let go. And know that we're okay. That the pain is not from missing someone, it's from feeling like you didn't tell them enough. But we know what we mean to you. Both of us. Especially now." She peered at him lovingly. "You have to help someone else. And learn to be happy again. Until it's time."

"I don't know how to do that."

His wife glanced over his shoulder at Angela. "Then let someone help you."

***

Joe's time lasted longer.

Time enough to hold and kiss his wife and long enough to remember how it felt to hold his daughter in his arms. To feel the softness of her skin and remember the sweetness in her smell. To tell her how perfect she was. How being her daddy was the greatest thing he had ever done. Had ever felt. And how he thought of her, how he thought of them both, every single day.

Just as she thought of her daddy.

It also made their inevitable fading easier. Barely. But not before he kissed her a thousand times and memorized the feel of his lips on her tiny cheek. The way she giggled as she playfully pushed him away.

And enough time for Joe to tell his wife just how much he loved her. How much he missed her. And how sorry he was for his mistakes. As was she.

When all had finally faded, including the sky above back to its original pale azure blue, Joe Rickards finally turned around to see Angela waiting patiently and smiling.

"You okay?" she asked.

It took him several long seconds to answer. "I don't know."

He turned back around to examine the area. The crystal tower was once again how they had found it. Translucent and quietly ensconced within its surrounding copper-colored rock walls.

Wiping the last tears from his eyes, Joe stretched them open and grinned. "Well…Morton is not going to believe this."

86

The climb out was shorter. Different. Every step feeling lighter. Or easier, passing through the tight squeeze and back up the long winding path as though the Earth's gravity had somehow weakened.

But it did not last.

When they finally neared the small plateau, they could see more people waiting than when they'd left, and two of whom looked to be holding weapons. Someone was on the ground.

As they drew closer, Angela's eyes narrowed, just before realizing who it was lying in the dirt. "Oh my God!" she screamed and began running.

When she and Joe reached them, she glared at Karl Ottman, who was patiently standing next to Fischer and Becker over the very still figure of Mike Morton.

She dropped to her knees and rolled him onto his back, checking his breathing. Finding none, she quickly grabbed one of his hands, searching for a pulse.

Tears returned to her eyes as she looked helplessly at Joe. "He's not breathing!"

Joe checked both wrists and, finding nothing, peered up at the elderly Urcaguary, who merely shook her head without a sound.

"What did you do?!" Angela screamed. "You son of a bitch! You killed him!"

"It may not surprise you," Ottman said, looking down at her with no sign of remorse, "that your friend was uncooperative. And apparently not up to the climb."

Fischer then dropped something on the ground next to them with a tiny rattle: Morton's bottle of nitroglycerin pills.

"At least his heart wasn't."

She jumped to her feet, only to be struck down by the butt of Becker's rifle. In the same instant, Joe was on top of Fischer, seizing his gun and smashing an elbow into the German's broad nose, sending him stumbling backward, blood streaming from each nostril yet still managing to retain his hold of his rifle. Becker delivered a blow to Rickards' kidney, followed by another between his shoulder blades, causing him to slump to the ground.

Joe groaned and rose back to his feet. He lowered his head and charged Becker, wrapping his arms around the younger man's legs and driving him to the ground. Joe scrambled on top and punched his face repeatedly, stopping only when he felt the barrel of Fischer's rifle press forcefully against the base of his skull.

He turned to find the barrel move around and stop between his eyes.

"Go ahead," Rickards seethed. "I've got nothing to lose."

Fischer sneered through blood-covered teeth and suddenly pointed the gun at Angela. "How about now?"

"Would you like to continue struggling, Mr. Rickards?" asked Ottman. "Or are you coming to your senses?" When he didn't respond, Ottman added, "Your friend is dead. A sad reality, but true. Shall we move on?"

"I'm going to kill you," Rickards seethed through gritted teeth.

Ottman shrugged. "Perhaps. But not today. Today, you're going to tell me what you saw."

Rickards did not answer, prompting the old man to turn to Angela. "How about you?"

She didn't respond, either.

He looked at his man Fischer. "It looks like our friends are becoming noble on us. How heroic." He reached down and abruptly grabbed Angela by her hair, pulling her to her feet. "Where is it?"

"How about up your—"

It was as far as she got before he forcefully slapped her and turned around to study the group of Quechua. "Maybe one of you speaks English? *Oder Deutsch?*"

"They don't," said Rickards. "You killed the only man who could talk to them."

"Then I guess we'll just have to take one of you. You did find it, didn't you? I can see it in your eyes."

"You don't need us," he replied.

"And what is that supposed to mean?"

"It means it's not far," he said, wiping blood from his lip. "Or hard. Just down the path. What you're looking for."

Angela gave him an angry stare.

Rickards shrugged. "It doesn't matter, he's going to find it anyway. This way no one else has to get hurt."

"How far?" demanded Ottman.

"Couple hundred meters. Through there. Same way we came back."

"And what will we find?"

Rickards exhaled and rolled himself painfully onto one side. "I couldn't explain it to you if I tried."

Leaving Becker standing over them with a finger across his trigger, Ottman and Fischer started carefully down the path, taking just minutes to disappear from sight into the canyon. Ottman noted with interest the copper-colored walls growing darker the deeper they traveled, marveling not just at the surroundings but the realization that what he had so long sought under the sprawling canopy of the Amazon forest was instead nearly fifty miles from its border. Where he would never have thought to look.

The two slowed when they spotted the narrow gap in the distance and then cautiously continued. Reaching it, Ottman briefly peered through the opening before motioning Fischer through first.

Once past, Ottman followed and came to a halt when he saw Fischer's short hair standing on end.

"Was zum Tuefel?"

Both continued forward until rounding an outcropping and spotting an open area on the far side with a strange column standing in the middle made up of a clear material.

They approached, studying the strange object before hearing sounds reverberating from along the walls and growing louder by the second.

The old man's eyes traveled upward, where flashes of light appeared above them and slowly began circling one another.

"Was...ist...das?"

The sound became a deafening roar, followed by a brilliant flash of light. Leaving both men standing and peering around the walls in stunned silence.

A bewildered Ottman raised his hand and studied it. Enthralled at the sight of swirling lights moving around and then through his tight thin skin.

Next to him, Fischer examined his own hands before suddenly looking up.

On the opposing side of the canyon walls a figure could be seen. Dressed in black clothing and moving toward them. A dark complexion, and even darker eyes, peering at them across the short expanse. Plodding. With a walk or gait that seemed slightly uneven.

***

After more than an hour, Rickards finally leaned forward and stood up from the ground, leaving Angela seated next to Mike Morton's still figure, his face hidden beneath a bright, colorful shirt borrowed from one of the Quechua.

Rickards peered at Becker, who instinctively raised his rifle.

"Getting a little curious?"

The German didn't respond. Instead, he watched Rickards turn around and face the canyon opening.

"Didn't take us that long."

"Shut up," spat Becker.

Rickards shrugged. "Just wondering what would happen if they needed help."

"They're fine."

He nodded, then dubiously glanced down at Angela. "Sure are taking an awfully long time."

Rickards continued pacing, past Urcaguary, who was now quietly sitting along with the others, until he reached the edge of the small plateau and looked down the other side, back toward the village.

"You should probably go check while you still have time."

Becker glared. "I said shut up."

"I heard you," replied Rickards. "But I don't think you're hearing me."

"What are you talking about?"

"I said, 'you should go check...before it's too late.'" With that, Rickards motioned down the hill.

A hint of nervousness crept over the German's face and he squinted. Then he stood up and approached apprehensively with his rifle aimed, until he was close enough to follow Rickards' gaze downhill.

His eyes shot open when he spotted more Quechua down below, all surrounding the base of the hill. Not dozens, but hundreds. *Several* hundred, all peering uphill and waiting.

Rickards turned to him. "You're probably going to need that other rifle."

***

When Becker reached the outcropping through the canyon, the strange sounds had already reached him. He rounded the corner and spotted the open area with a large, strange object in the center.

Just before it, two bodies lay on the ground.

Becker ran, calling to them in German, sprinting forward

with the rifle clutched tightly in both hands, only to find neither of the figures moving.

At all.

Neither Ottman nor Fischer. Instead, both lay face down with their arms at their sides.

When Becker turned them over, wide, dead eyes stared back at him. Their haunting open mouths were lined with dirt.

High above him, lights appeared in the air, leaving a stunned Becker wondering what the hell had happened. He was blissfully unaware, as both Ottman and Fischer had

been, of just how colossal, how utterly unimaginable, the trove of gold and silver truly was that was hidden just a few hundred meters directly below their feet.

EPILOGUE

I

The snow was falling again. Snowflakes outside the window tumbled almost in slow motion before settling softly upon the white ground, some falling only as far as the needle-shaped leaves from a nearby blue spruce.

And the silence, similar to that inside the room where a single person sat unspeaking, her head resting against the padded high-backed chair, mournfully peering out at the sky and absently watching the snowflakes and their journeys to Earth.

Barely in her seventies, the woman might be mistaken

for being dead if not for the extraordinarily faint movement of her diaphragm beneath a thick sweater and concave posture.

She was completely unaware of the large wooden door opening less than ten feet behind her, only moving when it was quickly closed with an audible *click*.

The woman's head barely turned, reflecting only mild curiosity as to which nurse it was.

When no one appeared, the woman turned more, spotting someone behind her, standing quietly and erect. Unusual, and prompting her to come alive and twist around.

When she saw who it was, her eyes froze, partly from shock and the rest from bitterness.

"What...are you doing here?"

The voice was low and masculine. "Happy holidays, Kathy."

"I told you not to come here," she answered coldly. "You're not welcome."

"I know."

"Then why are you here, in my room?"

He lowered a large, square, flat box onto the bed and opened it, revealing a dark green Christmas wreath inside.

"This is for you."

The woman stared at him angrily. "I don't want it!"

"I know."

"Get it out of here. And you with it!"

There was a pause, and the person behind her disappeared from view, walking back to the door. But instead of opening it, she heard another, deeper, click.

The door being bolted shut.

The woman now whirled around to the other side. "What are you doing?! I said, get out!"

Joe Rickards walked back and pulled a plastic chair toward him. He placed it in front of her and sat down. "I know you don't want me here," he said. "But I wanted to say hello. To make sure you're okay."

"I do not need you checking up on me. I told you to

never come back."

"Yes, you did," he said, leaning forward. "But I've come to make you a deal."

"Get out of my room!"

Rickards ignored her and shrugged. "The deal is that I will never come back. Ever. As long as you agree to do one thing."

There was no answer.

"If you do one thing for me, you will never see my face again. For as long as you live. You have my word."

"I'm not going to do anything for you. I'll tell them not to let you in."

"I'll just keep coming back," Rickards replied calmly. "I'm a federal agent. And half of the staff here are terrified of being harassed by anyone working for the government. I'll keep coming back," he said, "even if I have to climb through the window."

The old woman said nothing, glaring at him with seething green eyes.

"If you know me at all, you know I am not joking."

Her eyes narrowed. "What? What is it you want?!"

"I want you to come somewhere with me."

"Where?"

"It's significant. But when we return, if you never want to see me again, you won't. I promise."

She continued glaring at him, watching Rickards lean back in his chair.

"That's the deal," he said. "Otherwise, I'll keep coming back. Every…day."

"You wouldn't?!"

"You know how stubborn I can be. You told your daughter many times."

"Don't you ever mention my daughter!"

"That's the deal, Kathy," he said again. "Come with me or see my face every day."

"Why are you doing this?"

"It doesn't matter."

After a long, glaring silence, she answered, "Fine. Where are we going?"

Rickards nodded. "You're going to need a passport."

II

An exhausted Angela Reed fell into her chair and looked around her small apartment, feeling as though she'd been away for years. The normal comfort of her home somehow felt slightly amiss.

She scanned the room. Her small kitchen, clean and neat, the living room with two small leather couches and TV, even the artful decorations and pictures upon the walls were all somehow different.

Strange.

Angela came back to the table, where she stared at her laptop for a long time before finally opening the lid and powering it on.

So much had happened and the world appeared so surreal. Everyone in her family was entirely gone. Even Lillian Porter, who was still missing and who would probably never be found.

It made Angela wonder if she was now seeing the world for what it was. What it had been all along.

She worked to push that solemn thought from her mind by focusing on the computer in front of her, now displaying a login screen against her favorite majestic background image of the Rocky Mountains.

She reached forward and typed in her password, then hit enter and waited as the system continued booting up. When finished, it automatically opened her email program and connected to her mail server.

Angela watched in a daze as one by one, the screen was populated by a full page of new messages. She'd started to look away when something caught her eye and she turned back to stare at it. One of the messages had a sender's address that looked different:

mmorton@spacejunkies.org

When her eyes finally parsed the characters, they widened with surprise and Angela shot forward, reading the address. Then again, and again. Making sure she hadn't mistaken something.

In a moment of apprehension, she reached forward and clicked the item to open the message, gasping when she saw it was indeed from Mike Morton.

She looked at the date on the email and her mind churned as she tried to piece things back together, wondering when he could possibly have sent it.

The night at his trailer. When she slept inside. Morton later told her he had looked her up online.

But he'd never said he sent her something.

Angela read the short note and looked at the attachment Morton had referenced--something he'd decided to send to her just in case.

Yet it was not until she opened the attachment that she was truly stunned. Shocked, in fact, as she slowly read through it.

Page by page.

It took over thirty minutes. And when finished, she leaned back in her chair, utterly speechless.

To: Angela Reed   <angela.reed@colorado.edu>
From: Mike Morton   <mmorton@spacejunkies.org>

Angela,

I found your email on the university's website after reading your profile. You are quite an accomplished anthropologist, just as I suspected.

It is now almost 3:15 am as I sit here staring into the fire's dying embers, wondering if perhaps there is a reason our paths have crossed. Yours, mine, and Joe's. I do not believe in coincidence, but I do believe in fate. My wife always believed we meet people when we're supposed to meet them.

As I mull the facts over, I now believe that what I've been searching for all this time is the same thing you and Joe are trying to find.

Which brings me to this email.

I don't know why, but I trust you. Just as I trust in my wife's memory. And if all of this truly is for a reason, then I need to give you something important. A copy of my data from the CERES prototype satellite. The prototype I helped design and that detected the strange energy anomaly I've been looking for.

Attached to this email is the satellite's original data dump, which I have saved for decades. Most of it is in binary form and will be unreadable to you. But the rest is not.

This information is not to be shared with anyone. The two exceptions being myself and one other person noted within these pages. A colleague with whom I worked at NASA

Reading this should convey just how important this data is. Because there is more than just one location where these energies converge and reach the Earth's surface. Places where I am certain the very laws of physics will be affected. Possibly in ways that have never before been observed.

And thus ends this old man's oration. I must now get some sleep, before I reveal to you what I found out about your ALMV10 cipher.

Mike Morton

The Desert of Glass

Prologue

July 1977

There was no sound.
No crickets, no insects, no anything…
but dry, dead air.

Utter silence. Unmoving. Slowing time and existence to a crawl through endless days of searing heat and suffocating air followed by long, empty black nights.
No movement of any kind.

Until it happened—
Almost instantaneously.

Grains of sand began to move across the trembling ground a split second before a massive explosion of sound and speed. Overhead, it was sudden, thunderous, and gone as quickly as it came.

Barely three hundred feet above the ground, with hands gripping the control column like vices, a lone pilot peered intently through the cockpit window into the darkness in front of him, feeling every vibration traveling up through his trembling arms.

The aircraft was under enormous strain, pushed to its limit by twin turbojet engines at the tail of the craft, sending it hurtling forward just below the speed of sound, ensconced in total and utter darkness.

All navigation lights had been turned off, including the interior lights, leaving the only illumination of the pilot's face coming from the instruments themselves, the only lights keeping the small cockpit from pitch blackness. Except perhaps the dim scattering of stars across the ebony sky above.

A thousand kilometers was all he needed. Due East. Below the radar horizon. Enough to give him a fighting chance.

Fear coursed through his body, down his arms in the same path as the vibrations and into his hands, which remained wrapped around the controls in a death grip. He was fearful of making the slightest mistake, as it would take almost nothing at his velocity and altitude to slam the aircraft directly into the earth at full speed.

His thoughts briefly drifted to the rest of the craft behind him—to his cargo. He almost turned his head as if needing to verify it was still there.

Don't look! Pay attention!

He squinted tighter and continued peering through the tiny windshield, searching for anything in his way.

But he knew the truth. At this speed, anything he saw would hit him before he could even react, leaving his desperate plight fixed solely upon hope and prayer.

Hope that there was nothing in the way.

And the prayer that he would reach salvation in time.

What the lone pilot could not know, what he couldn't see, was the sky behind him, which was also black and dotted by a multitude of faint stars appearing like a giant shimmering blanket overhead, with more than enough twinkling lights to hide what was approaching from the rear.

Navigation lights from another jet.

In the lead cockpit, the man released one hand long enough to wipe the sweat from his forehead before immediately returning it to the controls, blinking wide and staring into the night. Each passing minute gave him another minute of hope.

If he could just—

He never heard the launch of the missile behind him—or its impact when the entire Learjet instantly exploded into a brilliant ball of orange flame.

1

Present Day

The mighty Pacific winds buffeted the small car as though trying to push it from the narrow gravel road upon which it was traveling alone, struggling through continual waves of dust clouds passing over the plains of Baja. Over thirty miles of barren hills and valleys before the powerful gusts finally rising up and over the open waters of Mexico's Gulf of California.

The car didn't surrender. Instead, it held its ground and stubbornly continued along the dirt-strewn road until reaching and turning onto an abandoned set of worn tire tracks heading toward the distant cliffs.

The tracks grew less visible as the small automobile

wound back and forth over rugged terrain, reaching with difficulty the remnants of an old structure severely damaged but still technically standing in its own relentless fight against the elements.

The white car stopped and remained for several moments before the driver's side door opened, and Joe Rickards stepped out onto the hard ground.

Dressed in a light jacket, jeans and boots, he fought against the mighty wind to force his door closed and stood for several minutes staring at what was left of the old house. He then stepped out from around the car and approached. The house's entire roof was collapsed, with half of it missing entirely. What sections remained were wedged between several stone walls that managed to remain standing against all odds. Windows whose glass was broken and missing remained embedded within the stone in empty wooden frames.

Debris was scattered everywhere—large stone chunks down to small rocks and pebbles covered the entire stone foundation, obscuring what appeared to be broken dishes and a plumbing conduit.

Behind the structure lay perhaps another mile of rolling hills which eventually dropped off and began a meandering descent to the aqua-colored waters of the gulf several hundred feet below.

Rickards studied the abandoned dwelling and gradually began to circle, viewing it from all sides, his brown hair whipping wildly in the wind.

He stepped forward to move onto the house's foundation but stopped himself, deciding against it. He didn't want to desecrate the place any more than it already was.

Twenty-six years.

Twenty-six years had entirely destroyed the house, along with the family who'd once lived there.

He stepped back and scanned the horizon, finding nothing but dry grass waving under the forceful breeze.

With hands in both pockets, he turned back to the remains and continued staring.

Loss was painful, but regret was forever.

2

Several days later, Angela Reed found Rickards on a bench in Denver's Bear Creek Park, quietly overlooking a small playground filled with children scampering about, squealing with laughter and chasing one another in a game of tag.

Angela slowed several feet from the bench when Joe turned and glanced up at her.

"I've been trying to get ahold of you."

"Sorry," he replied. "Been a little busy."

She stepped forward and eased herself down onto the other half of the bench. "Everything okay?"

"As well as it can be."

"When you disappear, you really disappear."

"Sorry," he said again, briefly glancing back at the playground. It used to be his daughter's favorite.

Angela lowered her large purse beside her and watched the children with a smile. "How did it go with your mother-in-law?"

"Interesting."

"Just interesting?"

He thought a moment and turned back. "She was more than a little reluctant. But I convinced her."

"How?"

"I told her I'd just keep coming back to visit her until she agreed."

"I'll bet that did the trick," Angela said with a laugh. "And?"

"I took her," he said simply, "to Bolivia."

"And did she go in?"

"Eventually, but it took a while. She thought I was insane."

"And?"

"Well, she doesn't think I'm insane anymore."

"What happened?"

He gave a soft shrug. "She went in—and came out thirty minutes later crying."

Angela inhaled. "What did she see?"

"I don't know. She wouldn't say."

"At all?"

Rickards shook his head.

"So... you have no idea what—?"

"No. But something happened. After that, she didn't hate me anymore."

"Well, that's good."

He nodded solemnly. "Yeah."

They both fell quiet, listening only to the sound of the children playing.

"Are you back to work?"

Rickards shook his head again. "I quit."

"You quit?"

He raised his head and looked at her. "Kind of hard to go back. Things are too different now."

"I can understand that."

"How about you?"

Angela nodded beneath a head of light-brown hair. "I'm back teaching at the university. But it *is* different." She looked out over a group of pine trees, their needles twinkling in the light spring breeze. "Surreal, really. It's as if very little in the world matters anymore."

"Yep."

"I turn on the TV and listen to the news, and it all feels so, I don't know, juvenile. Everyone just arguing over things that don't matter—at all. But they don't know it."

Rickards gazed absently at the ground. "That's about it."

She grinned and brushed a strand of hair behind her ear. "Half the time my students ask me a question, and I just want to answer, 'Who cares?'"

Rickards smiled.

"I feel strange," she went on. "As if I'm in this place between the life I've lived and the life I'm supposed to live now."

"I get that."

"You're probably the only one who does, which is why I've been calling. I was worried something had happened to you."

"I just needed some time."

"I'm happy you're okay."

"You don't have to worry, Angela. I'm not... you know."

She watched as a couple strolled past. "Well, that was *one* of the reasons. To make sure you're okay." She turned and picked up her purse. "The other reason was to show you something."

"What's that?"

She reached in and retrieved a thick manila envelope.

Rickards looked at her curiously and then at the envelope until she pushed it forward and into his hands.

He took it and studied it before flipping it over. "What is this?"

Angela didn't answer. Instead, she motioned to the envelope and waited until he'd opened the flap and pulled out the top piece of paper.

It took only a moment for his expression to change and his eyes to widen as he read the paper.

He didn't speak, but instead read the entire page. Then, when he'd finished, he sat in stunned silence.

"Is this real?"

"Yes."

"From Mike Morton?"

"Yes."

"How is that possible?"

"Look at the date on that email. He sent it the night we met. I'm guessing he had a satellite connection or something."

"But…"

"I know. I couldn't believe it, either."

Rickards repeatedly blinked at the sheet before finally pulling out the rest of the papers inside, page after page filled with what looked to be computer data and mathematical computations, including images from different maps.

He turned to Angela. "How long have you had this?"

"Since I got back."

"Have you told anyone?"

"No one else would believe me. Only you."

"And this is why you've been calling me?"

She winked. "One of the reasons."

3

"Something tells me you haven't been idle," said Rickards.

She grinned. "I've located the person Mike references in his letter."

"Who is it?"

"An old colleague who worked at NASA with him. Maybe on the same project."

"Mike said no one else believed him."

Angela shrugged.

"So who is he?"

"His name is Leonard Townsend. He's retired and teaches college math and physics."

"Have you contacted him?"

"No."

"But you plan to."

"I was waiting to talk to you first."

Rickards returned the pages to the envelope and sighed, leaning back against the wooden bench. "Another location."

"Sounds like it."

"That does what?"

She shook her head. "I have no idea."

After a long pause, Rickards took a breath and exhaled slowly. "I say leave it alone."

"What?"

"Angela," he said, turning, "you *do* understand the significance here."

"I do."

"Are you sure? Because what we already know is enough to change everything."

"I understand that."

"Then you also understand it's only a matter of time before others find out."

"Yes."

He held up the papers. "And you still want to find this?"

"Mike obviously did."

"Mike didn't even know what the first one *was*," exclaimed Rickards. "What it was *or* what it could do. This is big, Angela—bigger than either of us. Jesus, it's bigger than *all* of us."

"I know that, Joe."

"Really? Because it seems to me as if maybe you don't."

"What's that supposed to mean?"

"What I mean is this thing is beyond…"

"What?"

Rickards struggled for the right word. "I don't know—*comprehension*. And it's dangerous. What happens when everybody else finds out?"

"And uses it for something bad?"

"Exactly."

"I don't see how they could do that."

"Anything can be exploited, Angela. *Anything.* Every object on this planet has been used for something terrible at one time or another."

"Just because something can be abused doesn't destroy the good it can do."

"You're an anthropologist. You, more than anyone, should understand what people are capable of. How many times has a country, or a race, wiped out another, be it oil, land, or just ideology? Don't tell me you think this would be any different."

Angela contemplated before finally answering. "Yes. I'll admit it has and does happen. A lot."

"But now—"

"Let me finish," she said, cutting him off. "Yes. You're right," she acknowledged. "You're right. History is littered with terrible acts against one another. Without a doubt. Will it ever change? I don't know. Maybe it will, and maybe it won't. But good God, Joe. Look at the world today. Look at the fighting and the vitriol. It's everywhere! Is this our future? Is this the way you *want* the world to be? Because I don't."

She took the envelope and shoved it back into her open purse. "The world is lost, Joe. *Lost.* No one knows what's real anymore. No one tries to listen. It's as if the whole world is trapped in some constant, never-ending fight with itself where no one ever wins. They just incessantly attack each other."

"You're making my point for me."

"No, I'm not," she said. "Here we are, you and me, sitting on a park bench knowing something no one else knows. Something that could fundamentally affect people's lives, change them deeply, right down to their cores, and we think it may be too dangerous? Too dangerous for what?

Do you really think it could make things *worse* than they are now?"

"Angela—"

"No. Say it, Joe. Say you think the greatest potential discovery—maybe *ever*—is actually going to make things worse."

"What I'm saying," he replied slowly, "is there is something powerful about that place. About that thing. And sooner or later, someone will try to exploit it. Harness it. Use it for their own self-interests."

"So, then *no one* should benefit? Because eventually someone will exploit it?"

Rickards sighed.

She softened her voice. "What do *you* want the world to be like?"

"It doesn't matter what I want."

"How can you say that?"

"Because I don't have any incentive to make it any better. Not anymore."

"None at all?"

"No."

Angela looked around. Her gaze stopped on the playground again and she pointed at the playing children. "Not even for them?"

There was no answer.

"What if your daughter were still here?"

Rickards suddenly shot her a stern glare. "Don't!"

"You said yourself this is bigger than all of us. You, me, anyone."

"That's not what I meant."

"Then tell me this," she said, looking back at the children. "With the path this world is on, do you think things will be better for them... or worse?"

4

Hard polished gray tiles stretched the entire length of the long hallway, creating a loud echo from the woman's heels as she walked.

Nearly every door she passed revealed another elderly patient lying in bed or sitting idly in a wheelchair with old, frail hands folded limply in their laps. Some shook uncontrollably, all against a backdrop of distant coughing.

These patients were all in their final waning days and years. Heads down. Sitting and waiting.

With each door the young woman passed, she briefly glanced in—sympathetically and respectfully—before eventually slowing as she reached the second to the last door, every one of them painted in a muted beige amongst perfectly matching walls.

She glanced in through the small window and, seeing nothing, reached forward to pull open the door, suddenly jumping when it was immediately pushed open from the inside, revealing a black-bearded man dressed in a light tunic and white skull cap.

Squeezing through the door, he promptly greeted the woman.

"A 'Salaam Alaikum."

"Alaikum a 'Salaam." The woman nodded and bowed respectfully, speaking in Arabic. "You were the one who phoned me?"

"Yes, yes. Thank you for coming. We do not have much time."

The young woman, dressed in a plain red dress instead of a traditional hijab, stepped back and peered curiously through the window again. "Time for what?"

"Please," the man answered, widening the door behind him. "Come. He is very weak."

The woman cautiously followed, unsure of what or who was waiting on the other side of the wooden door. She'd been told almost nothing on the phone, only that it was an urgent matter and she needed to come quickly. Even in modern-day Egypt, when an imam summoned, you were expected to respond.

Inside the small room was a single hospital bed occupied by an older man. Tubes ran from his left arm up to a hanging IV bag, while a mask over his nose and mouth fed his thin, frail body fresh oxygen.

The man remained motionless, watching with a pair of sunken eyes as she entered the room.

"Sit down. Please," urged the imam, who circled the bed and took a seat on the opposite side.

Uncertain, the woman stepped over to the empty chair and eased herself down.

After an uncomfortable silence, she introduced herself in a polite tone, unsure how well the man could hear. "A 'Salaam Alaikum. My name is Mona Baraka. I am a journalist—"

The religious leader interrupted with a reassuring gesture of his hand. "It is okay. He knows who you are. He is the one who asked for you."

With some difficulty, the patient raised a hand and pulled the oxygen mask from his mouth, briefly licking his lips and inhaling before speaking in a low, raspy voice.

"Thank you," he said weakly, "for coming."

"You're welcome," Mona replied, glancing briefly around the room. "What, exactly, am I here for?"

With a heaving chest, the man glanced at the imam to his left, who answered for him. "Tawbah."

Mona blinked and turned back to the old man, studying him.

Tawbah was the Islamic word for 'repentance.'

"My name is Abasi Hamed," he began, inhaling between

sentences. "I was born and raised... in a village outside Kharga."

Mona's brief hesitation went unnoticed by both men before she reached into her handbag to retrieve a small audio recorder. "May I record this?"

Hamed, the older man, nodded.

It wasn't the first bedside confession for which she'd been summoned. Quite the contrary—though rarely did they prove to be newsworthy. They were often little more than an unburdening from the person facing the certainty of the great beyond, even from some of the most ardent and faithful believers. It was something to help them feel at ease with their indiscretions or regrets. While these deathbed confessions were critical in helping another human clear their conscience, it was hardly justification for Mona to suddenly drop whatever she was working on. Regardless, she gave a polite smile and offered no hint of annoyance, quietly pressing the small round button on the handheld unit and setting it on her lap.

"I am," the old man corrected himself, "*was* a captain in the Egyptian Air Force from 1963 to 1995." His eyes rolled and peered at the ceiling as he spoke. "Accepted when I was twenty-four years old."

Mona thought for a moment. "You are now 82?"

The old man didn't respond, instead using his energy to inhale again.

"Yes," confirmed the imam.

Hamed nodded. "I served for thirty-two years. I flew F-16 Falcons and later MiG-23s."

Mona was impressed. "That is admirable," she said, but to her surprise, the old man merely shook his head.

"I have served my country," he replied. "Faithfully." After another short breath, he added, "*Mostly.*"

He watched while she glanced at the imam. "There are many things of which I am proud," he whispered. "But some of which I am not." Another pause to breathe. He was staring at her now. "By not proud... I mean *ashamed.*"

Mona Baraka was unsurprised at the change in subject. "What are you ashamed of?"

It took the man a long time to respond. "I participated in many battles… things they now call *conflicts*. The Romani ambush… The Battle of Suez… The Four-Day War. Many more."

"You served your country well."

Hamed did not respond.

"You need not be ashamed," she offered.

"We are all ashamed," he mumbled.

"If you were—"

The man held up a finger and suddenly coughed violently, prompting the imam to rise and hold a small towel to Hamed's mouth until he gently pushed it away.

"Listen," he said. "Before it is too late."

"Of course."

"Soldiers are not given explanations. We follow orders. That is all." His dark eyes had returned to the ceiling. "But some orders," he said, now almost whispering. "Some orders felt wrong."

"Wrong in what way?"

"I am no longer fearful," he said, changing topics. "My family is now gone. In Jannah." He turned back to the imam. "But for me… it will be Sijjin."

The Islamic equivalent of hell.

Mona followed his gaze to the younger man at his side, staring back at Hamed. "What did you do?" she quietly asked.

"I sought."

She frowned.

"I sought," he repeated.

"Sought what?"

"To know the truth of what I had done." His words stopped until his eyes returned to Mona. "Firing on an enemy you know is easy, at least during combat. But other times…"

"You did what you were told," said the imam.

"It will not be enough," the old man croaked. "Not in the eyes of Allah."

"It will be enough," the imam assured him.

Hamed feebly shook his head. "Not this." He turned back to Mona and said, "Sometimes knowledge is worse."

"What do you mean?"

He replied almost painfully. "In 1977, I shot down a private jet."

After a long moment, Mona asked, "Who was in it?"

Hamed's eyes became glassy as though he were staring through her. "*Allah.*"

5

She stared at him with a confused expression. "You shot down Allah?"

The old man nodded.

"What does that mean?"

"It means Sijjin."

The man was beginning to talk in circles.

"Who was on the plane?"

"I did not know," he mumbled, staring through her. "I could not have known."

When she looked at the imam, he shrugged and returned a blank expression.

"It took years," breathed Hamed.

"For what?"

"To find out."

"To find out what?"

Again, he inhaled deeply, desperate for oxygen. "Whose plane it was."

Now Mona leaned forward. "Who?"

"*Shaitan.*"

She looked to the imam for clarification but received none.

Demons?

"I don't understand."

Hamed coughed again, this time with more spittle, caught once again by the imam's cloth. "You will."

No sooner had the words left his mouth that the old man's eyes widened, and his chest heaved without warning.

Once, then twice, before collapsing back into his frail body. In an instant, his eyes, dark and sullen, became lifeless.

***

Hamed was gone. Two nurses were in the room within seconds and together made a final, desperate effort to resuscitate him, until finally giving up and checking his pulse one last time. One of the two women turned and glanced between the imam and Mona, standing back against the wall, while the other gently reached down and closed Hamed's eyes.

A stunned Mona watched in eerie silence as though she were disconnected from the scene in front of her, while the imam dutifully stepped forward and began reciting a prayer from his open Quran.

***

Immediately following the prayers, and without a word, Mona was led out of the room and down the small hospital's hallway until the imam found an unoccupied room.

He pulled her inside and closed the door behind them. "His Tawbah is complete."

Mona was still reeling. "What?"

"He travels beyond now... unburdened."

"But he didn't finish."

The imam seemed not to hear her. "His burden has been passed to you."

"I don't—"

The leader finally stared at her and replied, "You will carry this forward."

"Carry what forward? He didn't finish. He didn't tell me *anything*."

The imam reached into his tunic and pulled something out—a large leather binder, aged and tattered.

"What is that?"

"It is for you," the imam said, placing it in her hands. "His instructions."

"Wait, wait," Mona said, stepping back and blinking several times. "What is happening? What is this?"

"Here," he said of the binder, "are your answers."

"I can't. I was just—"

"You must take it forward now."

"Take *what* forward?"

The imam reached out and simply placed his hand on the binder. "This."

6

Joe Rickards sat solemnly and silently in his car, his hands resting on each side of the steering wheel as he waited behind a long line of cars at the intersection of East Colfax and Colorado Boulevard. It was a testament to Denver's rapidly growing population, now making daytime traffic through the city almost unbearable.

At the moment, it went largely unnoticed by Rickards.

Instead, he remained motionless, lost in thought over

what Angela had said to him, coupled with the memory of a recent conversation he'd had with a priest in Bolivia.

It had been a discussion about suffering and loss and the often-inescapable trap of misery. Of true regret. A trap from which no amount of time or grief could free a person. No amount of reflection or therapy. Not even alcohol.

For there were some parts of the human heart that simply would not let go.

Ever.

Unaffected by reckoning or penance, there were places where some wounds never healed, and the only hope was in everlasting diversion.

In all the years the priest had consoled people through pain and loss, the one thing he'd told Rickards that would help—the only thing—was *purpose*.

Purpose alone.

The soul's one and only path for escape from the black hole of true misery.

Purpose.

He thought again of the playground, remembering back to one of the many days he'd been there with his daughter, watching her laugh and play with the other children, running in and out through the metal poles of the play structure until coming upon a smaller boy who'd fallen. He'd sat in the soft layer of wood chips crying and calling for his mother.

The boy was unhurt, but Rickards remembered watching his young daughter wrap her tiny arms around him and help him up. It was one of the sweetest things Rickards had ever witnessed. His daughter's genuine, untainted care for someone she didn't even know still touched him to that day, still resonated with him.

How proud he was of that little heart of hers.

He was so lost in thought that he did not immediately hear it—a noise outside. There was a commotion somewhere in the traffic behind him, within the endless line of cars waiting to inch forward beneath the stifling sun.

What he eventually heard was yelling, followed by the slamming of a door, prompting Rickards to turn and look over his shoulder a few cars back to two men who'd climbed out of their vehicles and were continuing to yell at each other.

Both appeared to be in their forties or fifties. Rickards watched as one man approached the second, yelling and waving his arms in unintelligible acrimony, spewing vitriol until just a few feet away and mere moments before the second man suddenly lashed out, punching him in the face and immediately sending him onto the hard pavement like a large bag of sand toppling over.

Almost simultaneously, honks erupted from all directions as the light turned green and dozens of cars impatiently pushed forward.

Rickards leaned and checked his side mirror to watch the fallen man slowly rise back to his feet and stumble away, returning to his vehicle.

It was a minor clash lasting mere seconds, and yet, for Rickards, the brutality lay not in the skirmish itself but in the reality of it. The vitriol. Without choreography or TV-like glorification. An actual assault in broad daylight at a stoplight.

There it was. Vitriol. The word Angela had used.
Cruelty and bitterness.

7

She opened the door to find Rickards standing on her front step, pensive and sullen, staring back at Angela and her look of surprise.

"Okay."

She frowned. "Excuse me?"

"I said okay."

"What are you talking about?"

"I'll help."

Angela's face lit up. "Just like that?"

"Just like that."

"I'm... surprised."

"At finding me on your porch or that I've agreed to help?"

She grinned. "Both."

"Well, at least I didn't do it at seven o'clock in the morning."

***

Inside, Angela placed a glass of water on the coffee table in front of him and then walked around to the opposite side.

She sat, resting both hands on her knees and continuing to grin. "I still can't believe you're here."

He was slow to answer. "I've been thinking about what you said."

"And that convinced you?!"

Rickards picked up the water and took a sip. "Let's not beat a dead horse. I'm here."

"No beating," she mused. "Or flogging. I'm just happy you changed your mind."

"So, what all did you find out about Mike Morton's friend?"

"As I said, he's retired and teaches now. College level, following a long career at NASA, just as Mike did."

"I guess they take their work seriously. Where's he at?"

Angela beamed back at him. "That's the best part. He lives in Hawaii."

"Hawaii?"

She nodded. "Maui."

"Not a bad place to retire."

"Exactly. Who wouldn't want to live in paradise? Have you ever been?"

Rickards shook his head and reached for another drink. "You?"

"Once," she said, smiling. "It's beautiful."

"At least there's an upside, I guess."

"Right. But here's the thing… I was thinking it might be better not to call him first."

"Why is that?"

"Mike said this man Townsend was the only other person who should see the data, but we don't know what kind of relationship they had."

"You don't think they got along?"

"I really don't know." Angela shrugged. "But Mike did say everyone else thought he was crazy all those years. That may include Townsend. Hopefully not, but if it does, what if he shoots us down before we even get there?"

"Like on the phone."

"Right."

"Then case closed."

"Wait, that's it? Everything just stops?"

"If the guy's not interested…"

Angela folded her arms. "Uh, yeah. No. If he rejects the idea, he can do it right in front of us—*after* we've shown him Mike's data."

Rickards shrugged. "We could end up taking a long plane ride for nothing."

"I wouldn't call it for nothing," she winked. "They have movies on the flight. And peanuts."

8

A world away and late at night, Mona Baraka sat quietly in her Cairo apartment studying the contents of the strange binder given to her by the imam. Cracked and peeling at each corner, it now lay spread across her small kitchen table filled with several dozen documents, letters, and photos. Some were originals and some Xeroxed, with a few even appearing to be copies of copies, all in what first appeared to be random order, but upon closer inspection looked primarily chronological.

But she still had no idea what it was all supposed to be.

There were documents on more than a dozen international companies, along with some of their financial filings, five of which had gone out of business years ago. Then there were the barely legible, handwritten letters and almost a hundred different Xeroxed pictures and newspaper clippings. But there was no apparent connection to all of them. None that she could see.

Why didn't the imam just tell her what this was all about? Clearly, the old man had revealed more to him than Mona. So why not just tell her what she was searching for?

All she knew was that it had something to do with a plane in 1977, owned by someone, or something, that took Abasi Hamed years to piece together. But so far, she couldn't find a single reference to the airplane incident. Not even in the hundred or so photocopied articles. Did the old man think she could read minds?

And why her? There were hundreds of journalists in Egypt, many of whom were far more prominent, with teams of people or staff who could make much faster work of this than she.

Mona leaned back in her chair and sighed before rubbing her face and pushing her chair back from the table. She stood and strolled into her apartment's modest kitchen.

She opened a colored glass cabinet and withdrew a small

packet and teabag, filled the steel kettle with water, placed it on a burner, twisting the dial until a large puff of blue flame leaped out and promptly turned it down.

She leaned against the narrow counter and absently stared at the stove.

Why her? Why not one of the hundreds of male journalists who had access to so many more resources? Or even a man in her own office?

Mona's eyes wandered, and she spotted her dim reflection in the glass pane of the adjacent cabinet, her arms folded and a frown on her lips.

Life in Egypt was hard enough for a woman, especially one trying to establish a career. Between the incessant sexual harassment from her coworkers, the pressure from her entire family to get married and the constant derision from every corner of society for things as trivial as how she wore her hair, it often felt like too much.

Too much to make the constant struggle worthwhile.

Still watching herself in the glass, she reached up with her right hand and released the tight bun behind her head, letting her black hair fall around her shoulders in a private act of defiance.

She didn't have time for this. She already had too much work to do—assignments and stories that none of the male reporters wanted and likely no one would read anyway. All for a meager salary that barely paid for her tiny apartment.

How much longer could she endure it all? How much—

She suddenly stopped in mid-thought.

In the reflection, Mona slowly tilted her head, returning to a thought just a moment ago.

Why... Her?

One of the breaking stories currently being covered by multiple outlets was yet another corruption scandal, this one allegedly involving the Egyptian Prime Minister and two of his cabinet members. It was hardly a surprise to anyone, given the deep history of corruption in the country, but what stood out this time was the involvement of three different well-known journalists who'd participated in the coverup, skimming millions of Egyptian pounds through agricultural land ownership and reclamation fees. The story didn't just highlight another channel of corruption within the government but how easily journalists and reporters could also be bought.

The story had been going on for weeks and now suggested that at least two of the journalists involved had not been bribed but *blackmailed*. They were successful, well-known men with everything to lose if they didn't cooperate. Evidently, someone had something on both of them.

Which prompted Mona to ask her question one more time.

Why... Her?

Was it possible the old man—Abasi Hamed—wanted to give his information to someone who could not be blackmailed? Because in Mona's case, she had nothing to be blackmailed over. Literally. No scandals. No money. Not even a reputation to speak of. At least not yet.

She continued staring forward in a trance for a long time before suddenly turning back to the stove when her tea kettle began to whistle. She stepped forward and quickly took it off the flame.

Absently, she continued to ponder as she turned off the stove.

Could that be it? Could Hamed have chosen her because she had nothing to lose?

Pouring the water into a flower-covered teacup and placing the kettle back atop the stove, then through the trail of rising steam, turned to view the binder again on the table.

News and the momentum of a story could be highly unpredictable. So much so that the attention over the prime minister's allegations was already being overlooked following the new revelations about the three journalists.

Perhaps that was what Abasi Hamed was trying to avoid with her.

But if that were true, he had to have known the challenges she would face as a woman, just how little time and resources a single female reporter would have—especially if he needed a country controlled by men to believe whatever it was he'd given her.

Unless he didn't.

9

"Hello?"

"Omar, it's Mona. Are you awake?"

Following a long pause, the man finally replied. "Who is it?"

"It's Mona. Mona Baraka. Did I wake you?"

"Who?"

"MONA!"

On the other end, Omar Maher frowned and propped himself up on one elbow in his bed, emerging beneath a single silk sheet.

"Take it easy. I'm joking," he replied. "What time is it?"

"A little after 1:00."

Maher momentarily pulled the phone away from his ear and glanced at it. "In the morning?"

"Should I call back?"

"Why?" he sighed. "I was only in paradise, surrounded by my seventy-two Houri."

Mona smiled. "Sorry. I thought you might still be up."

"I am now. What is it?"

"I need some help from the smartest financial analyst I know."

"Of course you do. I'll make it easy. Gold and local

bonds."

"That's not the sort of help I'm looking for."

"How about some real estate? I have a nice pyramid I can sell you."

"I'm serious. I need help looking into some companies—international companies."

"This for a story?"

"Yes. And it may be important."

"Let me guess," he said, exhaling. "Someone, somewhere, did something bad."

"Are you done?"

Maher managed a tired smile. "I think so. How many companies?"

"Fourteen. I have a bunch of financial statements, but I don't know what to make of them."

"What kind of statements."

"I'm not sure. Maybe income statements?"

"Digital?"

"Paper. But I've scanned them."

"Okay. Send them over. How urgent is this?"

"It's hard to say until I know more."

"Fine. I'll try to take a look at them tomorrow if I can."

"Perfect. Thank you, Omar."

"What are friends for," he replied sarcastically, "but to wake up in the middle of the night for something that doesn't involve them at all?"

This time, Mona laughed. "I owe you a favor."

"You owe me a lot of favors."

"Then I owe you *another* one."

"Can I go back to sleep?"

"Yes. Thank you."

With that, the call ended, leaving Mona scrolling through her giant scanned file on her computer. Forty-two pages in all. Page after page of numbers and columns, several of which had been circled on different pages, presumably by Hamed. Different columns, different numbers and different dates.

On her screen, she clicked out of the file and back to her browser, where a picture of a much younger Abasi Hamed was displayed.

Taken decades before, he was dressed in a tan military uniform and a dark blue cap and was staring intently toward the camera. He was almost unrecognizable from the man

Mona had met in the hospital, except for the eyes. Those same dark, fierce eyes.

The Desert of Glass

Available on Amazon.com

FROM THE AUTHOR

I read once that it's only in times of crisis that you find out what's really important.

I've been wanting to write this story for a long time. And am releasing it now in what seems to be a world of surrealism.

Last year was a difficult one for me personally, and this year is proving to be a difficult one for all of us. And through both crises I've come to have my world redefined and refocused rather dramatically.

I've always enjoyed answering emails and connecting with readers on different levels. And I have been particularly touched by many of those people reaching out to check in on me, and make sure I'm okay under these dark times.

I've always asserted that I owe my readers a deep gratitude for supporting and allowing me to write for you. But I think it has become more than that. A deeper level of gratefulness that feels more akin to an extended family. Something I'm not sure I can ever fully repay.

Thank you. Thank you for the support, the friendship, and for the valuable time you have invested in me and my stories. Time which is finite for all of us.

Finally, being a self-published writer, I would deeply appreciate it if you could take a moment and leave a review or help spread the word for the book. Your support got me through last year. And I believe without a doubt, we can all get each other through this year.

Michael

Read Michael's Bestselling

Breakthrough Series

BREAKTHROUGH

LEAP

CATALYST

RIPPLE

MOSAIC

ECHO

Made in the USA
Middletown, DE
08 March 2022

62294678R00194